also by brynn bonner

Paging the Dead
Death in Reel Time

Picture Them Dead

Brynn Bonner

Pocket Books

New York London Toronto Sydney New Delhi

Pocket Books
An Imprint of Simon & Schuster, Inc.
1230 Avenue of the Americas
New York, NY 10020

First Pocket Books paperback edition July 2015

POCKET and colophon are registered trademarks of Simon & Schuster, Inc.

For information about special discounts for bulk purchases, please contact Simon & Schuster Special Sales at 1-866-506-1949 or business@simonandschuster.com.

The Simon & Schuster Speakers Bureau can bring authors to your live event. For more information or to book an event, contact the Simon & Schuster Speakers Bureau at 1-866-248-3049 or visit our website at www.simonspeakers.com.

Manufactured in the United States of America

10   9   8   7   6   5   4

ISBN 978-1-4767-7681-1
ISBN 978-1-4767-7683-5 (ebook)

To Adeline and August,
the apples of my eye

acknowledgments

Many thanks to my friend Wilma Romatz for sharing the story that inspired this one.

To Dr. Billy Oliver for information on burial practices and laws. Any errors in how his information was applied in this story are strictly my own.

To Margaret Maron for the title.

And to my family, always.

one

That was my grandmother's word for when a person is so stunned, it renders her slack-jawed and mute. I haven't experienced this many times in my life, as I'm a decidedly sanguine person, but at the moment, I was definitely thunderstruck.

As a professional genealogist, I've seen enough skeletons come dancing out of family closets to get an impressive conga line forming. But they've all been metaphorical skeletons. Until today.

I stood on a berm of red dirt in our potential new client's backyard, only a few miles from where I live in Morningside, North Carolina. I stared down into the hole the backhoe had ripped, and even though I'd been warned, I was shocked senseless. There was a skull grinning up at me, and while this was disconcerting enough, what really got me was the casket. It was made of glass in a milky green color and was broken in multiple places, the shards sticking out like spikes. The metal hinges were rusted and twisted and what was left of the lid had slid to the side. Tatters of rotted fabric sprouted from the pile of wreckage like desiccated seaweed. A jagged hole where the backhoe's scooper had hit left a handy window for our macabre game of peekaboo with the grinning skull. The whole casket had settled wonky. It canted to one side as if the occupant had rolled over in his big sleep and taken the casket with him.

"Dear sweet Lord, have mercy," my business partner, Esme Sabatier, whispered.

For the first time in weeks, she and I were in total agreement.

Esme's been my cohort in our genealogy research business for several years, but more than that, she's my housemate, my confidant, and my dearest friend. She's my family. We're great partners because we have complementary outlooks and skills. But the sprockets on gears are complementary, too, and if they don't line up just right, there's a lot of grinding. We'd been out of alignment lately.

This weird casket and its tenant were the most disturbing things Esme and I had witnessed today, but not the only jolt we'd had. We'd been snug in our beds this morning, minding our own business and trying to recover the sleep we'd lost over the past two weeks while on a job for a big Italian family in Maryland. We'd gotten in late last night, so exhausted we'd dumped our suitcases in the front hall and gone straight to bed.

A little after 8:00 a.m., which to my sleep-deprived brain was an ungodly hour, someone started mashing on our doorbell. I'd put my pillow over my head, but it didn't let up. Defeated, I'd hauled out and trudged downstairs, muttering old Sicilian curses I'd recently learned at whoever was leaning on the bell. I threw the door open to find Jennifer Jeffers standing on our front porch.

Jennifer is the last person in the entire population of our little town who would pay a social call on Esme and me. She dislikes us—rather intensely—for some reason neither of us can fathom. True, we hadn't met under the best of circumstances. Three years ago, one of our clients had been murdered, and for a brief time, Esme and I were deemed persons of interest since we'd been among the last to see her alive. Jennifer and her partner, Denny, had been the detectives on the case and had come to question us. We were quickly cleared, so I couldn't see why Jennifer would still hold that incident against us. Denny certainly hadn't. As soon as they'd eliminated us as suspects, Esme had become a person of immense interest to Denny.

But Jennifer is still so unfriendly toward us. We've tried being sweet to her, we've tried giving as good as we got from her, and we've tried analyzing every interaction with her to see if we could get any insight into the problem. Nothing had gotten us any closer to understanding what we'd done to offend her so much. These days, we did our best to ignore her.

Jennifer's the youngest person ever to make detective in the police department, and quite the overachiever. Her partner, Denton Carlson, is Esme's boyfriend, though that sounds like a silly term when you know them both. Esme is a beautiful Creole woman in her fifties and she's substantial and statuesque—over six feet tall in her stocking feet and fond of heels. Denny is the same age and is a Mack truck of a man. They are a formidable-looking pair.

I, on the other hand, am short and small, much like Jennifer Jeffers. When we'd first met, I'd had the brief idea we had some short-girl solidarity going, but she soon disabused me of that notion.

So, to see her standing on our front porch in off-duty clothes was a surprise. And what came out of her mouth after I gave her a puzzled hello was even more surprising.

"Hello, Sophreena. I hate to ask this, but I need your help. And Esme's."

I stood for a moment trying to process what she'd

said, thinking I must still be sleeping and that this was a dream, or a nightmare ramping up.

"It's not for me, it's for my dad," she said when I didn't respond.

"And what is it we can do for you, or him, exactly?" I asked hesitantly.

"It'll take some explaining," Jenny said.

"Oh, okay," I said, opening the door wider. "Come in. Would you like some coffee? I sure would."

"No, thanks," Jenny said, clearly uncomfortable.

As we went into the kitchen, I could hear Esme muttering as she descended from the mother-in-law suite on her side of the house.

"Who was that mashing that doorbell so early in the morning? Don't they have any—" She halted mid-grumble at the bottom of the steps and reared back as if a sudden wind had pushed against her when she caught sight of Jenny. She looked to me for an explanation.

"Jenny needs our help," I announced, raising my eyebrows as I turned to flip on the coffeemaker. "Or her father does. She was just getting ready to tell me about it."

"Is that so," Esme said, moving to the cupboard to get mugs and simultaneously giving me *What the hell?* eyes. "Well, let's hear about it."

"Have a seat," I said, turning back to Jenny. She stood, shifting her weight from one foot to the other, looking like she'd rather be getting a root canal.

"That's okay, this won't take long," she said. "I need to get back to my dad."

We waited, enshrouded in what had to be the most awkward silence ever, until the coffeepot gurgled and Esme snatched it up and poured. "You sure you don't want a cup?" I asked Jenny.

"Fine, if it will speed this up, I'll take one," Jenny said, taking the cup from Esme, who, with uncharacteristic ungraciousness, held it out only slightly, making Jenny come get it.

"Now, what's this about?" Esme asked as she settled at the table, making a fuss of rearranging the cream pitcher and sugar bowl.

Jenny took a deep breath and let the words explode from her mouth. "My dad bought a new place a few months ago, just outside town—the old Harper place. It's an old farmhouse and a five-acre plot of land. He's doing a lot of work on the property, wants to put in a big vegetable garden and a bunch of other stuff. It's this permaculture thing he's into. This morning he was using a Bobcat, you know what that is, right? One of those mini-bulldozer deals?"

I nodded. Esme rolled her eyes.

Jennifer's nostrils flared, but she went on. "Anyhow, he was excavating to put in a water feature and he hit something. He thought it was a rock but when he couldn't get the bucket loose, he went to investigate.

It's a coffin, a weird coffin. Made out of glass. There was no grave marker, and there was no disclosure about anybody being buried on the property. He wants to talk to you two about it."

"Why us?" I asked.

Jenny shrugged and took a sip of her coffee, examining the brew as if she suspected it might be poisoned. "Don't know," she said. "He just wanted me to ask if you'd come out and take a look."

And so we did. You can't dangle the words *glass coffin* in front of genealogists without arousing a certain level of curiosity.

Meeting Jennifer's dad was yet another surprise for the day. He wasn't at all what I'd expected. Jennifer is a straitlaced gal, conservative in dress, measured in her movements, and taciturn in speech. She's very self-contained.

River Valley Jeffers was not an uptight gentleman. He greeted us when we got out of Esme's SUV with an extended hand and a doff of his gimme cap. "Jenny's inside making some calls," he said. "She's trying to figure out what needs to be done from the official side."

He had a two-day scruff of whiskers and was dressed in well-worn blue jeans and an old Pink Floyd T-shirt, topped with a flannel jacket that looked soft from many washings. His gray hair was pulled back in a braid that hung a few inches down his back and the fan of wrinkles around his eyes documented a lot of time spent laughing.

"Jenny's talked so much about you two and how good you are at finding out things that happened years ago, I thought you'd be the ones to help me figure out who my mystery man is." He turned and pointed to a pile of dirt at the top of a gradually sloping acre of side yard and gestured for us to follow him.

"Maybe Jennifer's adopted," Esme whispered out of the side of her mouth.

"I feel bad about disturbing this fella's eternal rest," River went on. "Least I'm assuming it's a fella; kinda looks like he was wearing a suit coat when he went to meet St. Peter."

"And the coffin is actually glass?" I asked. "I've heard of those but never actually seen one. Have you?" I asked, turning to Esme, who didn't reply.

"Have you, Esme?" I asked again.

"No, sorry," Esme said. "I was still stuck on Jennifer saying you and I are good at what we do." She turned to River. "Is that really what she said?"

He nodded. "All the time. But listen, I'm not asking for a favor or anything. I want to hire you to look into this. I've wanted to know more about the history of this place anyhow, and now that I've gone and plowed up what I'm assuming is a family member of the folks who lived on this land, I feel like I really need to know more. Maybe he's got companions up there on that hill."

"Well," I said, "let's see what we've got here and we can talk more later if we think we can be of help."

Picking our way along the newly turned dirt where River was putting in not only a vegetable garden but also trees, flower beds, and an elaborate trellis structure was slowgoing. Esme, as was her wont, had worn high heels, this pair in a leopard-skin design and completely inappropriate for the terrain. She kept sinking into the loose earth and then having to extricate her footwear. As we walked, Jennifer came from the direction of the house and fell into step with us.

Arriving at the hole, we stood around the grave, a peculiar party of mourners, staring down at a stranger who seemed to be staring back, mocking us from his ruptured glass casket. After I finally got my wits about me, I looked away from the skull and began studying the characteristics of the casket. The glass was opaque in a color that reminded me of old green Coke bottles marbled with ivory veining. There was no burial vault, so the grave was likely an old one.

"You got everything all sorted out?" River asked Jennifer. "Is somebody going to come get him?"

She sighed. "I'm not sure. I keep getting passed from one authority to another. I'm having trouble getting to the proper people on this."

Something about the look on Jennifer's face made me feel bad for her. It was as if she felt she'd failed her father.

"I'm not sure I'd know who to call either," I put in, trying to make her feel better. "I've dealt with old graves before in family cemeteries, but they were always marked and registered. This seems like a job for maybe a crime analyst."

"We don't even know who this is, or how he died, or how long he's been here. Where's the crime?" Jenny snapped, then muttered under her breath as she turned to glare at Esme's feet. "Other than those shoes."

I watched Esme's face twist into a murderous glare.

"Jenny, darlin'," River said, reaching over to pat her back. "We've got enough negative energy here right now. Be sweet like your mama taught you."

Esme opened her mouth, no doubt to express the opinion that Jenny's mother had failed miserably, but I rushed to cut in.

"As I understand it from Jennifer, you weren't told about a grave on the property when you bought the place, right?"

"Right, nothing was said about it," River said. "I bought the place about six months ago when the lady who owned it had to go into a nursing home. I dealt with her lawyer; never met her. She must have been a good ol' gal, though. I understand she made a nice contribution to the Literacy Council when she sold the land."

"Claire Calvert, the head of the Literacy Council, lives just over there," Esme said, nodding her head in the direction of the rise beyond the open grave. "Maybe she scored a convert."

"Claire could talk you into funding a program to teach rocks to read," River said. "But she was pretty surprised about that particular contribution. She says she and the lady were neighborly enough, but not close."

"Would you mind letting me review your deed and title?" I asked.

"Glad to. It's not an imperfect deed, if that's what you're thinking. I've got a crackerjack real estate lawyer. But the papers are in my safe-deposit box, so I can't get to them until Monday."

We all looked up as a van came down the long gravel driveway, kicking up a cloud of red dust.

"Finally," Jennifer said. "That's the medical examiner." She marched off toward the van while Esme and I turned our attention back to the casket. "The glass is pretty if you can get over what it is," Esme said, tilting her head to one side.

"It is, isn't it? It's very ornate," I said. "And it must have been expensive. Whoever this was must have been highly regarded. I wonder why there's no marker."

"It's possible there was a gravestone at one time and it got destroyed," River said, glancing around. "We're too high on the hill for flooding, but we've had plenty of big storms come through this area over the years."

Jennifer walked back with a guy who looked all of twelve. He was red-haired and freckled and so slight he was having difficulty with his heavy case of supplies. When he got to the edge of the grave he looked down and gushed, "Wow, way cool!"

"This is Josh," Jennifer said with barely disguised disdain. "He's interning with the medical examiner's office."

"They sent a flunky," Esme whispered in my ear. "Guess Jennifer doesn't have much juice."

I shushed her, but she had a point.

"It's not cool," River said gently, "it's disturbing."

"Oh, sure," Josh said. "I just meant I never saw a glass coffin before. I'm supposed to take some photos and measurements."

"It's not a coffin," I said, hardly aware I was speaking. "A coffin has six or eight sides and is wider at the top, shaped more like a body. A casket is a rectangular box. This is a casket."

"Interesting," River said. "But whatever he's housed in, are you going to arrange to have this—him," River corrected, "disinterred and moved someplace?"

"Don't know if we can," Josh said. "There're all

these burial laws and stuff. Somebody way above my pay grade's looking into all that."

"And in the meantime," Jennifer said sharply, "what's my father supposed to do?"

"Nothing." Josh shrugged. "We're not supposed to touch anything or do any more damage. I'll cover the hole with a tarp when I'm done, and then you wait for the big enchiladas to get in touch." He set his case on the ground and squatted to release the latches. "Now, if y'all would step back, I'll get to work."

"I'm gonna make some more calls," Jennifer said, whipping her cell phone from her pocket. "I can't believe they sent Opie," she muttered as she walked away.

River accompanied us back to our car and we chatted for a few more minutes. I told him we'd do a little investigating and I'd let him know tomorrow if we could be of any help. We talked fees and I was surprised when he didn't blink. Esme and I don't come cheap. But we also don't take on jobs where we can't provide any value. Hard as it is for me to accept, there are some things that are simply lost in the fog of history.

As we drove home, Esme and I discussed whether to take on the job. "We don't have anything pressing right now," I said. "And, of course, I'm curious about that glass casket. But I'd also like to help River if we can. I like him."

"Me, too," Esme said. "I can't believe that man is Jennifer's father; they are nothing alike. Sometimes the apple does fall far from the tree."

"Maybe there was wind the day the Jennifer apple fell," I said with a smile.

Esme harrumphed. "Must've been gale force."

two

ESME AND I WERE LINGERING OVER OUR BREAK-
fast while reading the Sunday paper. This doesn't take
nearly as long as it used to, since the newspaper's getting thinner each week, but we still savor the ritual. I
especially appreciated this moment of quiet together-
ness since we've been getting on each other's nerves for
the last month or so.

Esme has lived in the mother-in-law suite over
my garage for years now. My father built the suite
with the intention of moving his mother here from
Missouri to live with us. But Grandma McClure died
suddenly before it was finished. Later the space had
become my mother's art studio. Since my mother's
death, it had served as a seldom-used guest room.
When Esme had moved here from Louisiana to join
me in my genealogical services business, she moved
in, temporarily, while she looked for a place. We soon

found the arrangement suited both of us and she stayed on.

Our friendship has grown and deepened over the years and now she's the closest thing I have to family. We get along splendidly, most of the time. But it's really no wonder we have friction occasionally, just like people do in blood families. First off, there's the generation gap. I'm mid-thirties and Esme's mid-fifties. Then there's the work process: I tend to be meticulous in my research habits, while Esme is, shall we say, rather casual with her interpretations, or at least she had been in the beginning. And finally, there's our personal style. I'm small in stature and dress plainly and practically. Esme's a clotheshorse, using her considerable body as a canvas. And she's got such a thing for shoes, she really should be in a support group.

And if all those differences weren't enough, we've got a complicated personal dynamic. She seems to think she has the right to mother me, which is a mixed blessing. I love it when I need mothering, but it chafes when her advice is contrary to what I want to hear. We've always fussed and bickered, but in a teasing way. Lately there's been an edge to it, at least coming from Esme.

"You gonna call River to tell him we'll look into his mystery man or do you want me to?" she asked.

"I'll call him," I said. "I'm thinking we should offer

him a set number of hours for a flat fee. I have a feeling it may be a financial hardship for him."

"Fine by me," Esme said, reaching for the arts and entertainment section. "Like I said, I like the man and I have a hunch we'd be researching this whether we got paid or not. I know how you get when you get a bee in your bonnet. Curiosity may have killed the cat, but it makes you come alive."

"True," I said, "but you can't tell me you're not curious, too. Maybe we can even get the others involved."

"Oh, you can bet they'll jump on this. What better secret could you present to a genealogy club than an unknown fella buried in an unmarked grave in a glass coffin"—she held up a hand—"I mean casket. They'll pounce on this like a lion after an antelope—unless it's overshadowed by all the wedding hoopla. Winston and Marydale tie the knot in less than two weeks."

Winston and Marydale were the senior members of our close-knit club of family history buffs. Marydale was another mother figure in my life. She'd promised my dying mother she'd look after me and she'd taken that pledge seriously. I'd been in high school when my mom passed and I honestly don't know how I would have gotten through the following few years without Marydale. My dad was great, but he was doing his own grieving, and sometimes I just needed a woman's counsel.

Marydale had been a widow for a long time and Winston had become single a couple of years ago when his shrew of a wife left him, to the disappointment of no one who knew and loved Winston.

All of us had been blindsided when Marydale and Winston announced—confessed, really—that their longtime friendship had taken a romantic turn. And since both were long passed being dewy-eyed youths, they'd been disinclined toward a lengthy engagement. Wedding plans had commenced immediately.

I was thrilled for them, but I was also a tiny bit jealous. I've recently had an epiphany about my own feelings for Jack Ford, another member of our group. But I'm not sure he feels the same and I haven't been able to get up the courage to tell him how I feel. I'd been collecting signs for months now, signals that he considers me more than a friend, but there hadn't been enough to make me risk making a total fool of myself by declaring my feelings. I'm in limbo. I don't like limbo.

The phone rang and I got up to answer it, which I instantly regretted. Jennifer Jeffers was on the line and I could practically feel the heat coming through the handset. "Did you two go running your mouths about what happened out at Dad's place?" she asked, skipping "good morning," "how are you," and "do you have a minute" to get right to the accusations.

"No," I said patiently, drawing out the word. "We

did not go running our mouths, bumping our gums, or prattling on either. We don't bandy about our clients' business, Jennifer."

"So Dad's a client. You've agreed, then? I hope you're not planning to rob him blind."

"Jennifer," I said, my patience circling the drain, "we had decided we'd work with your dad on this, but after this phone call, we might reconsider. What's going on?"

"I'm sorry," Jennifer said, the sharpness in her tone belying the words. "No, really, I am sorry," she said with a long sigh. "Somehow word has gotten out and people are swarming Dad's place, gawking. A few have left flowers by the grave."

"Isn't the area cordoned off? I thought Josh was securing it against the weather when we left yesterday."

"He did," Jennifer said, "but it's not like he posted an armed guard."

She loaded the last with enough sarcasm to make the phone heavy in my hand. I mentally auditioned several snappy comebacks, but decided to simply wait her out.

"Dad caught a couple of teenagers trying to peel back the tarps this morning. He ran them off, but people just keep coming. He can't be expected to keep guard and I'm on duty today since Denny's out of town."

"Maybe he could post some No Trespassing signs," I suggested.

Jennifer huffed. "Yeah, that'll take care of it, Sophreena," she said. "Listen, Dad really wants you involved in this and that's his call, but just do whatever it is you do as quick as you can, then step back, okay?"

I pondered an appropriate reply, but "up your nose with a rubber hose" didn't sound professional, and anyhow Jennifer had already hung up, leaving me listening to the drone of the dial tone.

I turned to see Esme shaking her head and tsking. "I wish I knew what in this world we do to get that girl's feathers ruffled all the time. I used to think she was just a bitter person, but I've asked around. She's not like this with everybody, mostly just us. And I tell you, I've had about enough of it."

I waved a hand dismissively, though I'd been thinking the same thing myself. While she wasn't universally liked, Jennifer had good friends who were loyal to her. And Denny thought well of her, too. Esme and I were both good people. Why didn't she like us?

A yoo-hoo came from the front hall and Marydale and Winston soon appeared in the kitchen doorway.

"Too late," Winston said, glancing at our plates. "I brought you apple fritters for breakfast, Sophreena, but we got a late start this morning. Marydale's been on the phone with her kids and me with mine trying to line up all our ducks for gettin'-hitched day. I'm beginning to think we should have just run off and tied the knot."

"Nonsense," Marydale said. "I want all our kids and grandkids there and all our friends, too. You don't want to share our happy day?"

"I do," Winston said, laughing. "And see how easy those two words come off my tongue? I'm just ready to say 'em and make it official, that's all."

Winston is a retired baker who can't seem to kick the habit and he's always bringing us fresh baked goodies. The aroma of those apple fritters was making me salivate and I quickly abandoned my half-eaten bowl of oatmeal.

"I hear you've been holding out on us," Marydale said, sliding into the extra kitchen chair.

"About?" Esme said.

"The glass coffin!" Marydale said. "Whoever heard of such a thing?"

"How did you hear about that already?" Esme asked.

"Word's all over town," Winston said, whipping out the kitchen stepladder we keep by the refrigerator to serve as his perch.

I heard the front door open again and knew instantly who'd be joining us. Colette Newsome, Coco to us, was a walking wind chime; the jangle of her many bracelets, anklets, and necklaces announced her arrival.

"Seriously, a glass coffin?" she said as she swept through the kitchen doorway, her gauzy skirt flaring as she went straight for the coffeemaker.

"Told you it was all over town," Winston said.

"I got three calls this morning," Coco said. "People have found out you two are on the job and since everybody knows we're friends, they thought I'd have the scoop, which I am aggrieved to say I did not," she added as she rummaged through the cupboard for her favorite coffee mug. "Not that I'd go gabbing about it if I did, but I like to be in the loop."

"There's no loop," I protested. "This all just came up yesterday. We hadn't even decided to take the job until a few minutes ago."

"Well, you know Morningside," Coco said. "We had little birds tweeting the trending news long before Twitter. Now dish."

Esme and I are big on confidentiality, but we'd long ago granted this group the highest clearance. We share freely with them and trust it will be kept in confidence. I gave them the short version of what we'd seen at River Jeffers' place.

"Ooh, creepy," Coco said. "No wonder everybody's imaginations are fired up."

"When you say everybody," I mused, "just how far has this gone?"

"People are already calling him the Forgotten Man," Coco said. "Emily Clemmons is trying to organize a community candlelight vigil for him at the graveside."

"Good Lord, no wonder Jennifer had her hair on fire

this morning. River's going to have people traipsing all over his place," Esme said.

"River can handle it," Coco said. "He's a really laid-back guy."

"You know him?" I asked.

"Oh yeah, we're buddies," Coco said. "We both took a class last spring from this old dude over in Carrboro on foraging for medicinal and nutritional plants. We've been foraging together since the weather's opened up. He's a sweetheart."

"I know him, too," Winston said. "We're in a Vietnam vets outfit together. But I wouldn't say he's laid-back, Coco. I'd say he just doesn't let things show."

"He and I went to grade school together," Marydale said. "His parents died when we were in fifth grade and he went to California to live with an aunt and uncle. He moved back here when Jennifer was in middle school. He'd lost his wife and apparently Jennifer was getting wild and he wanted her in a different environment."

"So you're going to help him find out who was in that coffin?" Coco asked.

"Yes, we'll dig around, no pun intended," I said. "There have to be records somewhere; this should be an easy one."

Famous last words.

three

I THOUGHT ABOUT THE SITUATION AT RIVER'S place all through Sunday mass. I was so distracted that Jack had to elbow me whenever it was time to kneel or stand. I've been a lax Catholic since my parents died, but as I get older I feel the need to be more dedicated. Issues of faith and spirituality aside, I like the ritual and feeling more centered helps me launch my week.

I knew River would be pleased to hear that Esme and I would be on the case, and I wanted to help him, but I knew dealing with Jennifer was going to be a gong show. When Denny was around she was civil, but he was out of town at a seminar. I felt confident I could cope with her if I put my mind to it. As for Esme, well, I'd just have to keep them apart as much as possible.

I was pulled out of my reverie near the end of the service when the priest began reading the petitions for prayer. "We ask your blessing on the Forgotten Man," he intoned, "though his earthly resting place has been disturbed, we pray that his soul is at peace with the Lord."

"Seriously?" I whispered to Jack, which earned me a giggle from a little girl who was watching us over her daddy's shoulder.

After the service, people took advantage of the beautiful spring weather to linger outside, gathering in clusters to chat. As Jack and I headed to my car, Emily Clemmons peeled off from a group and called my name. Emily is in her mid-forties, has an unruly mass of salt-and-pepper hair, and carries a bit of comfortable padding that she is forever trying to diet off. She's the go-to gal when something needs organizing: bake sales, funeral dinners, Easter egg hunts, Christmas bazaars, and sometimes events of her own creation.

"I'm so glad I ran into you," she said, reaching into her purse for a notebook and pen. "What can you tell me about this poor man they found buried at the old Harper place? I hear you and Esme have done some research; what have you found out? I'd like to know a little something about him before the vigil."

"Hello, Emily," I said, trying to hide a combination of irritation and amusement. "I'm afraid I can't tell you anything."

"Can't tell me or won't tell me?" Emily asked, giving me a playful slap on the arm. "I know how you are about that whole confidentiality thing with your clients."

"Well, there is that," I said. "But in this case I simply don't know anything. How in the world did you find out about this anyway?"

"Oh, Facebook," Emily said, waving a dismissive hand. "Somebody posted a picture of the coffin." She shook her shoulders in an exaggerated shudder. "Just gruesome. It breaks my heart to think about that poor man buried out there all alone for all these years and nobody even remembers who he is. Isn't that the saddest thing?"

I thought of telling her this was far from the saddest thing I'd witnessed. Whoever this person was, he'd been given a careful burial. It was sad that there was no marker, and quite frustrating for me as a genealogist, but Emily was ramping up the drama.

Alas, it mattered not one whit what I thought, as it seemed Emily's question was rhetorical. "Some people may think this vigil is unnecessary," she went on, "but I truly believe his spirit will rest in peace only if we let him know he hasn't been forgotten. Maybe you don't believe in that kind of thing, but lots of people do." Then she walked off, looking for fresh ears to talk at.

I needed no convincing about the existence of spirits. It was true that a few years back I would have tagged Emily as a crackpot, but since Esme came into my life, I've become a reluctant convert. Esme has the questionable gift of being able to receive communications from the dead—sometimes, about some things, often very obliquely, and usually the info is maddeningly enigmatic. When she first told me about this, after we'd become business partners, I'd questioned her stability. I mean, I'd seen plenty of people who were haunted, but only by memories. And I knew lots of families had ghosts, but that always meant unresolved issues or questions, not ghost ghosts. I'm a binary kind of gal. A thing is either off or it's on. I don't deal well with weasel words or nuances. And really, I'd no intention of keeping an open mind. But time after time I'd seen Esme do her thing and now I totally accept that she gets messages from beyond. Occasionally it gives us a huge advantage in our research, but more often it's an exercise in frustration.

"You wanna stop by Top o' the Morning for coffee and a Danish?" Jack asked, shaking his head as he watched Emily corral another group of recruits.

"Definitely. Caffeine and sweets are my favorite major food groups."

We decided to walk the few blocks from St. Raphael's, and Jack went in for our order while I grabbed one of the outdoor tables crammed into the little alley space beside the shop. I called River while I waited.

He answered, sounding out of breath.

"River, it's Sophreena. Did I catch you at a bad time?" I asked.

"Oh, hey, Sophreena. I'm not sure there is a good time this morning. I just had to go out and tell another bunch of people they can't be disturbing things around that grave."

"I heard you've had some looky-loos."

"Yeah. Can't blame 'em for being curious, it's a curious kind of thing, but I do wish they'd be more respectful about it. Things I took some care to plant are getting trampled. And some folks are going inside the tape that kid from the lab put up yesterday. People are literally crossing the line here."

"Isn't there anything Jennifer can do?"

"She's been by a few times and she ran off one couple, but she can't stay here all day and they just keep coming. She'll come back out this afternoon with some official police department signs to warn people off. Maybe that'll do the trick."

"I hope so," I said. "I'm calling to let you know Esme and I would like to find out whatever we can for you. We'll do a per-hour contract for three hours of research time to keep it economical. Is that acceptable?"

"Long as I have the option to renew, that's fine by me. This whole thing with finding the grave is really just the trigger—I've wanted to know more about who's lived on this land since the day I bought it. You may think I'm strange for saying this, but I believe you share your space with the ghosts of those who came before. Their culture, their hopes and fears, their living practices all sort of seep into the soil and grow in everything."

"That's a profound thought, River."

"Is that your polite way of saying I'm a nut job?" River asked with a chuckle.

"Not at all," I said, and meant it. "I'm a genealogist, after all. Of course I believe our heritage influences us. I'll make a courthouse visit tomorrow and you can get me a copy of your property deed then, too, right?"

"First thing in the morning," River agreed. "And there's an attic full of stuff here, might be something useful up there."

"I love poking around in dusty old attics," I said, "but let me see what I can find out from official sources first."

"Awesome," River said, sounding more like a teen-age skateboarder than a retiree. "If you could come out tomorrow morning sometime, I can give you a check. Or I could bring it to you, though I'm sort of afraid to leave home right now. Stupid, I know, but I feel like I need to protect our fella from the gawkers."

"We'll get the check when we see you next, no need for a special trip. But I would like to come out and have you show me the property lines and maybe take some photos to show where the grave is situated."

"Good deal. Other than a quick trip to the bank for the deed, I'll be right here, hanging out with Jimmy."

"Jimmy?" I asked.

"Fella needed a name. He seems to like it," River said. "Whole lot better than 'skeletal remains,' don't you think?"

I laughed. "Much better. See you tomorrow."

River Jeffers reminded me of my dad, whom I had loved fiercely. Jennifer clearly felt the same about her father and she was very protective of him. This made me think a little better of her—a very little better.

I'd just finished the call when Jack came out with two cups of coffee and two strawberry scones. I decided this was another sign I could add to my tally. Would a buddy remember your favorite pastry? And he'd doctored my coffee with just the right amount of cream and sugar. Double points.

"You get up with River?" Jack asked, giving me an odd look. Only then did I realize I must have been gazing at him like a doofus.

"I did," I said, reaching for my coffee. "I feel bad about charging him our regular fee considering the situation he's in. So we're going to give him the economy package."

"I wouldn't worry about that," Jack said, huffing a laugh as he dropped into the wrought-iron chair. "River's loaded."

"Sure." I laughed.

"No, really," Jack said. "You wouldn't know it looking at the way he lives, but he's got plenty of money."

"Family money?"

"No, I think he comes from a pretty humble background. He's a self-made man. He bought some little company back in the seventies. I don't remember what the original company made, some little molded plastic part for something. Guess he took that line in *The Graduate* seriously; you know, where Mr. McGuire gives the recent graduate advice and it's just one word, 'Plastics.' Anyhow, River had a knack for finding niche markets for parts he could fabricate quickly and economically and kept expanding the business. Eventually he got into making cases for electronics. Made a mint, then sold the company and bought another that made ecofriendly landscaping fabric. I use a lot of that in my business, so I helped him make his second fortune."

"So Jennifer's a rich kid? Maybe that explains the attitude."

Jack shook his head as he broke off the end of his scone. "No, he didn't spoil her. Not with material goods anyhow. River doesn't believe in excess. But he believes in the permaculture method like it's a religion. That's how I first met him. I went to a permaculture workshop. Thought maybe I could pick up some good practices for my landscaping business."

"And he attended the workshop, too?"

"He taught the workshop. Anyhow, he's got plenty of money socked away, I don't doubt, but he gives a lot away, too. He's got a thing for funding start-up ventures when he thinks somebody's got a workable and worthy idea."

"Okay, full price it is," I said. "Let's just hope we come up with something workable and worthy."

"This is getting totally out of hand," Esme muttered as she came into the workroom later that afternoon.

I reluctantly pulled my attention from the computer, where I'd been researching glass caskets.

"What's getting out of hand?" I asked.

"I just got a call from Claire Calvert."

"Claire? From the Literacy Council?"

"Do you know any other Claire Calverts?" Esme snapped. "I'm going over to her house. She needs somebody with her."

I drew in a breath, trying to ignore Esme's tone. "What's wrong? Is she sick?"

Claire was the survivor of an incident worthy of an Appalachian ballad. She'd been an active and admired young teacher in the mid-nineties. One night her husband, Quentin Calvert, had come home to find another man, Nash Simpson, in the house with Claire.

He'd gone into a jealous rage and there was a brawl. Claire had been seriously hurt, her injuries leaving her paralyzed from the waist down. Quentin had served an unusually lengthy sentence in the state penitentiary, but he'd been paroled a few weeks ago and was back in Morningside.

"No, not sick," Esme said. "She's just agitated."

"Please don't tell me Quentin Calvert is harassing her," I said. I'd heard a lot of talk around town and some people weren't happy he'd come back.

"No, Emily Clemmons is the problem. With all her good intentions that woman can sure misfire sometimes. She's taken her candlelight vigil on the road. River's place is posted so she's gone around on Claire's property, without permission, so she can get everybody as close to the grave site as she can. Claire and River are friends and Claire doesn't want him thinking she's had any part in this, but she can't get him on the phone. Where's Denton when you need him? He picked a fine time to go off on a law enforcement seminar."

"I hardly think Denny could have anticipated anything like this when he signed up for it, Esme," I said.

Esme had been touchy about everything lately, and I couldn't figure out what was at the core of it. When I asked, she maintained, grumpily, that everything was hunky-dory. But she definitely had a burr under her saddle.

"You want me to come with you?" I asked.

"No, you stay here and hopefully make some headway with the research."

I didn't argue. I like and admire Claire Calvert, but she and Esme are closer. They never let me get a word in edgewise when they're together. Besides, I was turning up fascinating stuff about glass caskets. Macabre? Yes. No apologies. Dead people are the stock-in-trade of my profession, so of course I'm interested in where and how they're housed for eternity.

One big thing I'd learned was that glass caskets had been a colossal flop both as a burial vessel and as a business. The Spanish flu pandemic had just ended and as always, there was no shortage of sleazeballs jumping to capitalize on people's fears. The manufacturers of the caskets made claims about how the sealed vessels would prevent the spread of disease, unsupported by anything other than their own advertising copy. The caskets themselves were expensive to produce and weighed in at nearly five hundred pounds, threatening to give the pallbearers hernias as they carried the casket to the grave site. Not to mention the glass couldn't take the pressure of six feet of dirt bearing down on it.

Also, there were plenty of financial shenanigans going on in this particular venture. The biggest company involved in "manufacturing" the caskets had perpetrated full-scale fraud. They printed up fancy brochures,

opened storefronts, and even set up a fake production plant. One particularly industrious gentleman in
Chicago staged an elaborate funeral with his not-quite-
dead-yet wife playing the starring role of the corpse. He
nearly suffocated her when he made the grand gesture
of sealing the casket at the end of the service. Waiting
until he'd gotten her into the privacy of the hearse to
open the lid and check on her, he found her turning
blue—and, I would presume, more than a little miffed.
But, hey, it did prove the things sealed.

In reality, a limited number of glass caskets were
ever made, which begged the question of how one
ended up in a North Carolina backyard. And, moreover,
who was the occupant?

I'd also found out a few things about the land River
Jeffers now owned. He'd bought it from a woman
named Charlotte Walker, who, as far as I could tell, was
still alive. Though if the info I had was up-to-date, she'd
be ninety-seven years old. I put a big question mark by
her name. I gulped when I saw how much River had
paid for the place.

I heard the front door open, and Winston called out
from the front hall, "Sophreena, Esme, y'all here?"

"I'm in the workroom," I shouted back, reluctantly
tearing my eyes from the screen when he appeared
in the doorway. He held up something rectangular,
wrapped in foil. "Lemon-zucchini bread," he said,

setting it on the table outside the workroom. We have an absolute no food or drink policy in the workroom, since this is where we sort, examine, and scan our clients' precious and often fragile family archives.

"You're baking? I thought you'd be too busy with wedding activities."

"Got a little case of nerves, I guess. Baking helps."

"What are you nervous about? You're not getting cold feet, are you?"

"No, no," Winston said, waving a lanky hand. "Not about marrying Marydale anyhow." He pointed to a chair and raised his eyebrows. I motioned for him to sit.

"I'm a little jittery about how the kids will all get along and how they'll all feel about it. I mean, they know one another and they're sort of casual friends already, but this'll be different. We'll all be family now. What if they don't cotton to one another?"

The kids were Dee and Brody, Marydale's grown children and the closest people I had to siblings. Then there were Winston's two grown sons in their early 40s, Forest and Jacob, their wives, and an assortment of grandchildren. My first instinct was to reassure him that they would all be one big happy family the minute they spoke the I-dos, but Winston has an excellent poppycock meter, so I didn't try to sell that empty promise.

"They may be a little slow to warm up at first, but Dee and Brody are happy about their mother finding loving companionship. I know that because both of them have told me so. Which isn't to say they weren't taken by surprise. We all were and it takes a little getting used to. Plus, they're accustomed to having their mother all to themselves, even if it is long distance. Be patient."

Winston nodded. "My kids were caught unawares, too. Especially since it had been such a short time after the divorce. I didn't like to talk to them about my relationship with their mother. I didn't want to dishonor her by talking her down. She's their mother, after all. But I suppose it was obvious to anybody with eyes that we hadn't been happy for years."

I pursed my lips. Winston's ex-wife, Patsy, was one of the most disagreeable people I had ever met. But I hadn't known her long. Maybe she'd been different back when Winston met and married her. And she was, as he said, the mother of his children, though she was no candidate for Mother of the Year, as far as I could see. I decided to deflect.

"You and Marydale will be very happy together, so your kids will be happy for you and with you. We all will," I said.

A slow smile spread across Winston's handsome face. He was tanned from coaching his grandson's T-ball team, and even more fit now that Marydale was orchestrating his diet and exercise. "You're right," he said, "it'll all work out. But, anyhow, the main reason I came by was to ask your opinion about something." He reached into the pocket of his powder-blue windbreaker for a gift box. "I got this for Marydale as a wedding present, but now I'm having second thoughts about whether she'll like it. Sort of relating to what we were just talking about. Maybe it's too soon. Tell me what you think."

I lifted off the top of the box to find a silver locket on a long silver chain nestled in a bed of tissue paper. I picked it up and admired the stylized engraved tree on the front.

"I was thinking of that as a family tree, you know," Winston said. "If I hadn't taken that class of yours and if we hadn't gone on with our family history club, I would have never gotten to know Marydale like I do now. We'd have stayed 'Howdy' friends is all. So that part's about us. Now open it up."

The locket was thick and had a small lever clasp on the side, and when I pushed the release, two hinged disks sprang out. I saw that it accommodated four photos instead of the usual two. Winston had inserted a photo of himself and one of Marydale into the central circles and family pictures with their respective kids and grandkids into the other two. I closed the locket and looked at the inscription on the back: *Winston and Marydale, we become family*, along with the wedding date.

"She'll love it," I said, placing it carefully back into the tissue. "It's perfect."

Winston beamed. "Good, then." He stowed the box away and pointed toward the computer. "You were in the middle of something. I ought to get on my way."

I told him what I'd been working on. "I've probably got about all I'm gonna get today anyhow. You don't happen to know a woman named Charlotte Walker, do you? That's who River bought his place from."

"I know of her," Winston said. "But I don't know her personally."

"You're using the present tense. Does that mean she's still alive?"

"Last I heard she was," Winston said. "She was a friend of my mother's, or leastwise an acquaintance. I'm not sure Miss Lottie had a whole lot of friends. She kept pretty much to herself. I believe somebody told me she was in that nursing home over in Hillsborough. Cottonwood, it's called."

"Yes, I know it. It's a nice facility. Was she married?" I grabbed a notebook and pen and started taking notes.

"Yes," Winston said. "Though I never knew her husband and don't recollect his given name. He died a long time ago. If I'm remembering right, she inherited the place, so she must have been a Harper. When I was young, that place seemed like it was way out in the country. The Harpers owned more land then and the place was a working farm, but it got cut up and sold off over the years. That bit River bought was the original home place."

"Got any candidates in mind for who might be in that glass casket?" I asked.

"No idea in the world," Winston said, shaking his head. "Everybody's calling him 'The Forgotten Man' now."

"Oh, I know," I said, and told him about Claire Calvert's call to Esme. "She's gone over there to keep her company and make sure the vigil folks don't bother her."

"Like Claire doesn't have enough to worry about," Winston said, shaking his head again. "I mean, the idea of the vigil is nice, I guess, but a little strange. It's struck a chord with people. Everybody likes to think they'll be remembered once they're gone."

I thought of the hundreds of ancestors I'd researched for clients over the years and how so many of them were revered. And even how some were despised. Either way, they were remembered. "It's a human thing," I said with a sigh. "Let's just hope someone remembers him as who he was or else he's going to end up being remembered for having been forgotten."

four

Monday morning dawned misty and foggy following a rain shower that swept through in the wee hours of the morning. My first thought was of the grave, covered only with a tarp, but then I remembered River saying they'd tented it when they posted his property.

Esme and I were up early, we'd eaten our breakfast on the run, and by 8:00 a.m., we were ready to make a quick stop by River's place to take a few pictures and get a feel for the property's configuration before heading to the courthouse.

On the drive over I admired how fresh and dewy everything looked, but I hoped the spring storms were done for a while. Marydale and Winston had planned for an outdoor wedding in the gardens at High Ground, the big estate on Crescent Hill that one of our former clients had left to the town. They'd have to move it inside if the weather turned foul. I told Esme about the wedding gift Winston had chosen for Marydale.

"Win is just the dearest man," Esme said. "Those two deserve every bit of happiness this world can offer. They're so good together."

"You and Denny ain't half-bad either, Esme," I said. "What's holding you two up from a march to the altar?"

"We're fine just as we are," Esme said, pulling her sunglasses from the top of her head and practically slamming them onto her face. "I've told you before, I'm never going to marry again. I tied myself to a man once in my life and it was nothing but heartbreak. I like Denton Carlson, but I'm not looking for a husband."

"Like him?" I said. "I think it's a little more than that, Esme."

"Okay, all right," Esme said, her voice singsongy. "You want me to say it? I do love the man. But he surely wouldn't love me if he knew about my gift. It would all be over. I like things just as they are."

"I don't suppose you've heard anything from the Forgotten Man, have you?" I asked in a teasing tone.

"Not a peep, Sophreena," Esme said sharply. "I wish I could choose who comes to me, but you know full well it doesn't work that way."

I ignored the jibe. "Well, anyhow," I said, "I don't think you give Denny enough credit. He's a special guy."

"He is," Esme said with a sigh. "But he wouldn't

understand this, Sophreena. He's a cop—he's trained to be logical and analytical. Roland was a musician and had an artist's outlook on life, so I thought he'd be open. But once he knew, he never looked at me the same way again. He started calling me Fruitcake as an endearment. He thought that was hilarious."

I tried to hide my surprise. Despite how close we were, Esme had never told me much about her short marriage. I knew he was a jazz musician and that she'd married him despite her parents' disapproval. And I knew the marriage had gone sour by the time he died in an auto crash, but that was about it.

"How was Claire last night?" I asked, changing the subject to see if I couldn't cajole Esme into a better mood.

"She was upset when I got there, but we reached River finally and told him what was going on and he reassured her. She was fine after that. I stayed on awhile anyway, just to visit. I found out the woman who sold River the property donated a big chunk of money to the Literacy Council in Claire's name."

"In Claire's name? That's cool."

"Cool, but surprising," Esme said. "They were neighbors, but Claire didn't know the woman well at all. I take it she was kind of a recluse."

"I think she's still alive," I said, and repeated what Winston had told me. "She'd be ninety-seven."

"We need to talk to her," Esme said. "The sooner the better."

"Yeah, I called the nursing home this morning, but they wouldn't even confirm she was a resident. Privacy issues. I think we should take a ride out there this afternoon."

Esme pulled onto the meandering gravel driveway that led to River's house, but only got a few yards before she came to police tape strung across the drive. She stopped the car and shut off the engine with a sigh. "I sure wish Denny would get home."

"Personal or professional wish?" I asked.

"Both. I can't believe I'm saying this, but I believe Jennifer needs him right now. She's gotten herself in a dither. I mean, it's an aggravation, but you don't see River getting het up over everything and it's his home." We opened our doors and climbed out. Stooping under the tape, we began to walk up the drive.

"Yeah," I said. "Jennifer should take a page from her dad, he's so chill."

Just then we heard loud, angry shouting. Quickening our steps, we saw River stalking across the yard from the direction of his house, yelling at the top of his lungs and gesticulating. "Enough's enough! I've had it. Get the hell out of here. Clear out, now!"

I looked to where River's attention was focused and saw a young woman lying on the dirt berm of the grave.

The tarp had been partially pulled back and her white arm stretched into the hole.

Esme and I reached the grave just as River did. "This is getting ridiculous," he said, pointing to the girl, whose long blond hair hid her face. "Now they're sleeping here?"

He reached down to shake the girl's shoulder. "You can't be here, miss. Wake up. Didn't you see this is taped off? You need to get out of here, right now!"

She didn't move, so River shook her again, a little harder this time. "Do you hear me? Are you stoned or something?"

Some of the dirt began to slide into the hole and the girl's head lolled to one side, half dangling into the grave. The left side of her head had been bashed in and there was a puddle of blood beneath her.

I don't know how long we stayed there, frozen, staring. It could have been a minute, it could just as easily have been an hour.

It's strange the things that go through your head when you've seen something that rattles your brain. I felt as if I were completely detached from normal human feelings, and any shame I might ordinarily have about judging her appearance was completely shut down as I took in every detail. I deduced she was a bottle blond, although it was hard to be sure if her roots were showing or if the blood had seeped into the hairline around her scalp. She had a small yellow rose tattoo on her shoulder that was stretched and distorted. Her hands were dirty, and her nails, which looked like they'd once been nicely manicured, were broken and ragged. She had on loose runner shorts and a tank top, with a matching jacket tied around her waist. I'd have guessed she'd been out for a run had it not been for her blinged-out flip-flops. I'd put her at late twenties, maybe early thirties. She was slender and pretty. I'd never seen her before, I was certain of that. I looked around for a purse or a bag, scanned her clothing for pockets, but didn't see any. She appeared to have gotten soaked at one time, and her clothes still looked damp. I had half an inkling that detail might be important, but couldn't quite string together why.

"I'd better call Jenny," River said at last. "Y'all try to back out in your own footprints; even I know that much about crime scenes." He looked behind him and stepped back into his own boot impressions and Esme and I attempted the same maneuver, though Esme had a harder time of it since she had on her stupid high heels again, and when she stepped into the impressions she'd already made, she kept sinking and almost falling over.

Once we were a fair distance away, the spell seemed to be broken and we all looked at one another, coming back to our senses.

"Do you know her?" River asked.

"No," I said, shaking my head.

"Me either. Had you seen her before?" Esme asked, the question directed at River. "Is she one of the people who came out to leave a tribute?"

"No idea," he said. "So many people were here in the last two days and I didn't see half of them, they came after dark. Could be she was one of them, but I don't recognize her." He fished his phone from his pocket and gave a quick nod in our direction. "'Scuse me for a second while I make this call to report a dead person on my property. Again."

five

IT SEEMED TO TAKE FOREVER FOR THE POLICE TO arrive and we stayed in our tight little trio, unconsciously taking one step, then another away from the dead woman, until finally I looked up and we were halfway back to Esme's SUV.

"You must be getting the idea this place is cursed," Esme said to River.

"Not the first time. Not when I plowed up poor Jimmy. But this," he said, gesturing toward the body with a wave of his hand, then reaching up to adjust his cap, "this is some bad juju. I don't think we need the cops to tell us somebody killed her."

"A fall?" I proposed, though I didn't have much faith in the theory.

"Off a skyscaper, maybe," River said. "But there's not one of those handy."

"Did you hear anything last night?" Esme asked. "Surely she would've screamed."

"There was lots of activity out here last night with the vigil and all. I came out once about sunset to make sure nobody was bothering my buddy there"—he nodded toward the grave—"but they all seemed content to stay on the other side of the fence, so I went back in the house and let them have at it."

"Who made that?" I asked, pointing toward the split-rail fence that separated River's property from Claire's. The handmade sign leaning against the fence read: IF YOU WISH TO LEAVE A TRIBUTE FOR THE FORGOTTEN MAN, PLEASE LEAVE IT HERE. DON'T GO ANYWHERE NEAR THE GRAVE. THAT'S THE LAW OF THE LAND AND OF COMMON DECENCY.

"I put that up," River said. "And I think it had some effect. Most of the stuff they left is over there, though a few folks thought they just had to have a look-see into the grave."

There were real and plastic flowers, a menagerie of stuffed animals, a host of handmade signs, and numerous wreaths tacked to the fence, along with enough candles to light up a small airstrip. Not to mention candy wrappers, burnt-paper candle guards, and the stubs of the tiny candles that had no doubt been passed out at last night's vigil.

"Here come the cops," River said. "Jenny's gonna be mighty upset by this."

Jennifer was behind the wheel of the unmarked car

assigned to her and next to her, I saw the outline of a
bulky figure in the passenger seat. At first I thought it
was Denny. I experienced a moment of relief before
realizing it was Lloyd Ramsey, Morningside's chief of
police. Ramsey's a nice enough man, but I wasn't sure
he was the brightest bulb on the Christmas tree. Denny
never trash-talked the man, but "He's a good adminis-
trator" was about the best accolade he could manage.

They both got out of the car, moving with some
urgency, Jennifer toward her father and Ramsey toward
the body.

"Dad, you okay?" Jennifer asked, glancing sideways
at her boss as she touched her father's arm.

"I'm fine, Jen," he said, his voice low. "Just go do
your job."

Jennifer double-timed to catch up with Ramsey.
He'd stopped near the body but he hadn't crouched
down for a closer look. I couldn't say I blamed him,
but I had to wonder if maybe he was feeling a bit inadequate. It was clear he hadn't been out in the field for
a while.

"This is a homicide," he said.

Thank you, Captain Obvious, I thought, literally
biting my tongue to make sure I didn't blurt it out loud.

"Call the medical examiner and tell him to get out
here," Ramsey said, tossing the words to Jennifer over
his shoulder.

I saw the muscles in her jaw clench, but she only muttered a "Yes, sir" as she pulled her phone from her pocket. She made the call, then traded the phone for a small notebook and pen. "I'm going to interview these three so we can clear the scene," she said, turning toward us before Ramsey had a chance to reply.

"Who found her?" she asked, pen poised over the page.

"We all sort of found her at once," River said, and explained how we'd converged on the scene.

"Did any of you touch anything?" she asked, looking first at me and then at Esme.

River raised a hand. "I did," he said. "I thought she was one of the tribute people and that she'd come out here to leave something, then dozed off. She was sort of on her side and it looked like she was sleeping. When she rolled we saw the blood and her head all like that."

"Did you touch anything else?" she asked, scribbling fast. We all shook our heads and she went on to ask about the time frame, what we'd observed, if we knew the victim, if we'd seen anyone else, all the typical questions.

"Okay," she said at last. "If we get any good footprint impressions we'll need your shoes for elimination purposes." She sneered down at Esme's high heels. "And if you think of anything else that might be important, call, but then you two already know how to insinuate yourselves into police cases, don't you?" she asked, her face deadpan.

"Jen," River said, his tone cautionary. "What is it you'd like us to do now?"

"Go on back to the house," she said. "Wait there. The ME may have questions for you. If he does, I'll call you. Otherwise just stay there until I'm done here."

"Us, too?" I asked, jumping in before Esme had a chance to start up an argument, which I could tell she was itching to do.

"Yes, all of you," she said, adding a perfunctory "We appreciate your cooperation" as her boss walked up behind her.

"I'll fix you a cup of coffee," River said. "You'll have to excuse the state of the house; I'm doing a little re-modeling."

This was my first clue that River was the king of understatement. The interior of the old farmhouse was a construction zone. The walls—the ones that hadn't been knocked down—were stripped to the studs and there were tools and supplies stacked everywhere. But the kitchen hadn't been touched. It was so retro it was in again. The turquoise appliances had to have been there since the fifties, along with the white metal cabinets and the deep porcelain sink. But there was a state-of-the-art microwave and a space-age coffeemaker that took up an entire section of countertop by the sink.

"How 'bout a cappuccino?" River asked, and we both nodded eagerly.

"So you're living here with all this going on?" I asked as he motioned for us to sit at the chrome and laminate dining table.

"I don't need much," River said with a shrug. "Kitchen works for as much cooking as I do right now. I'll redo it last, and if I time it right, it'll be done just as my garden starts coming in, assuming anything in my garden survives. The upstairs is finished, so I've got a nice place to sleep and a classy bathroom. During the day I'm mostly outdoors anyhow."

"You're not doing this all yourself, are you?" Esme asked.

"No, no," River said. "I've got a good contractor. I like to do the detail work myself: cabinetry, built-in bookcases, stuff like that. But it'll be awhile before we're ready for that, which is good, since the work-shop's not done yet." He motioned toward the kitchen window, and Esme and I craned our necks to see the skeletal rafters of an outbuilding going up in the corner of the backyard.

"You know, with all that's gone on here this morning, I've not had a chance to get the copy of the deed for you," River said.

"It's okay, we can use the time to figure out what we already know," I said, taking out my notebook.

"Okay," River said, pushing various switches and levers on the coffeemaker with practiced ease, "but that won't take long from my end, since I don't know much."

"Sophreena's good at getting information out of people that they don't even know they know," Esme said.

"Well, let's see. I never set eyes on Charlotte Walker," River said as gurgling noises came from the machine. "When I bought the place I asked questions about the family, just out of my own curiosity, but her lawyer wasn't the jawing type. Either he didn't know or wasn't inclined to say much. He always referred to Charlotte Walker as the Widow Walker, I guess because she'd been a widow for a long time."

"See, there you go," I said. "There's a bit of info we can use."

River grinned.

"How about relatives? Did she have living relatives?"

"Don't know," River said, getting cups and saucers from the cupboard. He held up a finger to signal an interruption and steamed the milk, which made a racket that filled the tiny kitchen. "I suspect she didn't have any kin, 'cause I bought this place and all the contents, kit and caboodle. I'd take it by that she didn't have anybody to leave it to. I kept a few of the things from the house because they were interesting or made me think of something from my own childhood, but I gave the rest away. Haven't tackled the attic yet; it's still stuffed full."

He fiddled with pouring and scooping and served up two aromatic cups before throwing the dish towel over his shoulder. "Nutmeg? Cinnamon?" he asked.

On any other morning that would've made me giggle. River looked like he belonged on a tractor, not acting as our barista.

He caught my smile and shrugged. "Coffee is important to me," he said. "I like to learn about things that are important to me."

He joined us with his own cup and I went back to my notebook. I jotted down the name of the lawyer. He might not be inclined to tell me anything either, but if I made some noise about the undisclosed grave, he might be forthcoming, if only to protect his vulnerable parts. I asked more questions about the property transfer and River answered patiently, though he didn't have much useful information. Then his phone rang and from his side of the conversation it was clear we were being summoned. I raised my mug and took one last satisfying gulp before reluctantly setting it down in its saucer.

When we got back to the tent, the crime scene techs were collecting the markers they'd used to identify details at the scene and the body was being loaded into the wagon.

Ron Solomon, the medical examiner, came over to

greet us. I've known Ron, now a burly man in his mid-fifties, since I was a kid. He and my father had been on the parish council together at St. Raphael's. They'd also been racquetball buddies and, despite being a decade apart in age, fast friends.

Like a lot of people who deal with death for a living, Ron has a dark sense of humor. "Tell you what, Mr. Jeffers," he said, after introductions were made. "I'm gonna give you a twofer. Since I was out here anyhow for the female, I had a look at your skeleton. He's got a hole in his skull, seems like it warrants a further look. I don't think he died of natural causes. Bad news for him, good news for you. We'll be transporting the remains back to the morgue."

"Well, I can't say I'm sorry to be turning this over to you," River said, "but I would like to know what you find out about the fella. I somehow feel responsible for him, crazy as that sounds."

"Not crazy at all," Ron said. "I get it. So does half the town, for that matter. But let's not get ahead of ourselves. Your part may not be over. A lot will depend on what we find out. North Carolina burial laws can be tricky, and family burial grounds are protected. We'll have to keep this area condoned off until we find out more. Sorry."

River sighed and Ron turned and motioned for us to follow him. "Just a few quick questions and I can let you folks be on your way," he said. "What are the odds we'd have two unidentifieds here in this same spot, huh? Probably fifty years apart, but still weird."

"What are you basing the fifty years on, Ron?" I asked.

He pursed his lip. "Nothing remotely scientific," he admitted. "They just look like old bones. I'll be able to run some tests later."

"Have you ever encountered a glass casket before, or heard of one being used in this area?" I asked.

"Nope," Ron answered. "I've read about them, but I've never actually seen one—never expected to, either. I think you can file that invention under 'seemed like a good idea at the time.' Unless you're a canonized saint or a banana republic dictator, I see no reason you need meet your maker in a display case. 'Course this one isn't see-through, but still, very impractical. I take it you're looking into that whole situation?"

"Yes, we're going to do some research for Mr. Jeffers."

"Good call," Ron said, looking back over his shoulder to grin at River. "My money's on Sophreena. She's a bull-dog once she gets her teeth into something, and with Esme on board, you got yourself the Dynamic Duo."

"So I've heard," River said with an amiable smile.

"Anything you can tell us that might shed some more light on how this guy got here, Ron?" I asked.

He stopped a few steps from where the young

woman's body had been found and turned as if to finish this conversation before he entered sacred ground. He tilted his head and thought for a moment, his bushy eyebrows bouncing up and down with the effort. "Well, I suppose you already know this land used to belong to a family named Harper. I think it passed on to Charlotte Walker sometime in the seventies, when Mrs. Harper died. I guess the Harper line died there, too. I didn't know any of them, but my grandpa was a farmer and he rented acreage from the widow Harper after her husband died. There used to be more than three hundred acres on this homestead. So I'm guessing whoever this man is, he'd be related to the Harpers in some way. Now, I did know the Harpers' granddaughter a little. Her name was Marla. Marla Walker. We went to Morningside High at the same time, though she was a couple of grades ahead of me and we definitely didn't travel with the same crowd. I was a nerd, which I know you'll find shocking," he said with a big grin, "and she was a wild child."

"Walker, not Harper? Does she live around here still?" I asked.

"No," Esme answered, shaking her head, then noticed the peculiar looks coming her way. "No," she repeated. "The way you put it sounds like she's deceased."

"Yeah, she is," Ron said, still looking at Esme, his forehead pleated into frown lines. And yeah, her name was Walker. Don't know how she was related to the

Harpers, but I assume she was king to them somehow. She left here while we were still in high school. Ran off with some boy as wild as she was. Bound for California, I believe, but I don't know where they actually ended up. I heard she died in a car crash, must have been about ten or twelve years ago."

"I guess that explains why she didn't inherit the place," I said.

"Doesn't explain why her kids didn't, though," Esme mused, and again she got a piercing look from Ron. "Assuming she had kids," she added quickly, giving me a sidelong glance.

"She did, I think," Ron said. "Although I can't remember for sure. Like I said, I didn't really know her that well and everything I heard about her after she left here was tidbits I picked up at class reunions and such. Sorry, that's about all I've got to contribute. Except one more thing that might mean something as you dig around in this, so to speak. Though it's hard to tell since your backhoe work kind of scrambled things," he said, turning slightly toward River, "I'd say the grave digging was an amateur job. The grave's not deep enough and there's no vault. There's no way they should have expected that coffin to hold up under all that pressure without one. And it didn't."

"Thanks, Ron. Will you let us know what else you find out?" I asked.

"I'll let Mr. Jeffers know," Ron said, "since he's the landowner. He can pass things on, or if he tells me you've got his proxy, you can check in with me."

River nodded. "They're acting as my agents. I'd like them privy to any information you'd be allowed to give me," he said, and I saw the first hint of the decisive businessman he'd been.

It wasn't until we were walking to Esme's SUV that the full impact of what we'd witnessed in the last couple of hours hit me. A young woman in the prime of her life had been literally struck down. The attack had been sudden and unexpected and presumably her killer was still out there, among us. My knees almost buckled.

Esme reached over, pulled my hand through the crook of her arm, and patted it. "Don't look back, Sophreena. Just keep walking. Life's got no reverse, we've got to keep moving forward."

Her warm hand was a comfort and I leaned into her as we walked.

"Were you getting something back there?" I asked after I'd made the arduous climb back into her SUV.

"Mm," Esme said. "Little something. Don't have the first idea who's sending the message, but I knew Marla Walker was dead and that she had kids. There's something off there about relationships. Unfinished business or something unsettled, don't know just what."

"That's pretty vague," I mused, drawing a family tree in my head to better understand the Harper lineage.

"Sorry I can't be more specific, Sophreena," Esme said with a sigh. "I wish this thing was all or nothing, and mostly I wish it was nothing, since it's costing me some precious things I might like in my life. But I don't get any say in it, apparently."

At the courthouse Esme and I took a few minutes in the lobby to plan. We decided on our usual strategy of divide and conquer. Esme would hit vital records, probates, and wills, while I combed land records and taxes.

"Okay," I said, "based on what I found out about the manufacture of glass caskets, I figure whoever's in that grave had to have been put there somewhere between 1915 and, well, long enough ago to have become 'old bones,' as Ron put it. Also, there was that full-grown longleaf pine tree so close to the grave that the roots had grown into it, so it probably hadn't been there at the time of the burial. I think we should narrow the timeline to, say, 1915 to 1950."

"That's reasonable," Esme said.

"And it sounds like the the Harper family owned the land back a long way, probably to land-grant days, but we need to concentrate on who was living there during our time period. Presumably that would be Charlotte Walker's parents."

"Sophreena, what are you forever preaching about presuming things?" Esme said, climbing into the saddle of her high horse.

I sighed. "That presumption contaminates your research. Slip of the tongue. I should have said our working theory is that the Harpers who lived on the land during that time period could be Charlotte Walker's parents and we need to be looking for the records that either verify or disprove that theory."

Esme nodded, satisfied she'd brought me back onto the straight and narrow. We decided on a meet-up time and each went on our merry way.

Four hours and three trips to the vending machine later, we met back in the lobby and compared notes.

"I think I found the right Harpers," Esme said. "Oren and Sadie Harper."

"Yes, that's them," I said. "And I verified how much River paid. Esme, that old farmhouse and a smidge over five acres of land went for a million and a half."

"Doesn't surprise me," Esme said. "Prices keep going up."

Since Morningside had undergone what some disgruntled folks called its "Disneyfication," home and land prices had steadily climbed, a localized anomaly in the national housing slump. A few years back, the

powers that be had launched an aggressive beautifica-
tion campaign and the small downtown area had been
forcibly infused with quaintness and charm. Faux old-
world facades had been added to buildings and public
areas had been elaborately landscaped. Everywhere
you looked there were wrought-iron fixtures and light
stanchions and enough slate and cobblestone to pave a
road to the Atlantic Ocean. Restaurants and boutiques
had sprouted up like crocuses, and a new spa hotel was
slated to go in near the championship golf course. Now
Morningside routinely makes top ten lists of the best
towns to live in. Realtors had been pestering me for the
past few years about representing me when I get ready
to sell my house. Which, unless I'm starving, will be
about the second week of never.

"Fly in the ointment is, I can't find any record that
Oren and Sadie Harper ever had children," Esme said.
"So who is Charlotte Walker to them?"

"She's not their daughter?" I asked.

"Like I said," Esme repeated, not bothering to hide
her irritation, "there's no record they had any children."

I glanced up at the clock in the lobby. "Still time
to get to the nursing home. How about we go see if
Charlotte Walker will tell us herself what she was to
the Harpers?"

six

I TRIED A DIFFERENT TACTIC WITH THE DESK people at Cottonwood. Instead of asking if Charlotte Walker was there, I simply asked for her room number, using the diminutive Winston had used. "We'd like to see Miss Lottie if she's up to having visitors today."

The attendants looked at one another. They seemed to be struggling to figure out how to deal with us. "Are you friends of Miss Lottie's?" one of them asked.

"Sort of," I lied. "She's actually a friend of a friend. I'm a genealogist," I said, veering back onto the righteous path. "I'm doing some research on her family." I handed over one of my business cards.

"I see," the attendant said, though I didn't think she did. She gave the other woman a meaningful look. "It's just that Miss Lottie's been here for nearly three years," attendant number two said, "and she's never had a single visitor."

"That's truly sad, isn't it?" Esme said, picking up the pen for the sign-in sheet and signing both our names. "What did you say that room number was?"

The attendants again attempted a mind meld and number one gave us the just-a-moment pointy finger and picked up the phone. "Let me call back and make sure she's in her room," she said, turning her head as she spoke into the mouthpiece.

"Where else would she be?" Esme groused out of the side of her mouth. "She's ninety-seven, she gonna be out painting the town?"

"Room Eighteen," the attendant said as she put the receiver down. "Right down that hallway."

There was a nurse outside the door of Room 18. "Miss Lottie is very excited to hear she has visitors today," she said, her voice a little too chirpy for me in my present state of upset, fatigue, and hunger.

The hospital bed had been cranked to a sitting position and a tiny birdlike woman sat nestled in the bed linens. She had on a satin bed jacket and her hands were folded primly in her lap. She looked very sweet.

As we went into the room she looked up and her eyes narrowed, focusing on Esme. "'Bout damn time," she said, her lips pinched into a tight line. "Did you bring my root beer?"

*   *   *

"She's a sundowner," I said to Jack that night, sliding a wedge of pizza onto my plate.

Esme had taken Claire Calvert out to supper and I'd been gazing into the fridge hoping dinner might materialize when Jack called to say he was on his way with pizza. I was happy we had the house to ourselves as I was recounting our visit to Lottie Walker. Esme hadn't found the whole thing nearly as amusing as I had.

"She's mostly lucid earlier in the day," I explained. "But near nightfall, she gets befuddled and cranky. She's got a thing for root beer, but their food services don't have it, so one of the attendants brings her a few bottles now and then. She mistook Esme for her root beer supplier and when we didn't have any contraband for her, the whole visit went straight downhill. The woman knows an impressive number of swear words."

"Did you find out anything useful?" Jack asked, picking off a piece of pineapple and throwing it onto a neighboring slice. I like pineapple on my pizza, he doesn't. But he'd gotten it anyway. Sigh.

"Not really, but I'm going back, earlier in the day next time, and without Esme. I think this woman probably knows some good information. I just have to figure out how to get it from her."

"And are you sure you're okay, from the other thing, I mean?"

"You mean finding a dead body first thing on a

Carolina spring morning?" I asked, trying to sound nonchalant.

"Yeah, that," Jack said, reaching over to rub my shoulder.

"No, I'm not okay. It was awful to see the way she died. I've been thinking about it all afternoon. And the fact that she was probably pretty close to my age and that we don't even know who she is makes it even worse."

"I saw Emily at the pizza place. She's already talking about organizing another vigil that will go on until the woman is identified. She's on a Forgotten Man and Forgotten Woman theme now."

I groaned. "I know Emily means well. I know they all mean well, but I wish they'd have some consideration for their living neighbors, too. They really upset poor Claire Calvert last night. That's why Esme's taken her out tonight, to get her away from the people camping out next to her house."

"They're on her property, uninvited. She could call the cops," Jack said. "I'm sure Jennifer would jump at the chance to clear them out."

"I think Jennifer would welcome an excuse to jail them all, but Claire doesn't want to alienate anyone. And the vigil people aren't the problem. It's the fence-jumpers. I think it makes Claire feel vulnerable to be there alone with all those people around."

PICTURE THEM DEAD   71

"Especially now, I'd think," Jack said, "what with Quentin being released from prison, although I don't know if I quite understand that whole dynamic. Did you know she went to visit him regularly while he was in the pen?"

"No, I didn't. Wow, you'd think she'd never want to set eyes on him again, wouldn't you?"

"I suspect that would be my reaction," Jack said. "But she's probably a more forgiving person than I am. I can tell you who is not happy about having him back in the community—Nash Simpson. Though I guess that's understandable. If I have my facts straight about how that whole thing went down, Quentin came pretty close to killing Nash in that fight. Nash would like Quentin tarred, feathered, and run out of town on a rail, and I think there are a few people around who'd agree with him. People love Claire Calvert, and they were out for blood when that happened to her."

"Do you remember it? I mean, do you remember when it happened?" I asked.

"Yeah, don't you?"

"Some of it, but I was so absorbed in what was going on with me at that time, I wasn't really tuned in to the outside world. My mother was dying and I wanted to spend every minute with her, and at the same time I was struggling to work out how I was going to live without her. It wasn't a good time for me."

"I'm sorry, Soph," Jack said, kneading my shoulder again. He took the plate from my lap and threw it onto the pizza box, then drew me over to put his arm around me. With his free hand he reached over to take mine and twirl the birthstone ring my parents had given me. It felt wonderful to be snuggled up like this, but this was always, always, when the elephant came strolling into the room. Our relationship had been stuck in the zone between friendship and romance for months now. And it seemed neither of us wanted to be the one to push it forward or try to rewind. Every time I steeled my nerves to bring it out into the open, I'd get two words in and choke. What if I screwed it up and lost Jack for good? There were signs, but on the other hand, what if I was completely misreading him and he was struggling for a way to let me down gently?

"Soph?" he said now, his voice sounding far away. "Can we talk about something?"

"Sure," I said, my heart thumping. "What is it?" I felt excitement, or dread, or maybe simple relief. Whatever emotional cocktail it was, it was making my pizza revolt.

Just then the doorbell chimed and I wished more than anything for a vaporizing gun to zap whoever was standing on the front porch mashing that button.

"Hold that thought," I said as I went to answer it.

I found all six feet five of Denny Carlson standing

on the front steps in the drizzling rain, a travel bag hanging from a strap on his shoulder. An airport taxi was pulling away from the curb. He held up a hand. "Tell Esme I know I'm supposed to call, but I just got in and my phone's dead."

I motioned him in, holding the storm door open as wide as it would go to accommodate his bulk. He dropped his bag in the front hall and shook like a dog.

"Esme's not here, Denny. She's out to dinner with Claire. I thought you weren't due back until Friday."

Before he could answer, Esme's SUV pulled into the drive, her headlights sweeping us as she maneuvered close to the house. She got out and ran to the porch, ducking inside as I pushed the storm door open again.

"Denton, what're you doing here?" she asked as she brushed water from her sleeves. "I thought you weren't due back until Friday."

"There's an echo in here," he said. "And welcome home, Denny, I've missed you."

"Yes, yes, that, too," Esme said, offering him a cheek to kiss.

"The chief called me back," Denny said as we all moved into the family room. "Because of the homicide, which I understand you two knew about before anybody else."

"How did Jennifer take it that the chief called you in?" Esme asked.

"About like you'd expect," Denny said, nodding a hello to Jack. "But truth be told, I think she may be relieved. Jennifer's a good cop, but she's too close to this one and she knows it. She wants to protect her dad, and that's how it ought to be, but somebody's got to be looking at the case with colder eyes."

"Let me fix you something to eat," Esme said, and my heart felt a tiny lilt at the prospect of them moving to the kitchen so Jack and I could get back to that thing he wanted to talk about. But that hope was squelched when Denny declined.

"A cup of coffee would be nice, if you wouldn't mind. This isn't an official visit. I came by because I wanted to see you, Esme. But since I'm here, I'd like you to fill me in on what you saw this morning—just a few questions. I know Jennifer took your statements, but I'd rather hear it from you two. I need to hit the ground running if we're going to clear this case quick. Unless I'm interrupting something here," he said, sweeping a hand toward the pizza box.

"No, no, it's fine," Jack said, though I silently begged to differ. "I need to get going anyhow. I've got a job over in Greensboro tomorrow. Need to be on the site by eight a.m. sharp. I'd better get some shut-eye."

"I'll walk you out," I said, jumping up from the ottoman.

I was still hoping we'd be able to pick back up on

the conversation we'd started, but the moment had passed.

"We'll talk later," he said, stopping to pull on his jacket. He gave me a brotherly peck on the cheek, which I enjoyed but also found woefully inadequate.

As I watched him run through the rain to his truck, I was quite put out with Esme and Denny. All I'd wanted was a little more time for Jack to tell me what he wanted to talk about. They'd ruined it. Or saved me, delayed an inevitable heartbreak. Who knew?

My mind kept jumping from one thing to another as I drove to the Raleigh-Durham airport on Tuesday morning to pick up Dee Thompson, Marydale's daughter. She was coming in early for the wedding so she could be a part of all the hubbub and was planning to stay a week afterward to help run Marydale's paper-craft shop while Marydale and Winston were on their honeymoon. Dee is the closest thing I have to a sister. Our mothers had been the closest of friends and we'd grown up side by side. We still stay in constant contact, mostly through texts, emails, and phone calls. I was excited about a real visit.

Denny's few questions the night before had turned into an exhaustive exegesis of every detail we'd observed when we'd found the woman at River's place. It

was what made him a good cop, and I usually appreciated his thoroughness, but I hadn't been in the mood.
I knew it was unforgivably callous, but I'd been more
concerned with Jack and the missed opportunity for a
talk that might have resolved some of our issues.

But now, in the clear light of day, I was thinking of
the dead woman, the image of her ruined face ingrained
in my mind. Who was she and why had she been at that
place at that time? She hadn't appeared to be carrying
anything to leave as a tribute, but maybe she'd already
left it by the fence. Was this somehow tied up with
the Forgotten Man or was it simply a bizarre conver-
gence of ill timing and bad luck? If the man who killed
her was someone she knew, it probably hadn't been
planned. If it had, he would have come with a more
efficient weapon than whatever he'd used to bludgeon
her. And what had he used? A rock? I didn't see any
bloody rocks anywhere near her. And why did I assume
the murderer was a man?

A stray thought hit me like a bolt out of nowhere
and I almost veered off I-40 into the breakdown lane.
River had been highly annoyed by the people invading
his property. What if he'd finally had enough? What
if he'd snapped? What did I really know about River
Jeffers? I knew he was a driven businessman and that
underneath his laid-back, man-of-the-land persona,
there was a wealthy man who could afford just about

anything he wanted and was accustomed to having his way. It was clear that establishing himself on this land according to his vision was important to him. How important? I pushed the thought away. It was ridiculous. Though I'd known River only a short time, I trusted my own judgment and I was convinced he was a good guy. A principled guy. A compassionate guy. I'd sooner suspect Jennifer, which might not be so far-fetched, I mused, considering how protective of her father she was. Then I caught myself. I didn't have the warm fuzzies for Jennifer, but she certainly wasn't a murderer. What was wrong with me?

I shook my head and tried to concentrate on something else. I hoped to get back to Morningside in time to go out to Cottonwood to talk with Lottie Walker again. She might be a little on the ornery side, but I had a feeling she was the key to finding out who the occupant of that glass casket was. I wanted to go without Esme, but I didn't want to have to explain to her why I didn't want her along, which was because she had no patience whatsoever with difficult people. Today was my chance, since she'd be tutoring kids at her church all afternoon. Kids were the exception to Esme's irritability. She had all the patience in the world when it came to the wee ones.

I'd spent two hours the previous evening poring over the copies of the records Esme and I had brought from the courthouse and the copy of the deed River had brought over yesterday afternoon. I hadn't found anything useful for identifying the Forgotten Man, but I now knew quite a bit about the Harper family's history in America.

Whoever Lottie Walker was, it was unlikely that she was the natural child of Oren and Sadie Harper, but clearly she had some sort of relationship to them. Why else would they have left her everything they had in this world? My single goal for this afternoon was to find out what Lottie Walker's birth name was. That would put me on a new trail. Anything else I found out I'd count as a bonus.

I managed to snag a prime spot in the parking deck right next to Terminal A and hustled inside so I'd be there to greet Dee. I joined the crowd at the bottom of the escalator and milled around, vying for a spot where I could see the top of the platform.

I spotted Dee's blond hair, styled in a new pixie cut, and called out to her as she descended. I'm not normally a big emoter, but Dee brings out the kid in me, and we were both squealing and hugging like teenage girls at a boy-band concert.

"Is that your only bag?" I asked, eyeing her compact carry-on.

"Yep, this is it," she said.

"Only you could pack enough for two weeks into that tiny bag," I said.

"I pack like the engineer I'll soon be," Dee said. "Everything has at least two functions and I can buy things here if need be. It'll still be cheaper than paying to check a bag."

Dee had an undergraduate degree in economics and had worked a short stint in New York as a financial analyst before deciding she was on the wrong career path. She'd found she was more interested in her brother's profession than her own. Brody was an architect, and the more he talked about his work, the more Dee became unsatisfied with hers. So she'd quit her job and gone to Chicago to get a degree in architectural engineering. She and Brody had plans to open a firm together in North Carolina once she graduated.

"We have our Genealogy Club meeting tonight," I told her once we were in the car. "You'll have to come. We've put together a really cool scrapbook for Marydale and Winston. It's beautiful, if I do say so myself. Lots of exotic papers, and I did all the calligraphy for it. All modesty aside, I do have a beautiful hand."

"You do," Dee said, "all modesty way aside, but is it supposed to be a surprise? How did you get all the stuff without Mother knowing? She knows the inventory in that shop like it's hardwired into her brain."

"Roxie ordered it all for me," I said, "off the books."

Dee's cousin Roxie came over from Chapel Hill every Thursday to keep the shop so Marydale could have a weekday off. She was a sweet gal, but a bit of a scatterbrain. When Marydale announced she was getting married Roxie had been floored and blurted out, "But you're old," before her brain could stop her tongue. She was never going to live it down.

"Oh, Roxie," Dee said. "Bless her heart. Yeah, I'd love to come to the club tonight. I want to see everyone, especially Jaaa-ack," she said, reaching over to poke me in the ribs.

I slapped her hand away, concentrating on a lane switch. Dee was the only one I'd confided in about my feelings toward Jack. "I can't take any teasing about that right now," I warned her. "Not after last night." I told her about our interrupted conversation.

"Sophie, you're torturing yourself," she said. "You've lived in this in-between long enough. You need to just put it out there and see what happens."

"And what if he doesn't feel the same way? Then it will be all awkward. I'm not sure we could ever get back to being just friends. It would be horrible."

"Well, you can't go on like this forever, either," Dee said, digging her sunglasses from her bag. "There's got to be tension."

"Yeah," I said with a sigh. "I've got tension, anyway. I'm not sure anyone else is aware of the situation."

Dee gulped a laugh. "Everyone else is aware, Sophie, everyone in the club and probably half the town. You know how Morningside is. And speaking of which, what is all this drama over that grave? A glass coffin? That's so creepy weird."

"And it just keeps getting weirder," I said. "When's the last time you talked to Marydale?"

Dee frowned. "Must have been night before last. Why?"

I told her about finding the body at River's place.

"Oh, my God, Sophreena, that must have been awful," she said.

I nodded. "On a scale of one to ten, it was about a seventeen," I said.

"Did you know her? Is it somebody from Morningside?"

"No, no clue who it is." I gave her a rundown on the facts, which didn't take long. "No identifying marks except a rose tattoo, and that's certainly not very unusual these days."

"A rose tattoo?" Dee asked.

"Yeah, on the shoulder. Only a butterfly would be more of a cliché, right? But at least she went for a more distinctive color, her rose was yellow, not red."

"Soph, I think I know who it is!"

seven

I ASKED DENNY TO MEET US AT MY HOUSE; I DIDN'T want to bring the taint of a murder investigation into the happy wedding kerfuffle at Marydale's. He pulled up at the curb as Dee and I were getting out of my car. I was relieved to see that Jennifer wasn't with him—I had enough stress in my life at the moment.

All of us automatically gravitated toward the kitchen, the room with the coffeemaker. I set a pot to brew while Denny talked with Dee.

"So you knew this woman?" Denny asked, pulling out his trusty notebook and clicking his ballpoint.

"Maybe," Dee answered. "I can't be sure and I wouldn't know her today if I met her on the street, but that tattoo, I can't imagine there would be that many women her age with a yellow rose tattoo who would have some connection to that place."

"Her name?" Denny prompted.

"Sherry. Sherry Burton. At least that was her name when I knew her. I don't know if she ever married."

"And when and how did you know her?" Denny asked, which was a question I wanted an answer to as well. Dee and I had known mostly all the same people when we were growing up, and I didn't remember anyone named Sherry Burton.

"When I was in middle school. I didn't know her well, but I met her a few times."

"I didn't know her at all," I said, and realized it came out like an accusation.

Dee frowned. "I don't think you ever met her. She was the granddaughter of the old woman who lived there, the one who was like a hermit. I've forgotten her name."

"Lottie Walker," I said.

"Yeah, that sounds right."

"How did you meet Sherry and I didn't?" I asked, setting steaming mugs of coffee on the table.

"She came to stay with her grandmother for a couple of weeks in the summertime. She had a younger brother, too, but I don't remember his name. Anyway, they came two or three summers in a row. It was always during the time you were visiting your grandmother in Missouri. I was looking for someone to hang out with while you were away, and Laney Easton had somehow met Sherry. I started hanging out with the two of them the first summer Sherry was here, but it didn't last long. My mother put the kibosh on it quick-in-a-hurry. She thought Sherry was too wild. But Laney's mother apparently didn't get the memo because Laney hung out with Sherry the whole time she was here. They were thick as thieves."

"Laney Easton, the village councilwoman?" Denny asked.

"The very same," I said. "Hard to imagine, I know, but we were good buddies way back then. Laney outgrew us and joined the in-crowd by the time we got to high school, but we were the three amigos there for a while."

"Now she's a power player," Denny said. "Youngest ever on the village council, on boards and committees and I don't know what all. So she'd know Sherry Burton?"

Dee nodded. "She did back then, at least. That first summer, while I sat home totally bored and waiting for Sophreena to get back from Missouri, Laney and Sherry and a couple of boys we knew from school were into all kinds of mischief, sneaking out at night and going on adventures. She got that tattoo when she was here. I don't know who she talked into giving it to her because she was clearly underage, but she managed it."

"And who were these boys?" Denny asked, scribbling in his notebook.

"Gavin Taylor and Bryan Mason. I don't know if Gavin still lives here or not, but I think Bryan is running the pro shop at the golf course. He was the last time I was home, anyway."

"He is," I confirmed. "Gavin's still here, too. He's a mechanic at Joe Porter's service station."

"Oh, I know Gavin," Denny said, packing a lot of meaning into the words. "And do you have any idea where Sherry lived or anything else about her recent life?"

"Not really," Dee said. "I think she had a pretty bad home life growing up. It seemed like her mother brought her and her brother here just to dump them and they hated it here. The grandmother didn't seem too thrilled about it either. She never did anything with them, as far as I could see."

Denny scribbled some more. "Okay, then, looks like the brother, assuming he's still among the living, would be the next of kin, unless she was married. No wedding ring, but that doesn't necessarily mean she wasn't," he said.

"I hope I haven't given you a bum steer," Dee said. "I mean, not that I hope it's Sherry, or that I hope it's anyone I know, or anyone at all. I mean, it's terrible that someone was killed like that." She looked over at me with a pleading look. "What do I mean, Sophie?"

"You mean you need to get to your mother's to prepare for one of life's joyful moments and let Denny get back to the cop work," I said.

"Guess that's my cue," Denny said, stashing his notebook and handing over his empty mug. "I'll let you know what I find out."

After we heard the front door close, Dee looked up at me, her eyes wide. "I don't think I've ever known anyone personally who died like that—before their time, and violently. It's really unsettling."

"All the more reason to get you to Marydale's and involved in something happy. You are happy about this, aren't you?"

Dee pursed her lips. "I am. But that doesn't mean I don't have a few reservations. I know Winston is a good guy, but I'm nervous for my mom. She's been on her own for a long time. This will be a big adjustment for her, and for Brody and me. But I know we'll work it out."

"That's what good families do," I said, trying to bat down the green-eyed monster rearing his ugly head. I envied Dee. Families were everything to me professionally, but I have few blood relatives left, and those are distant relations living in faraway places. Thank goodness I had Esme.

This time the front desk attendants at Cottonwood hardly even looked up from their paperwork when I signed the visitor log.

I hurried back to Room 18 and pushed the door open a crack. "Miss Lottie, okay if I come in?" I called in a half whisper.

"Come on in," said a voice both frail and irked. "Not like I have a choice about who comes prancing through here all hours. Who are you? You that girl that brings the books? I done told you I don't read no more. Bad eyes. Take your cart on to somebody who can still make out that tiny print. Don't know why they have to make it so small anyhow."

All this before I'd even set foot in the room. I explained again who I was and for a moment she seemed to understand. "Yes, I recollect, you came before. You wanted me to tell you a story, didn't you, little girl? Well, I don't know any stories, and besides, I'm tired. You go on now, go outside and play."

I sighed. Miss Lottie may have been a sundowner, but she wasn't too sharp at noon either.

Just then there was a smart rap on the door and Miss Lottie yelled out a "Come in" that didn't sound in the least welcoming.

"It's Carlos, Miss Lottie," a young male attendant said. "You want to go down to the dining room today or should I bring you a tray?"

"Tray," Miss Lottie said. "And a root beer."

"I've told you we don't have root beer," Carlos said, "but I can bring you a soft drink. They have cola and lemon-lime and I think they've got orange soda, too. Does one of those sound good?"

"Root beer or nothing," Miss Lottie said, pursing her lips and turning away from him like a petulant child.

Carlos gave me a wink and said, "Okay, then, I'll be back with your tray in a few minutes." He cupped his hand and whispered, "She's usually a little more sociable after she eats."

He was right. When he brought the tray, he asked if I'd like to help her with it or if he should stay. I looked at the tray stocked with fruit gelatin, some kind of chopped meat in gravy on a piece of toast, a mound of mashed potatoes, a carton of milk, and a glass of water. Of course I wanted Carlos to stay and feed her, but I figured doing it myself might help me build a bond with her.

It did, but it cost me. She complained about everything, from the way I held the spoon to the tone of my voice. She muttered under her breath about all my ineptitudes, punctuating the litany now and again by swearing at me. Man, she was a grumpy old lady. She ate like a bird, but still, she did seem to get a degree more civil with each tiny bite.

"Miss Lottie," I said, holding out a spoonful of mashed potatoes, "you grew up at the old Harper place, right?"

"Old Harper place," Miss Lottie repeated.

"Do you remember someone being buried there? Was there a family cemetery on the property?"

"No, I told the lawyer, I want to be buried at Plainview. That's where Howard is and I want to be laid out right by him. I bought the plot when I buried him. Stone's already there. All that's left is to put the date on when I go."

"I'm glad you have that taken care of," I said. "Are all the Harpers buried at Plainview, too?"

"Lord, no," Miss Lottie said, giving me a glare. "They were all Methodists, they don't go to Plainview. They get planted at Memory Gardens."

"All of them?" I asked, trying to sound casual. "None of them were buried on the old Harper place?"

"You're trying to trick me," she said, narrowing her eyes. "I grew up there. Lived there most of my life. Can't remember the time before I lived there. Fact, I hardly remember anything that came before that night. And can't forget a minute of what happened, though I surely wish I could."

"What night was that, Miss Lottie?" I asked, trying not to look at the mystery meat as I scooped up a bite and offered it to her.

"Is it night already?" Miss Lottie asked. "I get so mixed up in here. They forget to open my shades and half the time I don't know if it's night or day."

"No, it's still daytime, Miss Lottie," I said. "I was asking what you meant when you said you couldn't remember a time before that night. You were telling me about when you were still a girl and living at the Harper place."

"The Harpers are good people," she said. "Real good people."

"I've heard that about them," I said. "Did you grow up with Oren and Sadie Harper?"

"Sadie was a beautiful woman, wasn't she?" Miss Lottie said. "And brave. She had to do some hard things in her life, but she did what she had to do and I thank the Lord for that. I could have hated her for what happened in some ways, but I didn't. Not a bit of it. I loved her like she was my mother."

"What kind of hard things did she have to do?" I asked, excited that we finally seemed to be getting on some kind of track, a meandering one to be sure, but at least we had momentum. I scooped up another spoonful of the meat concoction.

She leaned over to take the bite, then immediately spat it onto her tray. "That's the worse thing I ever tasted," she squawked. "You trying to poison me?"

I wanted to point out that she'd already eaten two hearty spoonfuls of the sludge so she'd already be dead if I was trying to poison her, but we'd been trucking along so nicely and I was hoping I could get her back.

"No, ma'am, I promise I'm not," I said. "I'm sorry if it isn't good. Here, let's try a bite of the gelatin."

She accepted the quivering orange spoonful and seemed to enjoy it so much that she forgave me for trying to kill her with the mystery meat. She pulled a few impressive swallows of milk from her straw, then pushed the tray away.

"Miss Lottie, could you tell me your maiden name?" I asked.

"Gave it up when I married Howard. I was an old maid when I met Howard Walker. Thirty-three years old and never even had a beau. I never did think about myself the way he saw me. It was new and strange, and just mighty wonderful," she said, her eyes now staring off into the distance as if I wasn't in the room. "We run off and got hitched quick, and the next thing I know I've got a baby in my belly and Howard's got hisself killed down at the mill. I had no business raising a child. Some women ain't cut out to be mamas and the proof is in the pudding. Marla didn't turn out too good. She's always in one kind of trouble or another. The only time she comes around is when she needs bailing out of some mess. Oh Lordy, is she here?"

"No," I said, "she's not here, Miss Lottie. But I'm sure she'd love to see you."

Miss Lottie puffed out her cheeks and let out a whoosh of stale-smelling breath. "I 'spect not," she said.

"You don't know Marla if you think that. She'd as soon kick you as kiss you."

I wonder where she got that temperament, I thought. "Could you tell me your maiden name?" I tried again. "The name you were born with."

"Charlotte," she said. "It was my mama's mama's name, but everybody always called me Lottie, long as I can remember. I'm Lottie."

"And your last name?"

She looked at me and her eyes seemed to bobble along lazily in their sockets. Apparently an afternoon nap was about to happen, ready or not.

"Right, that was my name," she said, blinking very slowly.

"Yes, your maiden name, Miss Lottie. What was it?"

"Right," she said, the word slurring.

And she was out, her snore like the purr of a kitten.

The afternoon hadn't been a complete loss. I'd learned that Miss Lottie was indeed Marla's mother and likely the grandmother of the murdered young woman. But that raised other questions. If Lottie had living grandchildren, why would she give so much of the money she'd gotten from selling the place to the Literacy Council and not to them? Assuming she hadn't planned to leave something to them. After all, the woman wasn't dead yet.

Maybe she'd left them something in her will; that is, if the nursing home didn't eat it all up before she passed.

Esme was in the kitchen preparing a vegetable tray for the club meeting when I returned. I don't know why we continue to call ourselves a club. We have no real structure, no bylaws or rules, we're just friends. Still, we do set aside this time each week to work on our family histories and talk about our progress, and most Tuesday nights, we walk down to Marydale's shop after we eat and spend some time working on our heritage scrapbooks.

Winston's ex-wife, may she live out her life happily far, far away, called us the "Ancient History" club, and she didn't mean it as a compliment. She thought things from the past were best left there, not "dredged up for other people to paw over." And she'd really soured on the whole thing when Winston traced one branch of his lineage back to a slave woman.

"What do you want me to do?" I asked Esme. "Make some dip?"

"No, I'll do it. This kitchen is too small for both of us. You go on out to the workroom and see what I got done this morning."

"Okay," I said, though I couldn't figure out how the kitchen had gotten too small for both of us to work in it. We'd done it a million times. "You got my message, right? About Dee identifying the dead woman?"

"Yes, wasn't that something? Denny told me about it, too. I invited him to come tonight since this isn't a regular meeting."

"Good," I said. "What, specifically, did you want me to look at in the workroom?"

"I set up all the records we've collected so far for River's research and I got about halfway done with entering it into the database. I marked where I got to, maybe you can finish up before everybody gets here? And I went through that box of pictures and pulled out all the ones that were taken on the Harper place, for the scrapbook."

I'm normally the methodical one, but over the time we've worked together, Esme has become a conscientious record keeper. She'd set out the records, sorted the way I like them, and had even taped a long sheet of paper to the worktable so I could start a time line, one of my favorite tools. I picked up a ruler and a pencil and started ticking in dates. Eventually this would document everything we could learn about the Harper place, but for now I concentrated on the time frame from 1900 to 1950, since finding the identity of the Forgotten Man was the focus. I worked away on that for a few minutes, but then the guilt got to me. There was still a stack of records that needed to be entered into the genealogy program, so I woke up the computer and set to it.

I kept a close eye on the clock, since I knew I needed to tidy up the family room before our meeting. I finished with fifteen minutes to spare, but before I shut down the computer I ran the function that gives a display of everything that's been entered so that I could see what Esme had put in earlier. I glanced over the screen and hooted a laugh so loud it brought Esme to the doorway.

"What's so blessed funny?" she asked. "You scared me. I thought you were having some kind of fit in here."

"Miss Lottie's marriage certificate to Howard Walker," I said, pointing to the screen. "I didn't see this yesterday. Charlotte Wright and Howard Walker. Her birth name was Wright. She tried to tell me this afternoon and I didn't get it. Her name was Wright and I thought she was acknowledging that she understood my question. Anyhow, now we know her name. We just have to figure out how she's related to the Harpers."

Esme frowned and came over to look at the screen. She traced her finger along until she came to the marriage license info for Oren and Sadie Harper in 1915.

"I couldn't read this on our copy but I scanned it and put it through the guesser today," she said, using her euphemism for a piece of software we use that extrapolates to complete the text or image in old documents. We don't rely on what the guesser comes up with, but sometimes it can give us good clues to

pursue. Esme had the entry highlighted in yellow, a signal that the information was tentative. Oren T. Harper
had married Sadie Marie Wright in September 1915.
She was seventeen and he was twenty-one.

"So Miss Lottie is likely from Sadie's branch of the
family, not the Harper side. We need to switch gears."

"But, Sophreena, River tasked us with finding out
who's in that coffin, not with tracing yet another branch
of the family's history," Esme said.

"I know. But I think the answer to the question of
who is in that grave lies with Miss Lottie. If our time
frame is right, she'd likely have been alive when that
body was buried there. She'd have been a child but
maybe old enough to remember. And since we're not
having any luck with the official records, so far she's our
best shot. We'll have to go back to Cottonwood, probably a few more times."

"Not we, you," Esme said firmly. "I'll do the entry, or
make myself useful otherwise, but I can't deal with that
ornery old woman."

I could have said it takes one to know one.

But I didn't.

The club meeting was festive and mostly centered
around the upcoming nuptials, but we did manage to
get some business in. We all gave our usual reports

about what we'd worked on since the last meeting. Not surprisingly, Marydale and Winston had nothing to report because they'd been busy with wedding plans. Through having her DNA tested, Coco had found a long lost cousin who had some information about her father's side of the family. She was amused to find out her great-grandfather had been a gandy dancer for the railroad. "So I've got a fan dancer on my mother's side and a gandy dancer on my father's. No wonder I can't sit still."

Jack was finally getting back to working on his own family lines. He'd started the whole endeavor to find out if the family legend about being related to the infamous Ford who shot and killed the outlaw Jesse James was true. But when he got the proof, it put him in a blue funk for a while. I fully understood this, since I was going through something similar, as I reported to the group when it was my turn.

"I've had a breakthrough," I said. "I did a Skype interview with a woman who was a friend of my late grandmother, my mother's adoptive mother. She's elderly, but her memory is sharp and she remembered details I won't recount since this is a night for happy things. Suffice it to say, my mother's adoption was, as I suspected, quite irregular, almost certainly illegal, and, I fear, unethical. But now I've got some dates and names of other people involved and at some point

I'm going to make a trip to the Marshall Islands to see what I can find out. For now, I'm letting it sink in for a while."

"Can I have a turn?" Dee asked, raising her hand. "I know I'm just a visitor, but I'd like to report that I'm about to have a whole new family." She reached over to pat Winston's thigh, and I could have hugged her when I saw the smile spread over his rugged face. Marydale, too, was beaming.

Esme took that cue to give them our gift and Marydale burst into tears as she leafed through the book. The front part was filled with pictures we'd gathered of the two of them taken over the past few years; the rest of the book was filled with scrapbook pages we'd designed, waiting for new photos and memories. The remainder of the evening was spent reminiscing over the pictures.

Denny and Jack stayed on after everyone else had left. I almost invented some pretext to get Jack out to the workroom with me to see if we could resume our talk, but it would have been too obvious. The chatter soon came around to the topic that was never far from our minds these days, the murder at River's place.

"I understand you've been out to see the grandmother," Denny said. "Is she of sound enough mind for me to do a notification? We haven't been able to find any other kin."

"She comes and goes. Today when we talked she didn't even realize her daughter was dead. But she has moments when she's clear. You haven't been able to locate the brother?"

"Not yet," Denny said. "You get a full name or location on him in your poking around, you let me know."

"Any idea why she was killed?" Esme asked.

"Nothing solid," Denny admitted with a sigh.

"She must have died sometime after the vigil was over," Jack said. "Or surely somebody would've seen or heard something. And it must have been after that rainstorm came through. That was a hard rain. You think she went to the tent looking for shelter?"

The tumblers clicked. Of course, that's why it had been important that her clothing and hair looked soaked through.

"Could be," Denny said. "She died sometime in the mischief hours. Rainstorm moved through here about two thirty a.m. The ME puts time of death between two and four a.m. Now we've just gotta find out what evil creature was afoot in the land at that time."

"Have you talked to any of the people who were friends with her when we were kids?" I asked.

Denny nodded. "Talked to all three of them. Laney says she hasn't seen or talked to her in years, but Bryan says he kept in touch. According to him she bounced around a lot. Last he knew, she was a bartender down in Miami. They got together when he was there for a golf expo a while back. But he hadn't heard from her lately. We've contacted the department down there."

"How about Gavin?" I prompted when Denny didn't go on.

"Gavin was a little dodgier. He first said he didn't know her. Then he knew her but hadn't talked to her since they were kids. Then she wrote to him while he was undergoing his 'unfortunate incarceration' for auto theft. He swears, maybe a little too vociferously, that he didn't know she was in these parts until he heard about the murder."

"Are you saying he's a suspect?" I asked, almost laughing at the idea.

"You know the answer to that, Sophreena. Everybody's a suspect until they're ruled out. And since his alibi is that he was home in bed, alone, where any sensible person would be at that hour, I haven't struck him off the list."

"Well, she was staying somewhere," Esme said. "Did you check the local motels?"

"Gee, why didn't I think of that," Denny said with a laugh. "That sounds like something a cop might do."

Esme gave him a withering look.

He cleared his throat. "Yes, we checked all the hotels and motels, B and Bs, guest cabins, and rooming houses in a fifty-mile radius. We're on the lookout for cars that haven't moved in a couple of days and checking bus, train, and airline records. So far, zip."

The room fell silent for a moment until finally Esme spoke up.

"Well, she didn't fall from the sky," she said. "And she must have had more with her than what she was wearing. Sooner or later you'll turn up something."

Denny nodded. "I sincerely hope so."

"At least she's not the Forgotten Woman anymore," I said. "She's got a name."

"But I wonder who'll remember her," Esme said, her voice soft. "And whether they'll remember her fondly."

eight

I WAS AT COTTONWOOD BRIGHT AND EARLY THE next morning, sans Esme and armed with a six-pack of root beer.

"You're getting to be a regular," the desk attendant said when I signed in. "I think Miss Lottie is in the community room. You can visit with her there if you'd like, or if she'd rather have you to herself, you can push her back to her room. Community room's right down that short hall." She pointed to a wide entryway at the far end of the lobby, but I didn't need directions; all I had to do was follow the cacophony of voices accompanied by someone plinking away on a painfully out of tune piano.

Miss Lottie was sitting with three other women at a table in the corner and seemed to be, wonder of wonders, laughing merrily. She and another woman were in wheelchairs. The other two looked too young to be in a nursing home. As I approached the table, Miss Lottie frowned, but I had the sense it wasn't a grumpy frown, simply that she was concentrating. As the other women looked up, I introduced myself and told them I was a genealogist and was tracing the Harper family history and that Miss Lottie was helping me. All true as far as it went.

"I knew the Harpers," the other wheelchair-bound woman said. Her voice was strong and her big eyes were further magnified by thick lenses. "I knew them nearly a century ago, can you imagine that? We didn't live but a mile from each other, but that was a long way back then, when you had to do it on foot. It took us coming into this place all these years later to become friends, didn't it, Lottie?"

Miss Lottie nodded, but I wasn't sure she'd heard or understood.

"Maybe you can help me, then, too," I said. "What's your name?"

"I'm Ruth Wilkins. I can't say I knew Mr. Oren and Miss Sadie all that well; I was but a child. But they were friends of my mama and daddy's. I know they were good folks."

The other two ladies introduced themselves. The first was named Constance McNally and she looked far too young to be in a retirement home. When I said as much she explained that they lived in the apartments in the other part of the complex and that they came over to visit every few days. The other one introduced herself as Margaret Roman. She was petite and lively and had a dandelion fuzz of snow-white hair. She was excited to hear I was a genealogist, and I braced myself for a long recitation of her family's illustrious history, which is usually what I get when I meet an amateur family historian. But she surprised me.

"I just love family stories," she said, her smile the sweetest I believed I'd ever seen on a grown-up's face. "I come over here and talk to the people and write down what they remember about their families, then I give my notebooks to their family members later on when the person is, you know, no longer with us." She whispered the last words. "The families seem to appreciate it. It amazes me how many people don't ever think to do that until it's too late and then wish they had."

"Preach it, sister," I said, which earned me another smile.

"I've even done some of Miss Lottie's family history, haven't I, Lottie?"

Miss Lottie looked at her blankly.

"You remember I asked you about your birth date and growing up out at the farm and all," Margaret prompted.

"Charlotte Eugenia Wright Walker, born June sixteen in the Year of Our Lord nineteen hundred and seventeen. I was born at home in Maryland with an old granny woman the only one to help. I killed my mother coming into the world. Happy birthday to me," Miss Lottie said, setting her water glass down hard on the table, her expression dour.

"Now, dearie," Margaret said, patting Miss Lottie's hand, "it's a sad thing that your mother died in child-birth, but you oughtn't to say you killed her. That's not true."

"True enough," Miss Lottie countered.

"And what were your parents' names again?" Margaret asked.

"My mother was Eugenia, Eugenia Elizabeth Collins Wright. That was her name. She was real pretty. They say she had eyes blue as the sky and hair black as crow's feathers. That's about all I know of her."

"And what was your father's name?" I blurted before I could stop myself.

My mistake. Margaret's soft voice and gentle manner had been carrying Miss Lottie along and I'd broken the spell. Miss Lottie turned to me, her eyes narrowed.

"You'll not trick me, missy," she hissed. "We don't talk of my daddy. It was the war that ruint him. That and my mama dying. None of it was his fault, it was the war."

"Yes, I remember, you told me about him being in the war," Margaret said soothingly, not the least bit thrown by Miss Lottie's change of mood. "That was a terrible war, the First World War. Just awful."

"None of 'em are any good," Miss Lottie said, tilting her head as if thinking this over, "but that one was just pure hell for the ones in the trenches. It wasn't like now, where they drop the bombs from those robot planes. In that war, you had to look a fella right in the eye when you killed him. That does something to a man. It poisons his soul."

I leaned over and whispered a suggestion into Margaret's ear. She nodded and smiled at me, clearly proud to be taking the lead.

"Miss Lottie, could you tell me your daddy's name? And do you know when he died and where he's buried?"

"I could tell, but I won't," Miss Lottie said, jutting out her chin. "You're in with her and trying to trick me," she said, lifting her chin even higher in my direction. "I done told you I don't talk about that night. I made a solemn promise and I mean to keep it till I'm in my grave."

"That's fine, Miss Lottie," Margaret answered sweetly, though it certainly wasn't fine with me. What night? Promise not to talk about what? This was like waving catnip in front of a tabby's nose, then snatching it away.

"I'm not asking you to break a promise, Miss Lottie," I said, keeping my voice as low as I could and still have her hear me. "I just want to make sure your father's grave gets a proper marker, that's all."

"No marker," Miss Lottie said. "No, ma'am. That'd only lead to folks poking their snouts in our family business, and Uncle Oren says we'll not allow that. Nobody's got the right to judge until they've walked a mile in her shoes. It was the only choice, and I ought to know."

"Okay, no marker," I said. "I just wanted to check with you about it; your father is buried on the old Harper place, right?"

Miss Lottie looked at me, her eyes losing focus. It was as if someone had thrown a switch and the light went out. She looked around, confused, until her gaze came to light on a plate of store-bought cookies an attendant had brought over.

"Is there nobody in this place knows how to make a good apple pie?" Miss Lottie said, loud enough to be heard in the kitchen, which I was pretty sure was her intent. "Sadie makes the best pie you ever tasted out of apples from our orchard. They're small and nubbly, but sweet as a mama's kiss, and Sadie's crust is so light you have to stab it with your fork to keep it from floating off the plate. She always makes me a birthday pie instead of a cake. Is Sadie coming to fetch me soon? She'll be afoot, she never has learnt to drive a car. Maybe she's a-waiting for it to cool down outside. She said she'd come fetch me soon as she could get loose."

"I think you've lost her, sweetie," Margaret said.

* * *

I stopped for gas at Joe Porter's filling station. He runs the only station in town that still has full service, and I hate pumping gas. The stench gets into my nose and I can smell it for the rest of the day. It makes me queasy.

I was hoping to have a chance to talk to Gavin Taylor, and as luck would have it, he was the one who came out to fill my tank. I risked the fumes to roll down my window.

Gavin and I weren't exactly buddies, but I'd known him all through our school years. He was one of those guys who blended into the background, popping out now and again to do something truly impressive—or truly stupid—before receding into the background again. He'd been suspended and sent for counseling in his sophomore year for coldcocking the gym teacher. That sounds like a terrible thing unless you knew, as the students all did, that the gym teacher picked mercilessly on small, weak kids. One of those kids happened to be Billy Hayward, Gavin's next-door neighbor. Billy was a painfully shy, skinny kid who'd never have dreamt of talking back to a teacher. He'd left gym class each day for months with red-rimmed eyes and trembling legs. We'd had some class talks about bullying, but no one had ever given us guidance on what to do if the teacher was the bully. Gavin improvised.

"Hey, Gavin," I said, my voice nasal as I tried to keep from inhaling the vapors. "Haven't seen you in a while."

I'd almost said, "Since you got out," but saved myself from that foot-in-mouth moment. Apparently my hesitation hadn't gone unnoticed.

"It's okay, you can say it," Gavin said with a sigh. "Since I got outta the clink."

"Yeah," I said, "what happened with that whole thing, Gavin?"

He shrugged. "I just saw the car and wanted to drive it. I wasn't going to keep it or try to sell it or anything like that. I just wanted to drive that sucker, just once. A 1971 Chevy Camaro, a classic muscle car. Fully restored. It was just sittin' there, the sun shining down on it like it was in a spotlight. Seemed to me like it was beggin' to be put through its paces, so I borrowed it for a spin. Figured I'd have it back before the owner got off work and nobody'd be the wiser. Turns out the owner has a window office with a view of the street and felt absolutely no inclination to share the pleasures of his sweet ride."

"How long did you get?" I asked

"Six months, which was a gift. Could've been worse. But now I've got a record. Couldn't get my old job at the golf course back. I'm lucky Joe was willing to hire me."

"Remind me again what you did at the golf course," I said.

"I worked in the garage keeping all those carts running smoothly and spit-shined, ready for the rich folks to drive their fat butts around the course for their exercise. Bryan got me the job, but even he couldn't save my bacon after my unfortunate incarceration." The nozzle snicked off and he coaxed an extra gallon into my tank with a series of nozzle clicks.

"Joe's a good guy," I said once there was silence.

"Yeah, the man's solid. Truth is, I like working here better than at the course anyhow. Pay's not so good, but at least I'm working on real cars." He jerked his head toward the garage.

"How was it for you in there, Gavin?" I asked.

"Bad," he said. "I see now why sometimes people come out worse than when they went in. It's like a technical school for criminals. I learned about burglary, fraud, scamming, and fighting. I hope I don't ever use any of it. But I also learned a little about myself. The prison shrink informs me I have poor impulse control, can you believe that?"

"Hard to imagine," I said. "Listen, I wanted to say I'm sorry about Sherry Burton; I understand you were friends with her."

"How did you know—" He stopped and cocked his head back. "Oh yeah, you know the big cop, right?

Well, like I told him, I knew her when we were kids, but I haven't seen her in a long, long time. I was sorry to hear about how she died. It was terrible, but I don't know anything about it."

He was emphatic, maybe a little too emphatic, and I noticed he was no longer looking at me.

When I got home I went immediately to the workroom, where I found a stack of photocopies Esme had left for me from her morning courthouse excursion. Using the info she'd gotten on Miss Lottie, I was able to backtrack to her father, Samuel Wright, and after some digging I found what little there was of his military record. Samuel Wright had served in World War I, and from what I could find out about his unit, he'd probably spent some time on the front lines.

I had no proof that the glass casket held Samuel Wright's remains, but everything pointed in that direction and I figured it was time I called River to report the theory.

"So, run that by me again," he said, getting lost in my recitation of names and relationships. "This Samuel Wright ties into this place how?"

"He was the brother of Sadie Wright Harper, the wife of the owner of the property starting around 1910. Oren Harper, Sadie's husband, inherited it from his folks. Sadie and Oren had no children, and they left the property to Miss Lottie Wright Walker, who would have been their niece. I'm still digging, and as I said, I have no proof as yet that the remains you found were those of Samuel Wright, but he's our best candidate so far."

"Yeah," River said, "now all I'd like to know is how and why he ended up with a hole in his skull, buried in my yard in a glass coffin, the grave unmarked and undisclosed. Is his death related in any way to that young woman who died at his grave? Who would have been related to him how, exactly?"

"That's a lot of questions," I said with a sigh, my excitement about my theory waning in the face of all that remained unknown. "If I'm on the right track, he would have been her great-grandfather. You mentioned there might be some things in your attic we could go through. When would be a good time for us to do that?"

"How about tonight?" River asked. "I've got somewhere I need to be at five, but I should be back here by six thirty at the latest. I can rig some trouble lights up there and it'll be cooler after the sun goes down anyhow. Does that work for you?"

"You bet," I said. "I'll be there by seven."

I wasn't sure Esme would be able to make it, but at this point I didn't know whether to hope she'd be free to come along or that she'd opt out. I could deal with her irritability or Jennifer's hostility, but both at once was overload.

As if my thoughts had summoned her, Esme came in the front door. I went out into the hallway just in time to see her disappear into the kitchen with an armload of groceries.

"Need help?" I called. "Is there more in the car?"

"No, this is it," she called back. "Just picked up a few things while I was out."

I went to the doorway of the kitchen and told her what I'd found out and my theory about who the Forgotten Man was. "I was able to trace him with the help of the records you got me this morning. Thanks."

"You don't need to thank me, I was just doing my part," she said as she tucked a brick of coffee into the cupboard. "Did you call River and tell him?"

"Yes, and I set up a time to look through his attic. Tonight, about seven."

"That'll work," she said, "though it might've been nice if you'd checked with me first."

"Sorry," I said. "I just figured I could handle it if you weren't available."

"Yes, I imagine you could get along fine without me," Esme said, her tone brittle.

"What does that mean?" I asked.

She flapped a hand. "Nothing. I promised Denny I'd cook him supper, but we'll be done by then. It's fine."

I almost launched into a defense but I caught myself. I was getting tired of tiptoeing around Esme's shifting moods. "Good, then," I said.

"Good," Esme repeated. "Will you be here for supper? I'm making pork chops."

"Have plans," I said.

Actually, the only plan I had at the moment was to be elsewhere at dinnertime. Jack wouldn't be back by suppertime, but maybe I could pull Dee away from the wedding activities long enough for a quick bite. It wasn't that I didn't like spending time with Denny and Esme, but she wasn't herself right now. And anyway, I figured they needed to spend some time alone. From what I could see, her relationship with Denny was in danger of going into a death stall. There was no persuading her to share her biggest secret with him. I'd threatened to tell Denny myself, but she'd let me know quick-like-a-bunny—a very angry bunny—that there would be nuclear fallout if I did that. So they were stuck, just like Jack and me.

I was searching the workroom for my cell phone when it did me the courtesy of ringing. I retrieved it from underneath a pile of papers and saw Dee's number on the display.

"We must still have our Martian mild meld," I said. "I was just going to call and see if you wanted to go out for a quick dinner."

"That's why I'm calling you," Dee said. "Except you'll never guess who wants to take us out to eat. Laney Easton called, said she knew it was last-minute but she'd love to see us both and catch up. Talk about a blast from the past."

"Well, clearly it's you she's interested in seeing," I said. "I mean, if she'd wanted to catch up with me, all she had to do was give me a jingle. I've been right here."

"The way I understand it, your absence would be a deal breaker. She said if we both couldn't make it tonight, we'd just shoot for another time. She wants to take us to the country club."

"Can't do that," I said, not really keen on sharing the limited time I'd have with Dee on this trip. "I won't be dressed for the country club and it would have to be pretty early." I told her about my appointment with River.

Dee laughed. "I'll call her and give her your terms. Only you, Sophreena, would blow off the chance to have dinner with one of the town's muckety-mucks to go combing through a dusty old attic."

"Yeah, well, in most cases attics are more interesting than muckety-mucks."

I felt like I was back in middle school. Laney was gushing at Dee and me like we were her BFFs. We were reminiscing over crab cakes and salad at Mystic Café, a trendy new restaurant in Morningside's quaint downtown. I had mixed feelings about the place. It was cool and they served good food, but it had displaced my favorite hardware store, which had been driven to a low-rent strip mall way out on River Road. The eatery had been open only a week and there was a long line out front, but Laney had breezed right on past, speaking warmly to everyone in line as she towed Dee and me in her wake. People had smiled and chatted with her and no one seemed to resent her line jumping.

It was all coming back to me why we'd liked Laney Easton so much back when we were young. She was always smiling, always had a good story to tell, and had a deep-throated, infectious laugh. She put people at ease. I envied that talent and inwardly took a moment to analyze how she pulled it off.

Laney wore clothes well. Even dressed casually, as she was now, she looked as if every detail had been attended to. Her dark hair was precision cut in a style that was slightly longer on the sides, with straight bangs that just topped her eyebrows. Her nails were manicured and her jeans fit her slender body as if they'd been custom-tailored. A thin gold chain around her neck suspended a single pearl into the V-neck of her emerald-colored top, and her suede jacket dipped in at the waistline to follow her contours. I, on the other hand, was dressed in my attic-combing garb. And with me, hair grooming is a combat sport. I could have found Laney's appearance intimidating, but she didn't bring out insecurities in people.

She did, however, bring out a little jealousy when the talk turned to the times she and Dee had spent together when I'd been away at my grandmother's house for our annual summer visits all those years ago.

"That was when I sowed my wild oats," Laney said, laughing. "Pretty lame oats by current standards."

"Oh, I don't know. I remember hearing of exploits that involved a lot of sneaking out at night," Dee said, lowering her voice to a near whisper.

"Well, yes, there was that," Laney agreed, holding a finger to her lips. "My parents were so strict they would have locked me in my room until I was thirty if they'd known about that."

"Was this when you were hanging out with Sherry Burton?" I asked. "Sounds like you were good friends. I'm sorry about what happened to her."

"We were friends," Laney said, now solemn. "'Course, that was a very long time ago, but she played a part in my life and when someone you know dies like that, you feel the loss."

"Did you keep up with her over the years?" I asked. "Did you know she was in town?"

Laney looked at me and frowned. "You sound like Detective Carlson, Sophreena. Are you interrogating me?"

"No, not at all," I said, feeling my face redden.

"Relax," she said, reaching across to slap my hand. "I know you didn't mean anything by it. I lost touch with Sherry years ago. By the time she came for that last summer, I hardly saw her at all. My parents thought she was a bad influence, which she was," she said with a sigh. "But she was such fun. All we really did when we met up at night was go down to the little creek behind the Harper place and pretend we were part of some exotic tribe. It was all silly, innocent stuff."

"With boys!" Dee said. "Don't forget that part."

"With boys," Laney allowed with a smile. "But it was still innocent. Not that Bryan and Gavin wouldn't have liked it to be otherwise, at least where Sherry was concerned. They didn't give me a second look. Sherry was a tall, willowy thing with long, tanned legs and plenty on top. I wasn't any of those."

"Did she return their attentions?" I asked.

"She flirted with Bryan," Laney said. "But that was just to get him to do what she wanted. Gavin had a mad crush on her, but she didn't give him the time of day. He was a year younger and she treated him like a pesky little brother, though she already had her own pesky little brother. What was his name? I can't even remember it now. He used to try to hang out with us, but Sherry would always send him packing, and she wasn't very kind about it either. Poor little guy."

"Did Bryan or Gavin keep in contact with Sherry?" I asked. "I'm wondering why she would have come back here. She hadn't been out to see her grandmother, so that wasn't the draw."

Laney chuffed a mirthless laugh. "I assure you she wouldn't have come to visit her granny. Those two hated each other. I mean it. Hate, that's the only word for it. There was nothing storybook about them coming to her house for their summer stay. Granny Walker didn't want them and they didn't want to be here, at least Sherry didn't. But their mother just dropped them off. I mean, literally dropped them in the yard without even going in to speak to her mother. Is there some reason you're so interested in this, Sophreena?"

I told her about River hiring us to find the identity of the Forgotten Man. "And Esme and I were with him when he discovered Sherry's body. I guess in a weird way I feel responsible for her."

Laney's face softened. "That's kind of you, Sophreena. And I'd be happy to tell you if I knew anything that might help, but unfortunately I don't. Bryan's probably the one you should talk to. He kept in contact with Sherry, for a while anyway. He even hitchhiked out to Asheville once when she was staying out there somewhere with her mom and one of her several 'stepdads,'" Laney said, making air quotes. "Gavin may have stayed in touch, too, for all I know. But Bryan was pretty fixated on her. She was the bad girl he could never have brought home to mama. When I think about it, though, it was Sherry and Gavin who had the most in common. Neither of them had good self-control, or much judgment either. If I'd had to pick back then who'd wind up dead or in jail, those two would have been tops on the list. I know that sounds awful in light of everything that's happened, but . . ." She shrugged.

I caught a glimmer of the elegant watch on Laney's wrist and twisted my head to check the time. I was cutting it close. I made my apologies, urging Dee and Laney to stay on for dessert.

"Listen," Laney said, putting her hand on my arm as I got up to go, "I hope whatever you find out about the Forgotten Man turns out to be a good, uplifting story. You know he's gone viral now? He and his glass coffin are all over the Internet. And again, I know this sounds callous, but whoever this fellow was, he's putting the town of Morningside on the map. And if there happens to be mention in the media of our championship golf course or the new spa hotel that's going up with that spectacular view of the lake, well, Morningside can always use an infusion of tourism dollars."

nine

ESME WAS IN A GOOD MOOD WHEN SHE ARRIVED AT River's place. Spending time with Denny had clearly been beneficial.

We started the trek up to River's house but suddenly she stopped in her high-heeled tracks, all the happy leaking out of her like air from a punctured balloon. I followed her eyes and saw Jennifer's car.

"Play nice, Esme," I said, keeping my voice breezy to try to salvage what I could of her good cheer. "Remember, we're on the same side here. We all want to get to the bottom of this and let River get back to his peaceful life as a microfarmer."

As it turned out, Jennifer was in a good mood, too, at least for Jennifer. She answered the door with what could have been interpreted as a smile and led us back to the kitchen, where River was drinking some kind of wretched-looking tea. Jennifer's cup of more sensible cappuccino was waiting across the table.

"Ah, you made it," River said. "Would you like a cup of something before we tackle the attic?"

I started to decline. I'm trying to cut back on caffeine, but Esme accepted and the rich coffee aroma won out.

"You know," I said, glancing around the retro kitchen, "it'll be a shame to tear all this out. It's so cozy and I just love all this old-fashioned stuff."

"I've been telling him the same thing," Jennifer said, as if astounded we'd actually agreed on something. "This is my favorite room in the house."

River cocked his head and puffed out his lips. "Well, maybe I'll just put in a big outdoor kitchen and leave this one as is. I want a place where I can do some canning and preserving, but outdoors would be better for that anyhow. You two have me nearly convinced."

Esme motioned toward the coffee machine. "I don't suppose you'd teach me to work that contraption," she said. "I was thinking I might like to get one someday, but they look scary complicated."

I wondered where in my tiny kitchen she thought she'd put the monstrosity, but I enjoyed watching River lead her through the procedure. Esme laughed as she ladled on the dollops of foamed milk.

"Dad tells me you have a good theory about who the Forgotten Man might be," Jennifer said. She shifted in her chair before adding, "Good work."

"We still have a lot to find out," I said. "But it's a good start. Have you heard from Ron?" I asked, turning toward River.

He sighed. "No, I don't think Jimmy's a high priority. If he was a victim of foul play, it's not like they'll be putting out an all points bulletin for the killer. He or she is likely just as dead as Jimmy by now. But I sure would like to know more about him, and how he ended up out there."

A silence fell over the room and we all examined our cups as if the answer could be found in the liquid within. "River," I said finally, "before we completely lose the light, would you mind if we took a walk around the property now?"

"Sure," River said. "Fact is, I walk some part of the property nearly every day about this time. I like to sort of abide with it, you know? To learn all its contours and textures and to catalog in my head what needs to be done. I'd love some company."

Jennifer made a production of peering over the edge of the table at Esme's feet, but she didn't say a word.

Esme slid back her chair and reached for the over-size bag she'd stashed in the corner. "Just give me a minute," she said, her voice sweet as honey. She then proceeded to pull out a pair of the ugliest running shoes ever produced. Bright purple trainers with lime green strips and thick white soles.

We all stared and Esme lifted her chin to a haughty angle. "Just because I'm being practical doesn't mean I can't be stylish," she said.

We all laughed as Esme donned the neon clunkers. We were, if not best buddies, at least boon companions for the evening's stroll. The sun had only just disappeared below the horizon and the day teetered on the edge between day and night, the air soft and the light velvety.

"I'm pretty sure this is close to the original land boundary on this side," River said, pointing off toward the highway. "Or maybe the roadway went in later and the land was snatched up by eminent domain. But anyway, this side of the property runs to the highway, so you have to jump the road to get to the nearest neighbor, and the house on that property sits way back from the road. I haven't met the people who live there yet, but I'm told they've been there for generations, too, like the Harpers were here."

"I see your builders have made progress on your workshop," I said, noting that the structure now had walls and a roof.

"It's coming along," River said, adjusting his trajectory to walk toward it.

I hesitated, feeling a vague sense of dread. The last time we'd walked alongside River, we'd found a dead woman. Who knew what was inside the workshop.

As we approached, River pressed a button, which raised the garage doors and simultaneously turned on a bank of lights. Only building supplies and sawhorses were scattered about. It was then that I realized Esme had stopped in the yard and was holding her hand across her forehead in a gesture I recognized.

I went to her and spoke softly, so River and Jennifer couldn't overhear. "You okay?" I asked. "Are you getting something?"

Esme made a mumble in the affirmative, then bent down to retie her ugly shoe, as River and Jennifer noticed our delay and doubled back.

"Something wrong?" River asked, looking at Esme in concern.

"No, I'm fine," Esme said. "I just felt the urge to stop right here on this spot and enjoy the view," she said, giving me a coded eye signal.

"It is a nice view," River said, frowning. "But not the nicest on the property. Hey, maybe you were a water sprite in a former life. This is where the old well used to stand. Could be you felt the draw of the water."

"Well, nobody's ever described me as a sprite," Esme said, pulling herself up to her considerable height, "but I do love water." She smiled, but I recognized the signs. Esme's heightened sense of what was inaccessible to most of us took its toll on her. It gave her headaches and sometimes made her feel woozy.

We walked on, staying near the property line, River keeping up a running commentary on his plans for the place: an herb garden here, a chicken yard there, maybe an apiary just over there next year. "And here," he said, pointing to a row of newly planted trees along the rail fence that separated his property from Claire Calvert's place, "these are fruit trees and along there blueberry bushes." He walked closer to inspect the small saplings. "I'm happy these survived all the foot traffic through here," he said. "I call this optimism row," he added with a chuckle. "I'm hoping I'll live long enough to taste the fruit. But if I don't, I know Jen will get to enjoy it." He looped his arm around his daughter's neck and she gave him a beaming smile. It so transformed her, I almost gasped in surprise. She looked like a different person altogether.

"Did you know Claire before you moved here?" Esme asked, gesturing toward Claire's house.

"I did," River said. "Incredible woman. Terrible thing, what happened to her, but amazing how she's dealt with it."

"I wish she'd be a little more cautious," Jennifer said, staring at the house. "I told her if Quentin bothers her she could get a restraining order, but she insists she doesn't need one."

"Things are not always what they seem, Jen," River said. "Claire's a compassionate person, but she's nobody's fool; far from it. I imagine she knows what she's doing."

Jennifer shook her head. "In my line of work things are always what they seem, unless they're something worse."

I was expecting Esme to weigh in about now, considering how protective she was of Claire, but when I looked over at her I could see her mind was elsewhere.

As we all instinctively turned away from the still-tented grave site, River and Jennifer stepped out ahead and I reached over to touch Esme's shoulder.

She patted my hand and gave me a reassuring, if weak, smile.

"I don't know if you want to walk all the way down there," River said, pointing down a steep hill on the other side of his long driveway. "It goes down to a pretty little creek. It's rocky, uneven ground and it'll be full dark in a few minutes. I didn't think to bring a flashlight."

"That's okay," I said. "We'll save that for another day. Thanks for the tour."

"Proud to do it," River said.

Esme walked alongside River as we headed back to the house, and as I tried to make conversation with Jennifer, I heard Esme asking River more about the old well.

"He means that, you know," Jennifer said. "About

being proud to show all this to you. I think he's prouder of this place than of anything he's ever done, and he's done a lot of things in his life. He has it in his mind to create something here that can serve as a model to others. Now death and violence have intruded on it, twice. It's weighing on him."

These were more words than Jennifer had ever spoken to me, and they were deeply felt sentiments that she was choosing to share.

I was so surprised, I couldn't reply right away. I turned over in my mind what I should say, eager to preserve this fragile détente. "I get it, Jennifer," I said finally. "I do. I don't know if what I find will help, but I hope it does."

"I hope so, too," Jennifer said. "Dad's not a black-and-white kind of guy, he sees more shades of gray than most people. I think Vietnam did that to him. It's important for him to know the circumstances of what happened here. We'll solve the case of Sherry Burton," she said with absolute assurance. "You and Esme find out who Jimmy was and how and why he died. Deal?"

"Deal," I said, though with far less confidence.

Back in the house, I picked up my bag. "I've got dust masks and gloves in here. We'd better get on with it before it gets any later."

River guided us to the second floor, then opened a door that had concealed a set of steep, narrow steps.

As we lined up, he started punching buttons on a small display screen located on the wall nearby. At first I thought it was a fancy thermostat, but it seemed too big for that. He saw my curious look.

"Whole-house control," he said. "Lets me turn off lights, power down appliances, and adjust the heat and air. I like my comforts, but I can't stand waste. It'll turn off all the lights downstairs and turn them on again when we come down. There's a sensor on the door."

I looked to where he was pointing and saw a rect-angular electronic gizmo embedded in the door frame. "Cool," I said.

"I thought so," River said. "My company developed it."

"You mean you developed it," Jennifer said. "Your company was you tinkering in the garage back then."

River shrugged. "Concept was mine, but it took people smarter than me to make it work the way I wanted it to. Anyhow, onward and upward, ladies."

We made our way noisily up the wooden stairs and emerged into a huge attic packed chock-a-block with stuff. There was plenty of light and a fan brought in cool evening air from the outside. I was grinning from ear to ear. This was my kind of place.

Esme, on the other hand, looked horrified. When she's surrounded by the belongings of the deceased, she sometimes gets inundated with little scraps of mes-sages, images, and emotional spikes she calls surges.

The bombardment can leave her exhausted. She stood for a moment getting her bearings and then I saw her shoulders relax. Apparently this space was quiet for now.

"Nearest I can tell, the paper stuff is all over here," River said, directing us to the south side.

There was a lot of it and it was an archivist's nightmare. Crumbling cardboard boxes and moth-eaten cloth bags held reams of wrinkled yellowing paper.

"Tell you what," I said, looking up at River, "this is a little more than I was thinking we'd find. Would it be okay if I took some of it home to our workroom to go through? I'll bring it all back."

"Sure," he said. "I'll probably end up tossing it anyway unless you turn up any family members who might want it."

I snapped on rubber gloves and started to sort. Esme collected the chosen boxes and bags and stacked them at the head of the stairs. There were eight in all plus one that contained photographs, stored as carelessly as the documents. I cringed as the flap of the box fell away when I opened it. To me, family photos are treasures, and these had been treated like trash.

After I'd gathered everything, we wandered around the attic just enjoying looking at the items. Old bed frames, a wooden high chair, lamps, two chests with blankets and quilts inside, carefully wrapped in muslin, a dresser that was shabby chic long before that was a decorating trend, and a corner filled with old fishing tackle. My eye lit on an obviously handmade child's rocking horse; the wood had a patina of gray, and was split in places, probably from the heat in the attic. Was this a gift? Perhaps from a father to a beloved child? How I wish the things people leave behind came with their stories. This is why I urge clients to include information about their belongings in their family histories. We live among things; they're the artifacts of our lives. Soup ladled from a bowl you bought yesterday at your local discount store is a different soup from that taken from your great-aunt Matilda's treasured tureen, the one she received as a wedding gift and passed on to you because you'd always admired it. That soup nourishes you in a whole different way.

We were all strolling around lost in our own thoughts when our heads snapped up in unison in response to a loud crash from downstairs.

Jennifer moved immediately, but the rest of us had a delayed reaction. She was already at the bottom of the stairs, cursing the automated light that flooded the house when she opened the door. The rest of us started clambering down after her.

"Jen, wait," River called, but his words had no effect.

I heard pounding footfalls in the rooms downstairs as we each latched onto the banister and started down the staircase to the first floor. Just as we got near the bottom, a young man came streaking through the entry hall, his clothing rumpled and his blond hair sticking out in every which way. He didn't even look in our direction but yanked open the front door and bounded down the steps, running out into the night. A nanosecond later, Jennifer zipped by in hot pursuit as the outdoor lights, apparently also set on a sensor, illuminated the front yard.

The guy was young and fleet of foot, but Jennifer was closing on him.

"My Lord, that girl's fast," Esme said from behind me.

River was out the door, but with no hope of catching them. Jennifer, still several steps behind the man, grunted, launched herself in his direction, and tackled him, both of them bouncing along the ground before coming to rest in a tangled heap.

By the time we caught up, all of us panting and wheezing, Jennifer had his hands pinned behind him and was sitting on his back, peppering him with questions.

"Who are you and what were you doing in my dad's house?" she asked, not as a cop but as an indignant daughter.

"Who are *you*?" the man spat back. "And what are *you* doing here? That's a better question."

"I'm a police officer," Jennifer said, her breathing slowly returning to normal. "My questions trump yours."

The man made a noise and spat grass and dirt, then tried to twist around. "You sound familiar. Jennifer? Jennifer Jeffers? Is that you?"

She yanked at the man's hands, turning him onto his side so she could see his face. She frowned, but there was no sign of recognition. She looked up at her father, and River squatted down and twisted his head to look at the guy's face. "Who are you, son?"

"Luke Mitchell. This is my grandmother's house. Where is she and who are you people?"

ten

"I CAN'T BELIEVE YOU BECAME A COP," LUKE Mitchell said as Jennifer set a glass of water in front of him. He picked up the end of the towel he had slung over his leg and dabbed at his ear. It was raw-looking, but it had stopped bleeding.

"And I can't believe you became a criminal," Jennifer said dryly.

"Well, not professionally," Luke said with a lopsided grin. "I used to come and go from that window all the time. That was my bedroom when we stayed here in the summertime. But someone seems to have made some changes." He looked to River and apologized for perhaps the hundredth time.

"How is it you didn't know your grandmother had sold the place?" River asked.

"You don't know my grandmother, do you?" Luke asked. "We're not what you'd call close. And even if she'd been inclined to let me know, which she wouldn't have been, she couldn't have reached me in the past year. I'm an anthropologist, or I will be when I finish my degree. A professional anthropologist," he said with a nod toward Jennifer. "I participated in an experiment with three other anthropology students and some native peoples on an atoll in the South Pacific. It's isolated, and other than a satellite phone for medical emergencies, we've been living completely off the grid for a year and two months now. I just got back to the States a few days ago."

"That sounds really interesting," River said, leaning forward. "Living completely off the grid, you say?"

"Dad," Jennifer said, lifting her eyebrows, "not really the most important aspect of the conversation right now."

"Right, sorry," River said.

"You really don't remember me, do you?" Luke asked Jennifer. "'Course, I understand why you wouldn't. I used to challenge you to swim races at the public pool—loser buys the winner a Coke—which was stupid, since you always beat me. You were fast. Still are," he said, his hand going to the scrape on his cheek where he'd face-plowed when she tackled him.

"So you got back to the country and came to see your grandmother?" River asked. "And, what, you came in through the window for old times' sake?"

"Well, no," Luke replied, frowning. "I knocked at the kitchen door, but nobody answered and I figured Grandma was already asleep. She's deaf as a stone. So I let myself in the way I used to."

"You didn't see all our cars here," Jennifer said, nodding in the direction of the driveway, "or notice the construction going on?"

"I parked on the roadside and took the shortcut in," Luke said, pointing toward the main road. "I wasn't supposed to let anyone know I was here. Nobody but Grandma, anyhow."

"What do you mean you weren't supposed to let anyone know?" Jennifer asked.

"My sister left a message with my old roommate. He gave it to me as soon as I got home 'cause she said it was urgent. She wanted me to meet her here. I wasn't to tell anybody I was coming nor let anyone know I was here until she talked to me."

"Your sister," Jennifer said, her back stiffening.

"Yeah, well, my half sister. I don't think you ever knew her. She didn't hang around the pool much. We're not close either, but she called me, so maybe that's gonna change. Anyhow, I guess she's not here yet, eh? Unless you tackled her, too, and have her hog-tied somewhere." He glanced around and made a show of looking under the table, a teasing smile on his face.

Jennifer looked stricken, and I remembered Denton

saying how much she hated making family notifications. Apparently Esme remembered, too, because she reached across the table and put her hand over Luke's. "Your sister is Sherry Burton?"

"Yeah," Luke said. "You know her?"

Esme shook her head. "Never had the pleasure. I'm afraid we have some bad news for you, Luke."

"What a horrible thing to have to break to someone," Dee said as we sat around our kitchen table the next morning, assembling the favor boxes for the wedding reception. "How did he take it?"

"It was odd," I said. "It was almost as if he'd been expecting the news, but at the same time he was stunned by it."

"I don't think I saw him but maybe once or twice. I guess he was an anthropologist in the making even back then. In the short time I got to hang around with Sherry, she complained about him spying on her. She'd say outrageous things, always loud enough for him to hear when he was skulking about, just to test what he'd do."

"What did he do?" Coco asked, opening up what seemed like the millionth tiny baker's box and inserting a piece of parchment before sliding it down the line for Dee to fill with chocolates.

"Nothing," Dee said. "I think she was testing him to see if he would tattle on her, but who would he have told? Their grandmother didn't seem to care what they did as long as they stayed out of her hair."

"That was an odd thing, too," Esme said. "He didn't seem to care much either way when we told him his grandmother was still alive. I guess he'd assumed when he finally figured out that she didn't live there anymore that she'd passed, but when we told him she was in the nursing home, he just made a sort of *huh* sound."

I heard the front door open and the voice that called a hello made me smile, followed immediately by a sigh. Jack. Jack, of the unresolved conversation. Jack, here, where the room was full of people.

"Hey, what's going on?" he asked as he stood in the doorway inspecting the assembly line.

"Wedding prep," Esme said. "And you're in the wedding party. Pull up a chair."

"Nah," Jack said. "I'd like to help, but you know I'm all thumbs with this kind of stuff. This is women's work."

He put up both hands as four heads swiveled to give him the stink-eye. "Bad joke," he said, "but I really can't help. I'm supposed to be on the job. I just brought by a load of mulch and some liriope sprigs for your front beds, Sophreena. Want me to unload them in the usual spot?"

"That would be great," I said.

"Okay, then, I'll try to come by this weekend and help you with the beds."

After he'd gone, Dee tilted her head and winked at me. "Some guys bring roses, your guy brings mulch. Isn't that sweet?"

"Roses die, mulch lasts, just like friendship," Coco said, reaching to squeeze my shoulder.

I felt comforted by the comment for a moment. Then I began to wonder if she knew something I didn't. Was she trying to warn me not to expect that Jack and I were anything but friends? Had he confided in her about his feelings?

I got up from the table, a little more abruptly than I'd intended, tipping over my chair with a loud clatter. "'Scuse me a minute," I said, feeling my throat tighten as I righted the chair. "I changed my mind about where I want him to put that mulch. I need to go tell him."

"Jack!" I called, once I was out on the front porch. Again it came out with more urgency than I'd meant and Jack's head snapped up in alarm. He'd just been putting the tailgate of the truck down and he let it fall.

"What is it?" he asked, starting toward me. "What's wrong?"

"N-nothing," I stammered. "I just"—I motioned vaguely toward the truck—"thought, last time the mulch was fresh, and stinky, so maybe we should put it alongside the fence in case I don't get to it this weekend."

"Sure," Jack said, frowning at me suspiciously. "You want to show me where?"

I stepped over to a totally arbitrary spot along the fence. He pulled up and started shoveling the mulch into a neat pile, steam rising from the heat of the decaying matter as it hit the cool morning air.

"What was it you wanted to talk to me about the other night?" I asked, trying to keep my voice casual. "We never did get a chance to finish that conversation."

"No, we didn't," Jack said, shovel poised in midair. He glanced off toward the house. "We need to talk, but not now. You've got things to do and I need to get on the job. You want to get some supper tonight?"

"Yeah, that would be good," I said, trying to read his body language. He definitely looked uncomfortable. "When and where?"

"Five thirty? Gallagher's? We can find a quiet place outside. It's time we talked."

"Sounds great, I'll meet you," I said. I tried for a carefree amble back to the front porch, but my legs had gone to jelly and I was wobbling like a drunken duck. I had the image of Jack's face burned into my retinas, that solemn look when he said we needed to talk. It was not a happy face.

Once the last box of chocolates was stickered, ribboned, and packed into the box to be delivered to the refrigerators at High Ground, everyone dashed off to take care of other details and I was free to get back to work.

Well, free, except for thoughts and worries about Jack trying to worm their way into my head. So much for my stupid collection of signs. I kept hearing Jack's voice when he said we needed to talk. When had those words ever meant anything good?

I did a Scarlett O'Hara and willed myself to think about that later. I was determined to concentrate on tracking down Samuel Wright. I went down several virtual paths that led to brick walls before I finally got lucky. A woman named Ginger Holderman, who was apparently descended from a man named Virgil Wright, had posted on one of the genealogy message boards looking for information on Sadie Wright Harper, her ancestor's sister. She noted that she had info on Virgil and the other sibling in the family, Samuel Wright, which she'd be happy to share if other descendants were interested.

I wasn't a descendant, but I was most definitely interested.

I posted immediately, asking her to contact me to exchange information and then went back to searching databases. To my surprise, ten short minutes later I got

an incoming message ping from Ginger. We exchanged
a few pleasantries, then got down to business. She sent
me a long string of attachments: scans of documents,
handwritten notes, and transcripts for oral histories,
along with several very old and faded photographs.

Ginger had kept careful records of her sources and
had labeled everything clearly. The vast majority of the
information was about Virgil, her direct ancestor. The
information she had on Samuel was more loosely documented, but she was careful to identify which information was undocumented by using wiggle words like
"family lore has it that" or "according to what so-and-so
can remember."

I thanked Ginger and promised to return the favor
by sharing everything I turned up about the Wright
family in my own research. This is one of many things
I love about family historians; they are almost always
pleased to share.

I printed out the documents and spread them
on the worktable, stacking them in rough categories.
Then I started going through the boxes we'd brought
from River's house. Normally Esme and I would work
together on these tasks and I felt a little lonely doing it
by myself, but I was glad she was the one helping with
the wedding. I wasn't really in the mood to think about
happy couples right now. Not with the way things stood
with Jack.

I weeded through a box of old bills and receipts from the 1950s, finding little of interest unless you counted the shock of how much grocery prices have soared since then. I got sidetracked by a faded receipt from the Piggly Wiggly supermarket: milk, 43 cents a half gallon; coffee, 93 cents a pound; sugar, 43 cents for five pounds, and Ivory Soap, 29 cents for two bars. Man, talk about nostalgia.

I kept going, determined to empty the box. More ephemera, bills from Southern Bell and the Electric Co-op, receipts for farm supplies, but then something of note, hospital bills, itemized services identified as the maternity ward. I did some quick mental calculations. This would have been when Lottie Walker gave birth to her daughter, Marla. The bills were addressed to Howard Walker, care of Oren Harper. What did that mean? Was the couple living at the old Harper place with Oren and Sadie even then?

Suddenly I remembered what Lottie Walker had said about how early in the marriage her husband, Howard, had died. In a mill accident, wasn't it? And very close to the time their child was born. Before or after? Could it be Howard Walker in that grave? But no, Lottie had clearly said he was buried in a cemetery. Hadn't she? I tried to recall my first conversation with Miss Lottie. Had she been lucid then? I made a note to check on Howard Walker's final resting place.

The second box was older stuff and more interesting. Bills and receipts, yes, but also letters, a scattering of photos, and some small booklets that had been used as a sort of log to mark down important dates. Seed companies and fertilizer manufacturers had given out these small memo books by the thousands back in the day as a promo item. They turned up in the ephemera of almost every client I'd ever had, at least the ones from the south. There were three of them here and the handwriting looked feminine. The info was scant, but that was better for me. I didn't have to wade through a lot of extraneous stuff.

The first memo book started off with a page marked 1938 and a list of dates, moon phases, and instructions on what to plant on each day: May 2, waxing crescent, put in leafy vegetables and flowers that produce above the ground—lettuce, sweet corn, cucumbers, and spinach. May 7 will be first quarter. Put in all vegetables with inside seeds—tomatoes, beans, peas, peppers, squash, and pumpkins.

I flipped through all three tablets quickly and found a name inscribed on the inside front cover of the third, Sadie Harper. The handwriting was the same throughout the three tablets so I decided it was safe to assume all three belonged to Sadie.

Interesting though her plans for moon planting might have been, they weren't helping me get to what I wanted to know. I flipped through the little notebooks again, rapidly scanning each page. I stopped when I came to this terse entry: *Eugenia was delivered of a baby daughter yesterday. The child lives but Eugenia did not survive her ordeal. May she rest in the Lord's peace. A sad and joyous day.*

There were notations about Oren and Sadie taking the train to Baltimore for the funeral, then a few pages later: *Samuel and the baby will arrive on the four o'clock train, Hillsborough Depot. He has named the child Charlotte as Eugenia wanted. He has shipped his things and what little they had for the baby. Will need to see what we can buy or borrow for her.*

I unrolled the time line I'd started for the Harpers and ticked in these dates, then went back to unloading the box, more systematically now. I came upon another notebook, this one the larger old-fashioned composition-book style with a black-and-white faux marble cover that had faded to gray. This was not a diary but rather a commonplace book for Sadie Harper: grocery lists, calendar events, chores, and reminders were all written with no regard to category or format.

Near the front there was a list of recipes for home-made baby formula, several were crossed through with a note beside it giving the reason for its rejection: spits up, makes her colicky. At the end of the list was a note-to-self: *Go see Hershel Watkins about getting a nanny goat and have Louise show me how to milk it. Doc says goat's milk may be best.*

There were more notations about the best treatment Sadie had found for diaper rash, which was to leave little Lottie's hindquarters exposed to the sunlight for half an hour every morning. There was doctor's advice about putting the baby on a schedule (feed every four hours), and a granny woman's counter-advice on the matter (feed her when she's hungry). There were instructions for treating croup and disturbing advice on how to deal with teething—put a little paregoric or whiskey on the gums and rub them hard with your thumb.

Apparently Sadie Harper, who had no children of her own, had worked hard at acquiring child-care skills.

Notations regarding Samuel's ill health and declining mental state were numerous at first, but steadily decreased as I leafed through the book. What did that mean?

I looked up at the clock and was amazed to find it was after four. I'd gotten so absorbed in what I was doing that I'd lost track of the time, not to mention that I'd finally been able to let go of the anxiety about my upcoming talk with Jack. But now the worry was back with a vengeance and my stomach cramped.

I dashed upstairs and made myself presentable, fussing a little more over my appearance than I normally do. Maybe Esme's fashion sense was rubbing off on me, or maybe I just didn't want to get dumped while looking like a schlub. But really, I wasn't going to get dumped, was I? And could you even be dumped if you'd never been together? I couldn't believe I could've gotten the signals that wrong. Still, Jack had looked so solemn this morning.

I slicked on a bit of lip gloss and squared my shoulders, examining myself in the mirror. "Stop obsessing," I told my reflection. My reflection ignored me.

When I arrived at Gallagher's, fifteen minutes early, I snagged my favorite table in one of the outdoor nooks that had been carved out of every available inch of land surrounding the restaurant, which had once been a private residence. We'd have plenty of privacy, though at this point I couldn't decide if that was a good thing or not. I might be less likely to fall apart if I knew people were watching. I put down my notebook to save the table and went inside to order. This was the way Jack and I always operated—whoever gets to the place first orders for both—so why did I all of a sudden feel weird about it? Like I was being a bit too cheeky by choosing for him, though I knew, without one scintilla of doubt, he'd order the spicy chicken wrap. That's what he got here, every time.

I put in our order and went back outside to make notes on what I'd discovered today while I waited for Jack, while I waited for Fate.

"Sophreena Suprema!"

I didn't need to look up to know who it was. Bryan Mason had stuck me with that nickname back in high school, a little teasing attention as a favor to the nerdy girl. I'd hated it, yet liked it a little, too. It was all very confusing, as so much is when you're in that stage of life.

"Hi, Bryan," I said, hoping he'd nod and keep on going.

It was a vain hope. He came over to the table, pulled out the other chair, and flipped it around to straddle it. "How are things with you?" he asked. "Still running that research business? What was it, some kind of paralegal thing?"

"Family history," I said. "I'm a genealogist."

"Yeah, yeah," Bryan said. "I knew it was something like that."

There followed an awkward silence, a phenomenon I'm usually very good at waiting out, but in this case I wanted to get the chitchat over with so Bryan could move along. "And you're still out at the golf course? Running the pro shop?" I framed it as a question, though I knew he was.

"Yep. Been out there nearly ten years now. Geez, can you believe it? We're like respectable adults now. Seems like only yesterday when we were getting into mischief at Morningside High."

"Well, some of us were getting into more mischief than others," I said.

"Right. Right," Bryan said, his face split by a big grin.

"Listen, Bryan," I said, figuring I might as well capitalize on this opportunity, "that was so upsetting what happened to Sherry Burton, I'm really sorry. I understand you two stayed friends over the years."

"Well, not close friends or anything. We'd exchange email every now and again and we got together when I was down in Miami a while back. But yeah, it's horrible what happened to her."

"Do you know of anyone here who had problems with her?" I asked, deciding I might as well cut to the chase.

"Here?" Bryan said, as if the idea had only now occurred to him. "I seriously doubt anyone from around here was involved. Nobody here would have had any reason to hurt Sherry. Miami, now that's a different story. She was living large down there. We met up at the bar where she worked, really swank joint, but something about it didn't seem entirely kosher, if you know what I mean."

"No, I don't know," I said, pointing to myself. "Nerdy girl, remember? Spell it out for me."

Bryan shrugged, looking off toward the entrance. Bryan had always been a bird-on-the-shoulder conversationalist, his eyes routinely wandering to the space beyond you in case someone better came along. "I think they may have been selling stuff they weren't licensed for, things of the pharmaceutical variety." He cocked an eyebrow, clearly trying to determine if his meaning was penetrating my thick skull.

"Dealing drugs, you mean," I said. "And you think Sherry was involved?"

He shrugged again. "She worked there, and she seemed to be living well for a bartender. She invited me back to her place; it was pretty swank, too."

"So you're saying she was living beyond her means?"

"Definitely," Bryan said. "And you know that old saying about lying down with dogs and getting up with fleas." He shook his head as if the very thought of it made him sad. "I hate what happened to her, but I have a sick feeling she probably brought it on herself."

I saw Jack just then. He was on the porch scanning the outdoor spaces. I called to him and he came over, giving Bryan a cool greeting. Bryan greeted him back like they were best pals, then got up and motioned Jack into the chair with a flourish. "Meeting friends," he said, jerking a thumb toward the door. "Best not be late."

"What did he want?" Jack asked once Bryan was out of earshot.

"Nothing," I said. "He saw me sitting here and came over to say hello."

"I doubt that," Jack said. "He doesn't do anything without an agenda."

"No love lost for Bryan, then?" I asked.

Jack frowned. "I don't know the guy all that well." He turned toward me, crossing his arms on the table-top. "Did you order?"

I told him I had and waited, wondering if I'd be able to eat anything if we had the talk now.

Jack didn't seem in a hurry to get to it either. He was clearly uncomfortable, and as we made mind-less small talk, my sense of impending doom steadily heightened. I could hear the theme song from *Jaws* pounding in my ears.

A silence fell and Jack let out a big sigh, lacing his callused fingers together. He seemed about to get into it, but just then our waitress came onto the porch hold-ing a laden tray and shouting my name.

She arrived at our table, all perky, and deposited plastic baskets and cups onto the table. "Anything else I can get for you?" she asked, smiling in that 'please leave a decent tip' way seasoned waitresses do.

I looked over the spread and automatically asked for ketchup. I'm not a ketchup gal myself, but Jack seems to think it's a must-have condiment for every meal. The waitress produced a bottle from her apron pocket and took her leave.

I'd thought I was too tense to do anything but

nibble, but the aroma of my meatball po' boy made me salivate, and I figured if this was to be my last meal as a happy woman, I might as well dig in and enjoy it.

We ate, and the ritual seemed to relax us both. I savored every bite, thinking to delay the inevitable, and used the time to convince myself that our friendship could weather this. Things might be awkward for a while, but we could get back to the comfort we'd felt with each other as buddies. We could, I was sure of it. Probably.

"You want to tell me what's crossways with you and Bryan?" I asked.

Jack shrugged, forking up the filling from his wrap that had plopped into his basket. "Probably just me being touchy. We do some work out there, not the golf course proper, as they have their own grounds crew, but we take care of the areas around the clubhouse. I run into Bryan now and again. You'd think he owned the place. Gives out orders to my crew without checking with me and sometimes isn't very civil about it."

I nodded. "He's always been like that. He's not mean, he just doesn't get that he's insensitive. Which I guess makes a kind of sense, doesn't it? He'd have to be at least somewhat sensitive to realize he was being insensitive, ergo . . ." I let my voice trail off, and Jack threw his head back and laughed.

"That's why I love that we're friends, Soph," he said, the chuckle dying out. "You and your circular logic."

I felt the po' boy threatening a return trip. Friends. Oh, dear God, I was about to get the *We can still be friends* speech. I wondered if he'd tack on the *It's not you, it's me* line to cap off the humiliation.

Jack looked up and saw the expression on my face. "What's the matter?" he asked, looking around to see what might be amiss.

I gave him a tight smile. "You said we needed to talk. So let's talk." I put down what little remained of my sandwich and wiped my fingers, now eager to get it over with so I could go home and wallow in my misery in private.

"Yeah, that," Jack said, taking a gulp of water. After three false starts he finally began. "We've been friends a long time, Sophreena. And I hope we'll stay friends, no matter what."

"Sure, we will," I said, struggling to keep my voice from quavering.

"I hope so," Jack said, dragging his hand down over his face. "It's just that sometimes in a friendship one person might want something the other person doesn't have to give and once that's clear, it gets awkward and you feel uncomfortable and . . ." His voice trailed off and he squirmed, scratching at his neck.

"Look, Jack," I said, feeling almost as bad for him as I did for myself, "just say what's on your mind. It's okay, really."

I was amazed that I sounded so calm. Inside my head I was screaming and making lists of chores that required vigorous physical activity that I could tackle over the next few days to work out the heartbreak. There was a mulch pile to distribute, patio furniture that needed scrubbing down, a workroom due for a thorough file purge.

I was so absorbed I didn't hear what Jack said next. I looked up and saw the pained expression on his face and struggled with what to say to let him off the hook, but I couldn't come up with anything, not anything that wasn't a total lie anyhow. I wasn't okay. And I wasn't likely to be okay any time soon.

"Well?" he said. "Would you say something?"

I took in a breath and began haltingly. "I meant it, Jack, we'll still be friends, but I may need some time."

Jack looked miserable. "I knew I should have kept my mouth shut. I'm really sorry, Soph. I guess I mis-interpreted the situation. I thought I was reading your signals, but I guess it was just wishful thinking. But I couldn't go on the way it was either. I had to tell you I wanted more than friendship and let the chips fall where they may. And I guess they have."

"You . . . excuse me? You what?"

Now it was Jack's turn to put up a hand. "It's okay, Soph. I'll get past it, but I had to know where I stand. I didn't say anything before 'cause I didn't want to screw up our friendship, but you can't live on hold forever, so now it's out there"—he held both hands out toward me—"and you know, and clearly you don't feel the same, so it'll be weird for a while, but we can salvage the friendship, right?"

Our perky waitress chose that moment to appear at our table. "Dessert for you two?" she asked, starting to clear away the detritus from our meal.

"Yes," I said, matching her smile. "We'll both have a slice of your chocolate cheesecake. We're celebrating."

Jack frowned in confusion as she walked away.

"Now, let's finish our talk," I said.

eleven

I WAS WHISTLING BRIGHTLY WHEN ESME CAME downstairs the next morning. She was decked out in her walking clothes and seemed pleased to see I was ready to go.

"You're happy this morning," she said. "You find out more last night? You know for sure who the Forgotten Man is, or was?"

"Nope, no closer yet, but I'm hopeful. I'm ready to go if you are."

"I am," Esme said, eyeing me suspiciously. "Would you like to tell me what's gotten into you? Why am I not forced to holler myself hoarse to get you to come down and get out the door? Wait a minute, didn't you go out with Jack last night?"

"I did," I answered, trying to keep my face neutral. "We went to Gallagher's."

"And?" Esme asked, narrowing her eyes at me.

"And," I said, bending over to tie my shoes, "it was good. Everything's always good at Gallagher's."

"Sophreena," Esme said, drawing out my name.

I was delighted when the phone rang at that moment, and I jumped up to answer it. I wanted to keep the Jack secret a while longer. It was such a delicious secret.

"Sophreena, this is Margaret Roman. We met the other day out at Cottonwood. Do you remember me?"

I mentally sorted through the people I'd met at Cottonwood, linking names with faces, and bingo: Margaret, the amateur genealogist.

"Of course, how are you?" I said, hoping to keep it brief. In addition to being very generous, amateur genealogists can also be very long-winded. While I admire the enthusiasm, it's hard to maintain rapt attention through the litany of begats in their own family trees. It's worse than grandmothers armed with purses full of grandbaby pictures.

"I hope I'm not calling too early, but I wanted to tell you about an interesting conversation I had with Ruth Wilkins' brother, Cleve, last evening. You remember Ruth?"

Oh Lord, it was going to be one of those days. I covered the mouthpiece lest Margaret hear my groan. "Ruth?" I asked, feigning interest.

"Ruth Wilkins. She's the lady at Cottonwood who

said she knew Miss Lottie when they were girls. Do you recall?"

I did recall, and suddenly I didn't have to feign interest.

"Well, Cleve is younger than Ruth. He's got a much better memory and he loves a good story. You know the type. Anyway, he told me some things about the Harpers that I think might interest you. None of this is documented, you understand. I mean, it's not official, but it's pretty entertaining."

"I'm all ears," I said eagerly, grabbing a notepad from the kitchen drawer.

Margaret laughed, a pleasant bell-like sound. "Oh no, dear heart, I couldn't do the story justice. I was wondering if by chance you'd be free for lunch. Cleve would like to meet you and pass on what he knows."

I sighed. I'd hoped to finish going through the boxes from River's attic today, but this sounded too promising to pass up, so I made the date.

"I thought today was to be a workday," Esme said as I put the phone back on the base. "If I'd known we could go off and play hooky, I'd have made lunch plans myself."

"It's a working lunch," I said, determined not to let Esme rain on my parade. "You should come, too." I explained to her who we'd be meeting and why.

Placated, Esme set about filling our water bottles while I did a few hamstring stretches. I had a feeling

I might even be able to keep up with Esme's stride on our walk today. Giddiness, it seemed, was energizing.

"If we're able to get the definitive proof about Samuel being the Forgotten Man, do you think the hoopla will die down?" I asked as I finished my last stretch and took my water bottle from Esme.

"I very much doubt it. If you could let it be known why he was buried in that glass coffin, and if it's a reasonable explanation, then they might tire of the story and move on to something else. Look at what's happened with Sherry Burton's murder. People were all stirred up about it until they found out who she was and that she was on the run from drug dealers."

"Who says that?"

Esme shrugged. "Word about town. Rumor is she crossed somebody down in Miami and they hunted her down. Terrible, but it's plain old crime, nothing to do with them."

We were just heading out the front door when the phone rang again. I craned my neck around the doorjamb and saw Ron Solomon's number on the display.

"Thought you might like to know my findings on your skeleton-in-residence at the old Harper place," he said. "I wish I had unlimited funds and one or two more lab assistants, in which case I'd be studying this one for a while, but since I don't have either, I'm calling this a homicide and wrapping it up."

"Any estimates on the time frame?" I asked.

"A frame, yes, but not a date," Ron said. "Like I say, if I had unlimited funds, but I don't."

"Okay, well, if I told you I have reason to believe the man died in the mid-1920s, would that square with what you've found?"

"Why?" Ron asked, drawing out the word.

I told him what I'd learned about Samuel Wright. "I don't have the whole picture yet, but would that be consistent with your findings?"

"Spot on," Ron said. "Now, Sophreena, share and share alike, eh? You'll let me know when you find out more, right?"

"Sure, Ron," I said, putting a little faux snark into my voice. "So you want my tax dollars and you want me to do your job?"

"That'd be nice," Ron said.

Top o' the Morning was doing heavy business when Esme and I stopped by for our mid-walk coffee. We hadn't indulged in this ritual in a while, and it was fun, so far at least. Esme tried to wheedle more out of me about Jack, but I held strong, even though I was about to burst. I was dying to tell her, but at the same time I wanted it all to myself for now.

After Jack and I had finally worked out what each

of us felt, we'd talked for another hour, promising each other we'd take things slow and be very low-key about it. Grinning like a possum and chattering at Esme like a deranged howler monkey didn't honor that agreement.

"Well, would you look at that!" Esme said, stopping short on the sidewalk in front of the coffee shop.

I followed her gaze to the cluster of outdoor tables and spotted Claire Calvert, talking with a man seated opposite her. I couldn't see his face, but I thought I recognized his curly hair.

"Is that Quentin?" I asked.

"Yes, it is," Esme said, her lips setting into a hard line. "Claire is sitting there having coffee with the man who put her in that wheelchair. Has she lost her senses?"

She didn't look crazy. She looked like she was enjoying the coffee, and the company. I said as much, but Esme didn't appreciate my assessment.

She huffed and we turned to head inside. She'd just put her hand on the door handle when the shouting started. Nosy Nellies that we are, we stepped over immediately to see what was going on.

Nash Simpson stood by Claire's table, glaring down at Quentin. "Why'd you come back here?" he asked, loud enough for people at the other tables to hear. "No one wants you here."

Claire started to protest, but Quentin patted the air in a calming gesture and smiled at her. "It's okay, Claire," he said. He got up slowly, pushed in his chair neatly, and walked away without a backward glance.

As he walked by us, Laney Easton came out of the coffee shop, laughing at something her boyfriend, James Rowan, had said. They both froze and I saw Quentin give them a murderous look before heading down the sidewalk, his calm gait now an angry stalk.

I looked back to see Nash Simpson still standing beside Claire's table. He started to speak to her but she turned her head away. He scowled and headed for the parking lot, stopping to talk to people at other tables as he threaded his way through. Some seemed to be giving him attaboys, but others were frowning and shaking their heads.

"You go get our order," Esme said. "I'll sit with Claire."

When I came out, Claire was dabbing at her eyes. People at other tables were staring but pretending not to, their gazes darting quickly away when Esme's piercing eyes did a sweep of the alleyway.

"It's because people care about you, Claire," Esme said soothingly. "They don't want to see you hurt anymore than you already have been."

"People shouldn't be so quick to judge," Claire said quietly, and let out a huge sigh. "Life is seldom simple and human beings are complex. Plus, I'm a grown woman and perfectly capable of deciding where and with whom I would like to have coffee."

Esme smiled. "Even angry you're grammatical, Claire."

"I am angry," Claire said. "Do you know how tiresome it is to be the perpetual victim? I am not long-suffering Saint Claire of the Wheelchair. I want to live my life by my own rules and my own choices."

"I think people just don't understand," I said, handing Esme her coffee. "Forgiveness is a laudable thing, but most of us wouldn't have it in us to forgive what he did to you."

"That's because people don't know the whole story, or the true story, though God knows I've been trying to tell it for years. There was plenty of blame to go around. Quentin has paid for his mistakes and I've paid for mine."

"But, Claire," Esme said, "you're in a wheelchair because of him. That's a high price to pay for whatever you think were your mistakes."

"And you think going to prison wasn't a high price?" Claire asked, tears starting to pool in her eyes again. "Esme, Quentin is a good man. You don't know him."

"That's true," Esme said. "But I know people don't usually go to jail unless they're guilty, of something anyway."

I barked an involuntary laugh. "You really believe that? How are things in Utopia?" This earned me a glare from Esme.

"Sophreena's right, Esme," Claire said. "Much as I want everything to be fair and to believe people will do the right thing, sometimes it doesn't happen that way. Quentin was insecure, he was jealous, he had a bad temper, he left his dirty underwear on the bathroom floor," she said, allowing a flicker of a smile. "But what happened to me wasn't all his fault. It's more complicated than people know and things lined up in a perfect storm of injustice on this case. James Rowan was just coming in as assistant DA. He and Quentin's older brother had been chums and James convinced Quentin to take a plea. It was a bad deal, a very bad deal. If it had gone to trial I don't think Quentin would have been convicted, at least not of the most serious charges, not after I testified as to what really happened. But James convinced Quentin he'd be in jail until he was an old man if he didn't take the deal."

"You want to tell the story to us?" I asked. "I'd really like to hear it."

"I'd be happy to," Claire said, glancing at her watch, "but it will have to be another time. I've got to get to work." She nodded toward a building across the street that had once been an old cotton warehouse. It had been reclaimed and divided into cool, industrial-style office spaces. The Literacy Council operated out of the bottom-floor office.

Claire had worked hard at keeping in shape during her long rehab and she worked her wheelchair with ease, her muscular arms spinning the wheels in practiced rhythm. Esme and I fell into step alongside her.

"How are things going with Sherry Burton's case?" she asked. "Have you heard anything? That is still so heavy on my mind."

"Did you know Sherry Burton?" I asked.

"Yes," Claire said. "Such a sad ending to what I suspect was a sad life. I was still in my 'save the world, let's all join hands and sing "Kumbayah"' phase that summer I first met her. She seemed like a girl who needed saving. Her brother was a bit lost, too. I tried loaning her books since she seemed to have a lot of time on her hands, but she wasn't much of a reader. Her brother read everything he could get his hands on, but Sherry had other priorities. She was like a feral cat; if you tried to pull her close the claws would come out. But sometimes if she saw me outside she'd come over to talk or have something to eat. I don't know if this was true or not—Sherry had a tendency to exaggerate—but she told me their grandmother literally locked them out of the house during the day, so sometimes she came over just to use the bathroom. She was a troubled girl. I tried talking to her grandmother about her, hoping Mrs.

Walker would get her some help, but I might as well have been talking to a stone. She said all they needed was fresh air for their health and chores to keep them busy, then she invited me to butt out. She was very clear about that last part."

"So you knew Luke, too?" I asked.

"Ah, yes, little Luke," Claire said. "He was a sweet boy. Now, he was a reader. Every time I saw him he had a book, which wasn't too often, now that I think about it. He was as quiet as a little ninja. They were definitely at-risk kids. So sad. I know it doesn't help her now, but I hope they get whoever did this to Sherry."

"I think the police have some good leads," Esme said. "I'm convinced it will end up being something Sherry was mixed up in down in Miami."

We said our good-byes in front of the office and Esme and I set out on the rest of our walk.

"Why did you tell her that about Miami?" I asked Esme as we rounded the corner, headed for home. "That's just a rumor."

"Well, first, I really am thinking that's the way it's going to play out," Esme said. "And second, Claire is out there all by herself. You remember how upset she was the night of the vigil. It's got to be very worrisome to her to be thinking about a woman getting murdered right next door and the killer still out there. I thought she'd rest easier if she believes it had nothing to do with her or this community. How would you feel if something like this happened near you and you were living alone?"

"Safety-wise, you mean?" I asked. "I've never been one to twitch at every sound and I feel pretty safe in my house. Half the time I don't even remember to lock the doors. 'Course, I'm not as isolated as Claire, nor as vulnerable."

"No indeed, you're just a regular warrior princess, aren't you, Sophreena?" This was said in a tone that was decidedly not teasing; and as if I needed further evidence that she was ticked off about something, she lengthened her stride and poured on the speed, leaving me panting and sweating to keep up with her.

This was really getting old.

It wasn't as easy as I might have hoped, but after an hour going through more boxes from River's house and another frustrating hour of filling out request forms and perusing records at the courthouse, I finally had the death certificate for Samuel Wright. Immediately the phrase "death by misadventure" caught my eye. I'd never seen that phrase on a document, but I knew I'd run across it in school. If I remembered correctly, it meant a death that is caused by another person, but without intention, malice, or premeditation and not liable to criminal charges.

There was no information on where or how the body was interred, but a bashed-in skull certainly qualified as misadventure in my book.

We had to rush to make lunch. Cleve Jemson was pushing ninety years old and was a born raconteur. He'd driven himself to our luncheon and was planning to go fishing when we were done. As Margaret had claimed, he had a phenomenal memory. "Can't remember where I put the car keys, the remote control, but I remember things that happened years ago like I was seeing it on a movie screen," he said with a chuckle.

"I had a good ear as a kid. Could always tell when the grown-up folks were talking about things they didn't want the young ones to hear. 'Course, that's when I listened hardest. Mind you, lots of this stuff happened long before my time. I only know the stories the old folks told."

"Margaret tells me you remember some things about the Harper family that might relate to the body found on the property," I prompted.

Cleve nodded. "Well, I'm short on facts, but I know there was some mystery about Samuel Wright's death. Something not to be spoken about but in whispers among a chosen few. Folks referred to that 'terrible night' at the Harper place. I eventually pieced together the terrible thing was Miss Sadie's brother dying, and it wasn't just that he died, but that it happened in some gruesome way. I don't know if it was a suicide or an accident or what. There was something not right about the man. I got that by the way they talked about him. And also, I remember talk about how the sheriff at the time was a friend of the family and took care of everything. People around did everything but canonize him after that 'cause everybody thought so highly of the Harpers.

"When the brother died they laid him out at home, real private like, which wasn't uncommon for that day and time, but I had the feeling this wasn't just private, but secretive. And there was lots of concern about Miss Sadie. I don't know if she was hurt or sick or what, but she was an object of both pity and awe. That went on for years after her brother died. For a long time I thought her name was Poor Sadie, since that's what people always said when her name came up."

There was a ruckus at a table across the restaurant and I looked over to see Nash Simpson with three other men. His line crew, I guessed by the way they were dressed. Nash was talking and his face was florid. "Paid his debt? He hasn't even made a down payment. What do you know about it anyhow, Stanton? We need to be rid of that whole family. Quentin and his no-count nephew. He's a jailbird, too, you know. Car thief. I say we invite 'em both to clear out."

This pronouncement was met with shrugs from the

other men. This was likely a rant they'd heard before. They hunkered over their plates and dug into their food.

"Don't pay him any mind," Cleve said. "Nash is trying to get folks all riled up about Quentin being back from the slammer, but I doubt he'll get any takers. Tragic what happened to Claire, but she's forgiven him, and something about that case just wasn't right from the get-go."

"Is he talking about Gavin Taylor?" I asked.

"Yeah, he's Quentin's sister's boy," Cleve said. "He was a good boy, but Lord, lately he's caused his mama all kinds of grief. Sometimes he don't have the sense God gave a billy goat."

twelve

"WELL, WE DON'T HAVE ANY MORE FACTS THAN WE had before, but we can call it anecdotal evidence, eh?" I said as Esme gunned out of the parking lot.

"I'm getting some anecdotes, too," Esme said. "From across the divide. I feel like I've been hit in the head with a hammer. I can tell you one thing, whatever happened at the old Harper place, it unfolded right on that spot where River said the well used to be."

"Okay, so let's go over what we've got. The man, let's call him Samuel, just for the sake of argument, didn't die of drowning. So how does the well factor in? Unless someone bashed in his head after he was already dead, which is, I guess, a possibility."

"No, not drowning," Esme said, frowning in concentration. "There was something round and shiny, and horrible loud noises. Lots of shouting."

"Okay, so probably something violent. You know, it's

weird that we haven't found anything about his death in the newspaper archives, not even an obituary."

"There's a lot weird about this one. All I can tell you is whatever happened, it happened right on that spot," Esme said firmly.

"Any ideas as to the, uh, messenger?" I asked.

Esme sighed. "A woman, as it almost always is. I guess men aren't big communicators even in the hereafter. But I don't know who she is and I don't even know how I know it's a woman. I'm just getting images this time, and some sounds. They only come in little flashes. It's so frustrating." She gripped the wheel tight.

My cell phone chirped and I saw it was Dee.

"Strange request," she said. "Laney called and she's wondering if you could get permission from River for her to come visit the place where Sherry Burton died. She says to tell him it's not morbid curiosity, but she knew Sherry and since she's heard there's no memorial planned, she'd like to pay her respects."

"Okay, a little weird," I said, turning the idea over in my mind. "When does she want to do this?"

"Late this afternoon if you can set it up," Dee said. "Then could you go shopping with me? I've got to get some shoes for the wedding. I don't have anything but outdoor boots, athletic shoes, and city walkers. I need big-girl dress-up shoes."

I hesitated. What if Jack called and wanted to do something later? Then I gave myself a mental slap. I'd always hated women who would dump a friend for a guy and here I was contemplating doing it already, this early in the still-green relationship. "I'll call River," I said. "If he says it's okay, we can meet around five; there's still plenty of light then, and you and I can hit the mall afterward."

"You're getting chummy with Laney Easton," Esme said after I gave her the scoop. "You know people are saying she may be our next mayor. Maybe you can resurrect that idea of starting up a heritage center now that you seem to be in with the powers that be."

It was a pipe dream and I knew it, but I hadn't been able to let go of the idea of starting a nonprofit that would provide a space and resources for people to learn how to trace their family histories. I'd floated the idea several times to various town officials and everyone I'd talked to was very enthusiastic about the idea, but not so much into the making it a reality part. And, as our business has gotten more successful, gods be praised, I've had less time and energy to pursue it.

"Maybe I'll mention it to her," I said. "I'm sure she'll get right on it."

"I'm surprised she can peel herself off James Rowan long enough to do anything with you. She's got a bad case of man-worship when it comes to that guy. I don't see it myself, but she seems to think he's God on high," Esme said.

"So you don't think a successful, handsome, well-bred, well-educated attorney who dresses like he stepped out of *GQ* and has a lot of very white teeth is a good catch?"

"I'm not judging," Esme said in a tone that let me know she was definitely judging, "but he's nearly two decades older than she is. And he didn't have any interest in her until she got on the town council. Convenient, since he's a politician. And lastly, he wears a pinkie ring, for jiminy's sake. I don't trust a man who wears a pinkie ring. I think she's setting herself up for heartbreak."

"I hope not," I said, and found that I meant it more than I would've thought. I always liked Laney. She could be thoughtless, and she did have a sense of entitlement like a lot of rich kids do, but she was so guileless about it you had to forgive her. And I was certain she genuinely cared about the town.

"I can't believe she wants to do a remembrance where Sherry Burton was murdered," Esme said. "I can tell you now, that's one sight I'd just as soon forget."

Esme and I spent the next two hours going through the rest of the boxes we'd brought from River's attic. She sorted while I worked on the time line we'd be using to construct the heritage book for River.

This book would be the same as the family heritage scrapbooks we offer in our deluxe services, except it would feature the land rather than the family tree. River wanted to know about the people who'd lived on the land, but he was also interested in what had been grown there, how the landscape may have changed over the years, and other land usage issues. Plus, I suspected he might want to assure himself that bodies weren't going to start popping up every time he dug a hole.

Land records are not my forte. Acres and hectors, plots and plats, land boundaries and shifting creeks and rivers, it all makes me cross-eyed after awhile. Which was why walking River's land with him had been helpful. Looking at the real thing helped bring the dry descriptions to life.

Esme was humming softly and I realized this was the first time we'd worked so companionably in a long while.

"This is nice," I said.

"Hmm," Esme said, which could have been interpreted in a dozen ways.

"I've missed it. We haven't worked much together on this project," I added, hoping she was ready to talk about what was bugging her.

"We don't have to do every single thing together, Sophreena," she said. "It's fine."

Okay, so she wasn't ready. Leave it alone, I warned myself. And for once I heeded my own cautions.

I looked quickly through the stack of info I'd printed off from Ginger Holderman. My eye landed on a point of interest and I flipped through the papers until I came to the one with the contact info she'd sent. I punched in her number, expecting to leave a message, but she picked up.

"I see you have your great-grandfather's occupation listed as mortician. What can you tell me about that?" I asked, purposefully leaving the question open.

"Creepy, isn't it?" Ginger asked. "I mean, that's not exactly like finding out you're descended from royalty or something, right? Do you think it's wrong to be sort of ashamed of your family tree? That's blasphemy, right? I mean, I know there are all these cultures where they worship their ancestors and all that, but it just seems a lot of mine make me cringe."

I laughed. "Mine, too. But you know, when you think about it, maybe if they'd made different choices, it would have altered everything and they would have ended up in a different place or gone to a different school or never met their spouses and had children, in which case you wouldn't exist."

"Oh, my God!" she exclaimed. "I never thought of it that way. Anyhow, you asked about Virgil. He was born on a farm just outside Durham and grew up in

North Carolina, moving from place to place, until he fetched up over in Hillsborough as a young man with big plans. He got involved in a scheme that went bad and moved to Baltimore to get away from his creditors. That's where he went to school to learn his trade. Geez, I'm getting the willies just thinking about what that curriculum must have been like."

"Do you know if he ever had anything to do with selling funeral supplies?"

"Yeah, it was something to do with that enterprise that got him in hot water. He was selling certificates for the Modern American Burial Company. I've got a copy of one of them. They're beautifully engraved. Honestly, they look like money. They sold some kind of special burial vault or something."

"Caskets," I said. "Caskets made from glass."

"You mean like Sleeping Beauty?" she asked.

"Not exactly." I shivered, having my own case of the willies. I described the caskets and asked if she had any other information about Virgil's involvement with the company.

"Don't think so, but I'll look through the stuff and if I find anything I'll send it along. Then, you know what? I think I'll lay off the genealogy for a while. I'm an aromatherapist, for God's sake. I can't be thinking about death and embalming or I'll ruin my nose."

"Probably best to take a break," I agreed.

I summarized the call for Esme. "And that adds another few ounces to the weight of our evidence. We still don't know the hows and whys, but I think we can safely assume Virgil Wright supplied that glass coffin and that it's his brother inside it."

Esme considered, then nodded. "What was that at the end about taking a break?"

"Oh," I laughed, "she's disappointed in her ancestors for failing to provide a more admirable pedigree."

"Amen, sister," Esme said. "I wish to all that's holy whoever my forebearer was who passed on this so-called gift had skipped that bequest."

"But then you wouldn't be you, Esme. And you do good things with your gift."

"At a cost," Esme said. "At a dear cost." After a moment she went back to unloading the last box we'd brought from River's house. "What do you suppose this is all about?" she asked, lifting a cloth-wrapped bundle out of the dusty cardboard box.

She held it out as if it might have a live badger inside and I followed as she carried it to the card table we keep set up in the corner, covered with bath mats and curtained off from the rest of the room to contain dust.

The bundle was about the size of a bread box and wrapped in a coarse linen cloth tied several times around with tobacco twine. I instinctively reached out and felt the sides. "Feels like books, maybe."

I turned it over carefully and switched on the light above the table. On the bottom someone had written on the cloth with a pencil, the letters now faded almost completely. I grabbed a magnifying glass and stooped to read, squinting to help fill in the gaps in the letters. *For Lottie, someday.*

I stood up, engaging myself in a spirited ethics debate. I'm happy to poke around in the possessions of deceased people. But Lottie Walker was still alive, and this was clearly meant for her. Had she ever seen it? Should I get her permission to open it?

"River bought the place lock, stock, and barrel, remember?" Esme said as if reading my mind. "This is his property now and he wants us to go through it. So let's open 'er up."

I allowed myself to be convinced, ethics trumped by curiosity. But I grabbed my camera first and took pictures of the bundle as we'd found it before we cut the string. Inside there was a photo album, some stacks of letters tied with the requisite pink ribbons, and three more of the small memo books I'd seen before among Sadie Harper's things. Esme set in immediately to wipe things off with antistatic cloths, but I went straight for the stacks of letters, flipping through them like a deck of cards to look at the return addresses. This sent dust motes dancing into the stream of light from the lamp. Esme said a swear word in French and I felt ridiculously happy to hear it. She sounded more like herself than she had in days.

The letters were from an Inez Wright. I went to the table and flipped through the things Ginger Holderman had sent, locating the woman on the Wright family chart. She was Virgil Wright's wife. She and her sister-in-law, Sadie Wright Harper, had apparently kept up a correspondence over many years.

Esme opened the photo album to the first page and turned it to show me the picture of a snaggletoothed boy of around six, with the name Samuel Lemar Wright written underneath in irregular block letters. Esme quickly flipped through more pages. There were images of a young Samuel in a baseball uniform, school photos, a few snapshots of Samuel and a young woman, several of Samuel in uniform, then a wedding photo of Samuel and Eugenia, labeled in handwriting full of flourishes. Then there were a few snapshots of Samuel and a baby, who grew into a toddler through the series of shots.

We were interrupted by the doorbell, which meant it wasn't one of the club or Dee. They all held with the old custom of "helloing the house" by letting themselves in the front door while calling out to find out where we were.

Esme went to answer and came back a few minutes later with Claire wheeling in behind her. "I don't mean to interrupt your work," she said, "but I thought

I'd swing by on my way home and see if you had a few minutes to talk." She glanced around the tables of Harper family mementoes and documents. "Well, as Coco would say, 'Crikey!' I never realized you two had such an operation going here."

"People accumulate many things over a lifetime," I said, "and we love people with pack-rat mentalities. We find out a lot by plowing through stuff like this."

"Well, I'll let you work; we can get together another time," Claire said, backing her chair toward the door. "I should have called."

"No," Esme and I said in unison, Esme hitting a low note and me the high.

While Esme went in to fix us tea and serve up the zucchini bread Winston had baked for us, I guided Claire into the family room. I cleared off the coffee table, tossing magazines, notebooks, pens, and stray receipts onto the easy chair by the window. I really needed to tidy up in here. I hadn't been carrying my half of the housecleaning chores lately. Maybe that's what had Esme so cross.

"At the risk of being the world's worst hostess," I said as Esme set the tray on the coffee table, "could we start right off with the story, Claire? I'm supposed to meet some people at five and I'm dying to hear this."

"And I'm eager to tell you," Claire said. "Right after it happened I told it over and over until I had no voice left, but I couldn't get anybody to listen to me. Then somewhere along the way I gave up trying to convince people. This was all before you came to live here, Esme, and close as we've become, I don't think I've even told you."

"No, I've never heard you speak about it. I thought maybe you didn't like to remember," Esme said.

"Well, it's not pleasant to remember that night, but it's important to set the facts straight. This is the way it actually happened, as opposed to what you've likely heard around town through the years. I was a young teacher, twenty-six years old and filled with idealism. Honestly, if you could have heard me talk about my call to teaching, it probably would've made you puke. I was obnoxiously evangelical about it. Quentin was working at a small manufacturing company that made electronic thermostats. We'd been married nearly three years and we'd just bought the house. Now, I grant you, we were not the romantic fantasy of happily ever after. We fought and made up and fought again. We gave in and held out and got over and saw through. We were both immature, but we were finding our way in making a life together. We were happy. Our own version of happy.

"A few days after school was out that year, I ran into Nash Simpson at the hardware store. I'd known him since we were kids. We went to school together, or at least we did when his folks bothered to send him. His family was dirt poor and didn't value education much. Anyhow, he pulled me aside and asked very quietly if I could teach him to read. He'd just gotten on at the power plant, sweeping floors and doing gofer jobs, but he could see a chance to make something of himself there, except he knew he needed good reading skills. So I told him I'd be happy to work with him. Then he laid down the rules. No one was to know. He was embarrassed about being illiterate. So I agreed it would be just between the two of us.

"Quentin was working second shift, so we made plans for Nash to come over to our house two nights a week for me to work with him, and all went along fine for a while. Our house was isolated—well, still is pretty isolated, but even more so back then. No one was likely to see his truck there and he wasn't married at the time, so he didn't have anyone to answer to as to his whereabouts. He was making good progress and I was feeling pretty self-righteous about my part in it.

"Then one night I heard Quentin's truck come roaring into the driveway while we were working at the kitchen table. He came up the back porch steps at a run and flung open the door and nearly ran over the two of us before he stopped. He was wild-eyed and redfaced. Quentin had always been the jealous type, and to my everlasting shame, I sort of liked it. I thought it meant he really, really loved me. Never occurred to me in my romantic fog that it also meant he didn't trust me.

"He demanded to know what was going on and I started to tell him, but Nash put his hand on my arm to stop me, reminding me with that one gesture of my promise. But it only made us look guilty of something else. I stammered some lame thing and then Quentin turned toward Nash and took a step. But here's the thing, the big thing. Nash swung first. He started the fight. He hit Quentin in the stomach so hard he doubled over and then the rage was let loose. They fought all over that kitchen, both of them snarling like animals. Somewhere in all the confusion I got knocked down, and my back struck the edge of our old dinette table, which had been turned over during the fight. My scream ended the brawl." She stopped and I could see she was struggling not to cry, her voice coming out in a strained whisper. "My scream ended life as we'd known it."

"Oh, Claire," Esme said. "Darlin', how awful for you."

"So you see," Claire went on, "we were all guilty of something. Quentin was hotheaded and acted before he thought; I was wrong to agree to keep things from him and to encourage him to feel jealous; and Nash was guilty of an excess of pride for not wanting to be open about his illiteracy and for starting the fight in the first place. I might have been able to calm Quentin down if Nash hadn't thrown that first punch. They arrested

Quentin that night while they were still working on me at the hospital. I was in no condition to tell them what had happened and Nash insisted on pressing charges."

"That's not the way I've heard the story at all," I said.

Claire nodded, her eyes swimming with tears. She wiped them away impatiently. "You'd think as many times as I've told this I'd be over the crying by now. Anyway, while they were still discovering the extent of my injuries, charges were being drawn up against Quentin, and they kept piling them on. First it was simple assault, then aggravated assault, then assault with a deadly weapon, which, by the way, was a turkey platter we'd gotten as a wedding gift. It was absurd. And to make matters worse, Quentin had been in a couple of scrapes when he was a kid and because he had a record, he came in under three strikes. James Rowan, curse his hide, was trying to make his bones as DA and wanted to show he was a law-and-order guy. Quentin was sent off for a seven-year stretch in prison."

I did the math. "But that means he should have been out . . ." I began, still calculating.

"Should have," Claire said, "but Quentin still had anger issues and things didn't go well his first couple of years inside. He kept getting weeks and months tacked on to his sentence for one infraction or another.

I couldn't go see him at all in those early years because I was struggling with my rehabilitation and he had to earn visitor privileges, but as soon as I was able, I started visiting. He'd thought during that whole time that I blamed him, and maybe there was a part of me that did, but gradually we got through it and he started taking his own rehabilitation seriously. He got into counseling and picked up some computer training and we started planning for a life together when he got out. But it's been a long road, and we're not newlyweds anymore. We're trying to get to know each other again. We've agreed to live apart for at least a year and try to work on things slowly."

"One thing I'm curious about," I said, thinking back over her story. "What made Quentin come home that night?"

"There it is," Claire said, nodding. "That's the big question. He got a call at work. His boss came and got him off the assembly floor, told him it was an emergency. The voice on the line told him he should come home quick if he wanted to catch his wife with the other man she'd been seeing behind his back."

"Surely there were phone records they could have checked to find out who placed the call," Esme said.

Claire nodded. "From the pay phone at the Kwik-Mart, plenty of pay phones around back then, remember?"

"And Quentin didn't recognize the voice?" I asked.

Claire shook her head. "He said it sounded like someone had something covering the receiver. The words were clear enough, but he couldn't even tell if it was a man or a woman."

"Who do you think it was?" I asked.

"Well, I've thought a lot about that over the years. Nash was dating Connie back then. She's his wife now. She had a really bad temper, and she still does, by the way. If she knew anything about him coming to my house, she'd have been really angry. And Quentin had some coworkers who didn't like him much and were always trying to shaft him in one way or another. I had a couple of ex-boyfriends who hadn't taken kindly to being rejected. Those are the only people I can think of, but honestly, I don't think it was any of them. To this day I still can't think of anyone with cause to do something like that. So, that's the story and I'm happy to have you two actually listen and believe, or at least I hope you believe me."

"I would never doubt your word on anything, Claire," Esme said. "And I hope you'll forgive me for some of the things I've said about Quentin. I spoke out of turn."

"What about Nash?" I asked. "What's up with him? He bears some fault in this, too. What's with his attitude?"

"Guilt, I think," Claire said with a sigh. "Or shame. He knows this might have gone differently if he hadn't thrown that first punch. And it was ridiculous to hold me to the pledge of not telling about tutoring him. But it's easier to make Quentin the villain. Quentin and I would like to stay here in Morningside and try to pick up the pieces of our lives. I love it here, and my work and my friends are here, but if things don't settle down soon, we may have to move away to get some peace."

"Well, we can't let that happen," Esme said. "You're needed here."

"I'm glad Quentin didn't move back in with me right away, and that he has an iron-clad alibi," Claire said. "Else they'd probably have tried to pin Sherry's murder on him, even though I don't think he ever even met Sherry or Luke."

"Luke is here, did you know that?" I asked.

"So they found him?" Claire said. "I knew they were looking for next of kin. Well, that's good. I'd love to see him."

"They didn't exactly find him, but since I need to get going, I'll let Esme tell you that story. Amazing how two siblings can grow up under the same conditions and yet end up such different people. Luke seems like a good guy."

"'Seems' being the operative word," Esme said.

thirteen

I DECIDED TO GO OUT TO SEE RIVER IN PERSON TO ask if he'd mind me bringing Laney to the grave site. In any case, I wanted to tell him what we'd found that afternoon and give him a look at the photo album so he could see what Samuel Wright had looked like.

I found him trying to put order back into his trampled garden beds. He looked up as I drove up the long gravel drive, stones popping out from under my tires. His frown disappeared when he recognized my car and he stood and peeled off his work gloves, stowing them in his back pocket as he walked over. I asked about Laney's request right off so I could text Dee the plan.

He hesitated, but then I told him Laney's reason for wanting to make the visit.

"Well, sure, that's fine," he'd said. "Poor girl oughta have somebody that knew her grieving for her, other than Luke, I mean."

"Yeah," I said. "About Luke, do you have any idea where he's staying? Claire would like to see him."

"Matter of fact, I know exactly where he's staying; right here with me," River said, giving a head jerk toward the house. "He'll be helping me out with some things around the place and the rest of his time he'll spend writing up his findings and analyzing his data for his dissertation. I got plenty of room, and after the conditions he's lived in for the past year, he doesn't mind a little construction dust."

"That's very generous of you," I said hesitantly, "especially since you hardly know him. What does Jennifer have to say about it?"

"I believe her exact worlds were, 'For Pete's sake, Dad, he's not a stray puppy,' but I may be misremembering the front end of that. Jennifer's got a foul mouth when she's riled. But she'll warm to the idea. Sometimes it just takes her awhile to come around to things."

I smiled, careful to keep what I was thinking from showing on my face.

"I'm a good judge of character," River said. "That's not a boast, it's a statement of fact. I like the kid, and frankly, he's got more claim to this place than I do."

"Well, I wouldn't go quite that far, River," I said. "This is your land now, you bought it and you own it."

"Yeah, but that's only if you believe you can own the land. I hope someday this place will become a part of my being, but right now we're just getting to know one another. For Luke it's different. Anyhow, if, as you say, this is my place, then I get to say who stays here, right?"

"Right," I agreed, wondering why Luke would choose to hang around this place. It didn't sound to me like he could have many happy memories of his time here.

"What you got there?" River asked, nodding at the album I held clutched against my chest.

I told him what we'd found. "I thought of taking it out to Miss Lottie, but technically it belongs to you, so I wanted to get your take on it. But it looks like I've caught you in the middle of something." I motioned toward the garden.

River shrugged. "Garden's not going anywhere. The land abides. Let's go inside."

As we walked to the house I told him more about the contents of the bundle we'd found and about the faded inscription on the cloth.

"I'd love to see it," he said, "but as far as the whole ownership thing goes, that's Miss Lottie's stuff if she wants it. And if she doesn't, maybe Luke would. It might mean something to him to know about his family and this land. I sense the boy has a powerful need to belong to something—a place, a tribe, or a cause, maybe. I imagine that's one reason he was drawn to his profession."

We found Luke in the kitchen putting ice into three glasses. "I saw you coming," he said. "Lemonade or tea, what'll it be?"

"You're a handy fella to have around," River said, slapping his gloves into a basket by the door.

"Homemade?" I asked, eyeing the lemonade pitcher.

"Is there any other kind?" Luke asked. "That's one thing I learned during the past year. Modern life has brought us many wonderful things, but processed food is not one of them. This was made with fresh lemons and raw honey."

No wonder River liked this guy, I thought. They were two peas in an organic pod.

We sat at the table and looked through the photo album together. River took his time with each page. "So this is Jimmy," he said when he came to the one of Samuel in his uniform. "I guess I have to start calling him Sam now. He's got a good face."

"Yes, he does," I agreed, looking at the photo more closely. Samuel had been handsome in a boyish way. Light-haired and blue-eyed, he looked much too young to be going off to war. "I see a little of you in his face, Luke."

"So, he's my, what, great-grandfather?" Luke asked.

"Yes, this is your grandmother Lottie's father. There seems to be some mystery surrounding how he died."

Luke took all of this in clinically, as if it were one of

his case studies. And indeed, it might very well end up that way. It seemed River had told him about the glass casket and Luke had started to research it immediately, thinking he might get an article out of it.

I heard the toot of a horn, Dee and Laney's signal. I chugged the rest of my lemonade, not wanting a drop to go to waste, and left Luke and River still perusing the photo album, speculating about each picture.

"Oh, Sophreena," Laney said as she slammed the door to her SUV, a Mercedes, naturally, "thank you so much for arranging this. I don't know how to explain it, I just felt I needed to see where she died. Is that weird?"

"No, it's not weird," Dee said after she'd slammed her own door. "Not real weird, anyway," she added after a moment's thought.

"People grieve in different ways," I said, figuring that covered all contingencies.

"I know, but it seems strange that I'm feeling so sad about somebody I haven't seen in years," Laney said. "You knew her, too, Dee. Is it hitting you like that?"

"I didn't really know her, Laney. I saw her only a couple of times before my mother reined me back in."

Laney nodded, looking toward what I now thought of as Samuel Wright's grave. "Is that where you found her?"

"Yes, I'll show you," I said, moving into the lead.

"But we can't go inside the cordoned area, and try not to disturb anything. We don't have a final ruling on anything related to the grave yet."

When we reached the area, I described to Laney how we'd found Sherry, and then we took a moment of silence, each lost in our own thoughts.

"She never had a chance," Laney said at last. "Really, not one chance to have a decent life. Her mother went from one man to another, and Sherry never had a real home or any kind of family support. I guess when you grow up like that you make bad choices because you feel you have nothing to lose."

"Maybe," I said, though I was thinking that Luke must have experienced the same upbringing, and from all appearances, he'd turned out quite differently.

"Oh, but she was so much fun," Laney went on. "I wish you could have known her. So wild and crazy, but there was something deep about her, too. She gave us all tribal names and we used to meet down there by the creek." She motioned toward a copse of trees at the bottom of the hill. "We'd chant nonsense we imagined sounded like some Native American tongue and tell ancient tales—ones we made up on the spot, mind you. Sherry used the red mud from the creek bank to draw symbols on herself and then she'd dance under the moonlight like she was in a trance. It was silly, but at the time it all seemed very exotic and exciting."

"Now, that's weird," Dee said. "I always thought of you as a frou-frou girl back then. Make-up, boys, clothes, all that stuff."

"By day," Laney said, "but by night I was an earth goddess. Well, okay, Sherry was a goddess, but I was maybe a wood nymph or something. Anyhow, that's what drew me to her games. I was able to be something I wasn't, something different. I'd think of everybody indoors playing computer games, watching TV, listening to CDs, while we were discovering the hidden secrets of the night, and I'd feel pity for those people. We took it so seriously. I can't believe I never got caught crawling in and out of my window. My folks would have grounded me for the rest of my life."

"Did Sherry ever get caught?" Dee asked.

Laney shrugged. "She wasn't what you'd call closely supervised when she stayed here," she said, turning to look again at the trees.

"Would you two mind? I'd like to go down to the creek to see if that little clearing is still there."

"We'll come with you," Dee said, but Laney was already moving out, as if drawn by a magnetic force.

"I'll run on down and try to find the place," she said. "I know you've got stuff to do. I don't want to keep you." And with that she trotted off down the hill. It struck me as I watched her run that Sherry had been wearing similar running togs when we'd found her. Lots of people ran out along the main road. Maybe Sherry had been out for a run and had the same idea Laney had, to revisit a place where she'd been so happy when she was a child. That might explain what she was doing out here. But surely she wouldn't have been running in flip-flops.

Dee and I loped down the hill, zigzagging to avoid potholes and the briars coiling up to claw at our exposed ankles.

"Down here," Laney called when we got to the creek. She spread her arms as we came into the clearing. "This is it," she said. "It's so much smaller than I remember. Gavin used to sit right over there on the other side of the stream, usually whittling something. He called them totems, but they just looked like little pieces of stick a dog had chewed. I suppose if you'd really let your imagination work, you could see an animal in one or two of them. Anyway, he'd make them and give them to Sherry like an offering." Then, pointing to a flat rock that jutted out over the stream, she said, "That was Bryan's place. He'd sit there and watch Sherry, practically drooling. He was the main storyteller. This little spot over here was like Sherry's stage. She'd predict our futures, or dance, or tell us about the different places she'd been with her mother."

"Where was your place?" I asked, looking around and trying to imagine the little tribe of children out here sharing ancient mysteries, or maybe a few purloined cigarettes.

"I was sort of a floater," Laney said. "I usually brought food I'd nabbed from the pantry at home and I'd pass it out and sometimes I'd think of a story, too, but mine were never as good as Sherry's or Bryan's."

She looked around for another moment, then let out a sigh. "Okay, well, thanks for indulging me. We can go now."

As we walked back up the hill to our cars, we talked of other things. Dee filled us in on how the preparations for Marydale and Winston's wedding were going, then teased Laney by asking if her wedding would be the next to take place at High Ground.

"Maybe," Laney said coyly. "I think James may be working up to a proposal. He's been dropping a few hints and my birthday is coming up. Could be I'll get a special present, say, in a package about this big"—she pinched her thumb and forefinger together to show the size of a ring box—"but you're not to tell that to a living soul. You'll jinx it."

Dee put a hand over her heart and I drew a zipper across my mouth. Laney laughed, then gave one last mournful look in the direction of the grave site before we walked back to our cars.

"Well, will you look at that!" Laney exclaimed after she'd opened her car door. "I thought I'd lost this forever."

Dee and I turned as Laney held up something shiny. I stepped closer and saw it was a silver bracelet with a single heart charm.

"I've searched everywhere and all this time it was down in the seat. James gave this to me for Christmas last year. He'll be so happy; he was upset I'd lost it."

"Did you step on it?" I asked, noticing the mud caught in the links. "I'd clean it up before he sees it."

"Oh no, I must have," Laney said, looking down at her dirty shoes. "I'll go shine it up quick so I can wear it tonight."

She put the bracelet in her pocket, climbed behind the wheel, and shot out of the driveway as if going to clean her jewelry was an emergency. If she'd had a bubble light and sirens, I had no doubt she'd have used them.

Clouds were gathering and the wind was freshening as Dee and I arrived at the mall. I rummaged in the trunk for an umbrella, but of course there wasn't one.

I was never a mall rat. Even as a teen I didn't care much for shopping. I've heard it said that when it comes to shopping, humans revert to primitive roles. The men go out looking for something specific, find it, kill it, and drag it home. Whereas the women constantly scan the surroundings searching for edible herbs and brightly colored berries to gather. I'm with the guys on this one. Get in, bag your quarry, and get out.

But tonight I was enjoying myself as Dee and I trekked from store to store searching for shoes that looked good and didn't kill her feet.

"You know," Dee said as we headed to store number four, "you promised me a full report of what went on with Jack the other night. I've been waiting for you to bring it up, but you're holding out on me."

"I never promised you a full report," I said, "but okay, I'll hit the highlights. I've got to tell somebody or I'm gonna burst." I told her about our initial misunderstanding and how we'd eventually worked it out. "We're going to take it very slow and see where it goes. But we're going to mark our beginning by going on a real date. He asked me to dinner at Olivia's on Sunday night."

"Olivia's," Dee said, her voice lilting. "Ooh, fancy. What are you going to wear?"

"Wear?" I repeated. "Huh, I guess jeans and a T-shirt won't do."

"Sophreena," Dee said suspiciously, "what are you wearing to Mother and Winston's wedding?"

"My dress," I said, then reconsidered. "No, I guess not, it's black, that would be like bad luck or something, right?"

"Your dress, as in singular?" Dee said. "Sophreena, even I have more than one dress."

I shrugged. "Rarely have the need."

"Okay, you do now. We're going to find you a dress. What's our budget?"

I mentally checked my bank account. We'd done pretty well for the past couple of months and we had two more big jobs coming up. I gave her a figure I felt comfortable with. She sighed. "Maybe we can find a good sale."

I ended up buying a linen sheath with a matching jacket in a mustardy color. I hadn't wanted to try it on because someone once told me nobody looks good in that color, but Dee insisted. "It's perfect for your eyes and coloring," she'd said. And once it was on, it did look different, more earth-toney and less hot-doggy. I bought not only the dress but also a pair of shoes with an extremely high heel, by which I mean nearly two inches. I gulped a little as the clerk rang up the transaction, but I figured I could get at least a twofer out of the outfit this week alone. I'd wear it on the date with Jack and then again to the wedding next weekend.

As we were leaving the store we ran into Bryan Mason—literally, in Dee's case. He came around a corner and nearly knocked her over as he was checking something on his phone.

"Dee!" he said, looking her up and down. "I haven't seen you in forever. When did you get into town?"

Dee greeted Bryan with a bright smile and there

followed the usual "how ya doing," "whatcha up to now," and scuttlebutt about mutual acquaintances. Then Bryan turned serious.

"Sophreena, I understand Sherry's little brother's in town. Does that mean there might be a memorial or something for Sherry?"

"He hasn't mentioned anything to me," I said.

Technically that was true. Luke hadn't told me anything, but actually, I knew exactly what Luke planned. River had told me he'd made arrangements to have Sherry's body cremated and was planning to drive back to Florida at the end of the summer and get a few of her friends together for a small remembrance ceremony. Understandably, he wasn't eager to make the trip right away, not until somebody discovered why she was killed and by whom. He wasn't even keen on people knowing he was here, but apparently the word was out.

"How'd you hear he was in town?" I asked Bryan.

He frowned. "I forget who told me. Heard it somewhere. Listen, Sophreena," he said, cocking his head to the side, "I'm kinda worried about Gavin. Being questioned by the cops about Sherry has got him all squirrely. After that whole stunt with taking the car, he's cop-shy, you know? And when he gets rattled he does stupid things. You know him, how he is. Me and him have been friends for a long time and I want to help him. Do you think he needs a lawyer or anything? I'd pay for it."

"I don't have any reason to think he needs one, Bryan," I said, a little surprised at this outpouring of concern.

"I hope you're right," Bryan said. "But would you keep an eye on him and let me know if you think he's in trouble?"

"Sure," I said, "but I don't think you need to worry." As I saw Bryan's shoulders relax, I thought I might have to reform my opinion of him.

"Well, it was good to see you two, and don't rat me out, okay?" He lifted the shopping bags he was carrying, all from the sporting goods store. He smiled sheepishly. "I can't afford to buy everything from the pro shop, not even with my discount."

"Your secret is safe with me," Dee said, giving him another dazzling smile.

We said our good-byes and once we were out of earshot, I turned to Dee. "Were you flirting with him?"

"Maybe a little," Dee said with a shrug. "Just for old times' sake, and because now I can. I had such a secret crush on him in high school."

"You never told me," I said.

"What part of 'secret crush' don't you understand, Sophreena? Anyhow, he was so cute and popular back then, I knew he was way out of my league. He's still a handsome guy and I feel I've risen a league or two since high school, so I can flirt with him now without getting all tongue-tied. And anyhow, it's sweet that he's trying to look out for Gavin."

"Yeah," I agreed. "Unfortunately, Gavin seems to need a lot of looking out for these days."

As we headed for the exit, a chain of rolling thunder seemed to be traversing the entire county. The rain was coming down in sheets and my car was at the far end of the parking lot. We decided a hot cup of coffee and a cinnamon bun in the nice dry food court was a much more attractive alternative.

"Do you think they'll ever find who killed Sherry?" Dee asked once we'd scored a tiny table among all the other shoppers waiting out the storm.

"I hope so, and I hope it turns out to be something to do with her life in Miami. I know that sounds terrible, but I'd rather it be about drugs or some bad choice she made there than something personal here."

Dee nodded. "Doesn't make her any less dead, but I see what you mean. You don't think Bryan or Gavin could have had anything to do with it, do you?"

I frowned. "I can't imagine what would be their motive, but then again, I don't know much about their relationship with Sherry. Laney makes it all sound pretty innocent, but I think there may have been a little more to it than she lets on."

"Yeah, I think so, too," Dee said. "But they were kids and that was a long time ago."

I nodded. "So, who else did Sherry know here? She knew Claire. I think we can rule her out. And she knew Lottie. Ditto."

"Luke?" Dee offered. "An inheritance thing, maybe? He didn't want to share?"

"I understand there's not much left to inherit when Lottie goes."

"Yeah, but did Luke know that?" Dee asked.

"Good question," I said. "Very good question."

fourteen

THE RAINSTORM REFUSED TO ABATE AND WE didn't leave the mall until closing time, making a mad dash for the car along with lots of other folks caught umbrella-less. The air was filled with shrieks and squeals as people were pelted with rain and frightened by the strobes of lightning and loud thunderclaps.

My hair was soaked and dripping down the back of my neck and my jeans were cold and plastered to me by the time I slid behind the wheel, but my new dress and shoes had stayed dry where I'd tucked them underneath my T-shirt.

I drove slowly to Marydale's house, resisting the impulse to swerve every time lightning lit the sky. I pulled up as close to the back door as I could get, and Dee splashed through a rivulet of water surging toward the street's storm drain.

It seemed to take forever to drive the few blocks to

my house. The rain was still coming down hard and I had to creep along, my neck craned toward the windshield, my hands clenched on the wheel. When I finally pulled into the driveway, I debated going on into the garage, but the car would leave puddles on the floor. I'd cleaned the place a few weekends ago and given the floor a new coat of paint. I didn't like the idea of that pristine expanse being sullied so soon, and I was already wet anyhow.

Once on the porch, I shook like a dog, then let myself in. I headed for the family room to leave my packages before going upstairs to shower and get into dry clothes. I couldn't wait to show Esme my new dress and shoes when she got home from her dinner date with Denny. She was going to flip out. She thinks I have no fashion sense at all, which is sadly true.

Just as I went through the doorway, a lightning strike hit very close by with a loud crack. I jumped as I fumbled for the light switch. Just as I found it and flipped it on, my eye registered a person sitting in the chair in the corner, then the lights blinked and went out, plunging the room into total darkness.

I stood frozen, my hand still on the switch plate. A thousand things went through my mind, all of them jostling for first place and setting off trembling in every muscle in my body. If I made a noise I'd give away my position, and the man—I was pretty sure it was a man—might lunge for me. Had I really seen a person or was it just the throw blankets piled in the chair? After all, I'd noted the room was messy just hours earlier. Did I hear breathing? Yes, but was it mine or someone else's? Every tiny movement set the shopping bags crackling and I was struggling to stand stock-still. My leg was starting to cramp.

I was supposed to be the coolheaded one, I reminded myself. A plan. A plan was what I needed right about now. How fast could I spin around and which route should I take out of the house? I could go for the kitchen and out the back door, but then there was the issue of the garden gate with the hinky hasp. Sometimes it took some jiggling to get the thing open, and that was in dry daylight. The front door would probably be better, but then I had to turn a corner very sharply and there was tile on the entryway floor. I'd have to be careful not to slip. If I went down he could be on me in a flash. I had visions of every nature show I'd ever watched where the hapless gazelle was brought down and devoured by a lion.

Another flash of lightning answered my question. Not blankets.

"Who's there?" I blurted before I could stop myself.

"It's me," a voice said. "Only me."

I didn't recognize the voice, and whoever it was had on a hoodie and was hunched over so I couldn't see hair or a face. Then the figure started to rise from the chair.

"Who's me?" I asked, inching backward into the doorway, one tiny shuffling step after another. I'd decided to go for the front hallway, and as the figure moved toward me, I turned and ran for it.

I dropped the packages and tripped on the shoe box and, as if my own thoughts had doomed me, I slipped on the tiles in the front hall and went down with a bang, landing unceremoniously on my backside. I slid into the wall, my head striking the baseboard with a thud.

I saw stars, then a bright light. Was I dying? I wondered idly if I'd be able to communicate with Esme once I went over. We should have prearranged some sort of signal. I seemed to be moving toward the light. But no, that wasn't quite right; the light was moving toward me. I struggled to focus and realized the man was kneeling beside me, a Bic lighter held in front of his face. He was staring at me wide-eyed, concern wrinkling his baby face.

"Are you okay?" Gavin Taylor asked. "Oh man," he half whispered, misery packed into his words. "I didn't think . . ." He slapped his forehead with the heel of his hand. "Why don't I ever think? I didn't mean to scare you. I was waiting and it started raining and your back door was open so I came in to wait. I was gonna call out when I heard you come in so I wouldn't scare you, but I fell asleep. I'm sorry, I'm really sorry."

"Gavin?" I said. Which was stupid, since that had already been established. "What are you doing here?"

Just then there was a pounding on the front door. I struggled to understand this sound. We had a doorbell, why was there pounding? Then I remembered we had no power to operate the bell. Gavin half stood, ready for flight, but I reached out and grabbed the pocket of his hoodie and yanked him back.

"Oh, no, you don't," I said, feeling my head to make sure it was still attached as I clung doggedly to his pocket.

"Who is it?" I called out, which sent new pain skipping merrily through my head.

"Sophreena?" a muffled voice answered. "Sophreena, it's Joe Porter. Sorry about the hour, but I need to talk to you a minute. It's important."

"Get the door," I told Gavin as I moved, slowly, into a sitting position.

"I can't," Gavin protested. "He'll kill me. Or at least fire me."

"Get the door!" I said through clenched teeth. "Or I'll kill you myself and save him the trouble."

I heard a conversation from near the front door, but the words were warbled as if we were all underwater. I stretched my jaw to make my ears pop and by the time Joe Porter was kneeling in front of me, his mackintosh dripping on the tiles, things were becoming clear, at least as far as my hearing went. But I was still in the dark, literally and figuratively, about what was going on.

After a little back-and-forth about the state of my head, whether he should call the cops, and did Gavin have a lick of sense, Joe helped me to my feet. We made our way back to the family room, Gavin leading, his lighter held high like a torch.

I asked Joe to make a fire in the fireplace while I grabbed a blanket and curled up in the chair Gavin had vacated, shivering from cold and released adrenaline. The chair was still warm, which I found both creepy and comforting. I told Gavin where to find the basket of utility candles on the bookshelf, and he set them out and lit them. It didn't exactly flood the room with light, but by the time Joe had the fire going, we could at least see one another plainly.

Joe and Gavin continued to bicker, but I still had no clue what was going on. Finally Joe took off his mackintosh and laid it on the hearth, then pulled up a chair in front of me, examining me closely and asking again how I was feeling.

"I'm fine," I assured him, and was beginning to believe it myself. I'd probably have a knot on the back of my head tomorrow and my tush was gonna be a bit tender, but my brain was tracking again.

"You told me to talk to her about it," Gavin said, a whine in his voice.

Joe nodded. "That I did," he said, "but I didn't say break into her house in the dead of night to do it, now, did I? Have you completely left the planet, Gavin?"

I held up a hand and raised my voice, which is small, but can be fierce. "Enough already. Will someone please tell me what is going on?"

Joe sighed. "Gavin's got something he wanted to ask your advice about. Just to go on record here, I believe him. He's a knucklehead and his own worst enemy, but I don't believe he's wrapped up in this murder."

This got my full attention and I looked to Gavin expectantly.

"Her clothes and stuff," he said. "They were in the trunk of my car. I didn't put them there. She didn't put them there, not as far as I know. Like I told you, I haven't seen the girl in years. But I opened my trunk to put groceries in last night and there it all was. I didn't know it was hers at first. I was thinking maybe somebody put their stuff in the wrong car, but then who could open my trunk? The car was locked. I had my keys. There was a purse, so I looked through it and found a wallet and her ID. That's when I freaked out. I was up all night, just pacing and thinking."

"Or not thinking," Joe muttered.

Gavin ignored the comment and started to reenact his night of pacing on the rug in front of the fireplace. "I swear," he said, "I have no idea how that stuff got in my car. Honestly, I had to read the name before I knew it was her. I didn't recognize her from the picture on her license. We were kids when I knew her and I didn't even know her all that well then."

I couldn't help but contrast Gavin's dismissal of his time with Sherry with Laney's nostalgic recounting of their nights spent in the forest primeval.

"Who else has keys to your car?" I asked.

"Nobody," Gavin said. "I only have one set. I bought the car used and it only came with one set of keys."

"Did it look like someone had broken into the trunk?" I asked. "Were there scratch marks or anything?"

"No," Gavin said. "It looked fine."

"Okay, just so I understand this," I said. "You had not seen Sherry Burton since she got into town. You haven't talked to her recently. You don't know how her things got into the trunk of your car. And you had nothing whatsoever to do with Sherry Burton's death. And I enter into all this how, exactly?"

"That's on me," Joe Porter said, shaking his head. "Gavin came to me with this first thing this morning. I know you and Esme are close to Denton Carlson. I thought you might advise the boy about how to approach this."

"Yeah, yeah, I definitely want to talk to the big man. Jennifer's the one who busted me for boosting the car.

She knows me, for God's sake, but she was harsh. And with Sherry getting killed on her old man's property, I hear she's really got her knickers in a twist. She'd have me strung up by sunset tomorrow, Old West style."

I felt a ridiculous urge to defend Jennifer, which was definitely a new phenomenon. "She's a good cop," I said, leaving it at that.

"Yeah, okay, maybe," Gavin said. "But I'd rather take my chances with the big guy. Joe said so, too."

"'Course, I didn't think about him coming over here and breaking into your house and scaring you half to death," Joe said with a sigh. "Not till time to lock up when I realized he'd gone AWOL."

"I didn't break in," Gavin protested. "I told you, the kitchen door was open. I used to come over here all the time when we were in high school, remember?" Gavin said. "Your folks were really cool about having us hang out here."

"Yeah, I remember," I said absently. I could have corrected him. It was middle school he was thinking of. By the time I got to high school, my mother was ill and our house had grown quiet and insular. But there were more pressing matters than his misremembered old times. "Where do you keep your keys?" I asked.

"In my pocket," he said, pulling them out of his jeans and holding them down to the candle's guttering flame to prove his point.

"Where do you keep them in your apartment?" I asked.

"On a hook by the door," he said.

"And you haven't lost them, or misplaced them recently?" I asked.

"Nope, I've got sort of a tic about it. I hang them up every time. Listen, Sophreena, I just want you to help me figure out how to talk to the guy about this and make him believe me."

"Well, if I'm gonna do that, we'd better get figuring. Because any minute now, Esme and Detective Denton Carlson are going to come in that door from their dinner date"—I waved vaguely toward the front of the house—"and I imagine they'll have some questions about what's going on here."

All three of us scanned the room, taking in the line of candles, my bedraggled appearance, Gavin's stark black hoodie, and the rubbery aroma of Joe's mackintosh drying as the fire crackled. It looked like some misbegotten séance.

"I am so screwed," Gavin whispered hoarsely.

Luckily for all of us, by the time Esme and Denny got home, the lights were back on and I'd had a chance to get a quick shower and pull on dry clothes. Joe, Gavin, and I had talked through a concise recounting of how and when Gavin had discovered the things in his trunk, and I'd made a list of talking points for him to keep himself on track, since he had a habit of coming off the rails when agitated.

The assessment of his prison shrink kept coming into my mind: "poor impulse control." Just how poor? And how good an actor was he? Or how good a strategist? He could have simply thrown the stuff away and who would have been the wiser? Of course, he could also be thinking, Who in their right mind would voluntarily come forward and link themselves to a crime if they had something to hide? Maybe a lunkhead or maybe a very, very shrewd fellow.

However, we agreed to skip over all that had transpired in the previous hour, and were ready for Denny, sitting in the family room like civilized people, sipping hot cocoa and conversing in normal tones.

As always, I admired Denny's meticulous questioning. He was firm and thorough without trying to trip Gavin up. He listened intently, asking follow-up questions I wouldn't have thought to ask. After an hour, he closed his notebook and made his usual show of clicking his ballpoint pen and stowing it in his pocket. It was a purposeful gesture. I wondered how many people he'd interviewed had assumed the questioning was over when he did that and inadvertently blurted something to their detriment.

But Gavin didn't relax. He sat, staring at his running shoes, casting an occasional sidelong glance in Joe's direction.

"Appreciate you coming forward with this," Denny said.

"You're not going to run me in?" Gavin asked.

"Nope," Denny said. "Are the articles still in your trunk?"

Gavin nodded. "I didn't take anything out."

"Good," Denny said. "We'll go over with you to collect it. And sometime tomorrow we'd appreciate it if you'd come in and make an official statement."

"He'll be there," Joe said. "I'll see to it."

fifteen

ESME AND I SPENT A COUPLE OF HOURS ON SATurday morning arranging proper archival files for the stuff we'd found in the bundle Sadie Harper had left for Miss Lottie. Esme began assembling the artifacts for the scrapbook on the history of the land. She's good at it; she chooses representative samples that illustrate the text, whereas I want to include everything, which is impractical and also makes the scrapbook tedious and messy.

Being a sucker for diaries and old letters, I tackled those. I started with the memo books. Sadie wrote down everything, from important historical information to grocery lists, all together in little booklets. She was succinct to an extreme. In one, dated August 5, 1914, she'd written one word: "War." But somehow that one word took in all the horror and heartbreak of the next few years. She noted the date of Samuel Wright's death and underneath had written: "May God have mercy on us all." How I wished I had some context for that.

Next I looked through the correspondence between Sadie and her sister-in-law, Inez, reading snatches aloud to Esme. Sadie and Inez had kept up a correspondence for years, and though I didn't have Sadie's half of the exchanges, a lot could be garnered from Inez's responses. She had a beautiful hand and a pleasing writing style, and best of all, she was a consummate gossip, especially when it came to Eugenia, Miss Lottie's future mother. I pulled out one from July 1915.

> *I saw Eugenia today downtown. She was with*
> *her mother, Dolores. I don't have much to say to*
> *Dolores, for too many reasons to tell here. Let us*
> *suffice it to say her nose is too high in the air to*
> *make congenial conversation possible. But I do*
> *think little Eugenia is a sweet girl, despite her*
> *parentage. She is modest and polite and dedicated*
> *to Samuel. That is clear. I have had the chance to*
> *observe them together on several occasions and I*
> *feel assured she will be faithful in every respect.*

Inez was clearly more upper-class than Sadie Harper, or at least felt herself to be. There were references in her letters to Sadie's life as a farmer's wife, where she managed to convey both admiration and condescension.

*I simply cannot imagine how you get it all done,
Sadie. It sounds as if life for you is little better
than for the pioneers. All that gathering and
canning and the husbandry of your animals,
cow-milking, churning and all such. You are
truly a marvel that you can live and thrive in
conditions that would finish off a woman like me
post haste. I am afraid we would simply starve
were it up to me to work as you do to provide for
you and Oren day in and day out. You must be so
worn down.*

"So Inez was a city slicker. Where did she live?"
Esme asked.

"Baltimore," I said. "Though I don't think it was
really what you'd call a hot urban center back then."

"Is there more about Samuel?"

"Yes, here's one where Inez is lamenting that he's
had to go for his training and in another she says he's
been shipped out, bound for Europe."

I got up to tick those dates into the time line, then
continued reading the letters, skipping over day-to-day
news, looking for more dates. "Oh, here's something;
this would have been after Samuel was overseas." I read
aloud:

*I know by now, Sadie, you have heard the tragic news;
Eugenia's parents, Dolores and Conrad, both gone in one*

cruel stroke, their beautiful home burned to the ground. In the way of small mercies I have been assured they had expired from the smoke before the conflagration took them (if the people who say so really have any knowledge of the matter). It is so very horrid. I suppose I should feel guilty about some of the things I have written to you about Dolores, but I did, after all, only say the truth and her passing does not make it any less so. Still, I am fearsome sorry she died and I feel so achingly sad for poor Eugenia. Now she must bear her grief alongside her longing and worry for Samuel. It is a cruel turn.

"This was Miss Lottie's maternal grandparents," Esme said, consulting the Harper family chart I'd constructed. "So she never knew them."

"Not them and not the grandparents on the Wright side either. They were both dead long before Samuel went away to the war."

"What became of Eugenia? Do the letters say?"

I quickly skimmed some more, then huffed a laugh. "Uh-oh, trouble brewing," I said, then read to Esme:

Dear Sadie, It is with a heavy heart that I must write to let you in on this. I fear our sweet Eugenia is lost. You know that she has gone to live with her Aunt Lavinia. Well, that lady, dare I even use the word, is turning out to be not a fit guardian for a young girl. Eugenia has gotten quite out of control. She has bobbed her hair and I am very afraid she is becoming a flapper. She has adopted

*that style of dress and goes out jazzing with her friends
and being a regular bohemian. I hear through the grape-
vine that she has even been seen smoking in public and I
suspect may be doing worse in private. I do wonder if she
will forget all about Samuel, and him in those dreadful
trenches over there fighting for his very life. I am sorely
disappointed in the child.*

"Oh, God forbid," Esme said. "A flapper."

"And bobbing her hair!" I said. "That hussy."

"Well," Esme said, "we can poke fun, but I'm sure
that was cause for scandal back then. Especially if she'd
given poor Samuel her pledge."

"But she did wait for him," I said. "They were married very soon after he came home. She got pregnant
with Lottie within a few months of the wedding and
she died giving birth, so, sadly, they only had about a
year together. There's a wedding photo in the album,
but it's still at River's house."

"What did River say about taking the stuff from the
bundle to Lottie Walker?" Esme asked.

"He's all for it," I said. "But he'd like copies. I
finished the report for River to give Ron Solomon. It
details everything we've learned that points toward
identifying the Forgotten Man as Samuel Wright. It
may affect whether River will be allowed to move the
remains. I'm going to take it out to him this morning.
You want to come?"

"Yes, I think I will," Esme said. "I still have something floating around in my head about that spot in his backyard. I'm probably just asking for a headache, but I'd like to walk around a little out there and see if I get anything more."

"Okay, good. But just so you know, I'll probably take this stuff out to Miss Lottie afterward. You want to go out with me or take your own car?"

Esme puckered her lips. "I'll go with you," she said. "I'd like to see how she responds."

"She knows what happened. I'm sure of that. She keeps saying things about 'that night,' so clearly something dramatic happened, but she says she'll take it to her grave, and I think she has the will to do just that."

"Well, the woman is ninety-seven years old. If we're going to find out anything from her, it'd best be soon."

"Yeah, well, hard as it is for me to accept, there may be things we'll never know. We'll have to settle for what we can get."

We worked quietly for a little while longer, then Esme spoke, her question coming out of the blue. "So do you think Gavin Taylor had anything to do with Sherry Burton's death?"

"What? No."

Esme looked over her glasses at me.

I sighed. "Okay, I hope he didn't. I'm trying to

believe he didn't. Gavin is like one of the lost boys," I said. "But I really do believe he's a good-hearted guy. He just doesn't think sometimes. He does stupid things, but I can't believe he'd do bad things."

"It only takes one moment of bad judgment to do a lot of harm," Esme replied.

"Has Denny said anything more about the Miami connection?" I asked. "Are they making any progress?"

"He hasn't said much," Esme said. "I think it's pretty clear she wasn't living like Rebecca of Sunnybrook Farm down there, but if she was into something that got her killed, I don't think they've nailed it down yet. And I don't think they're slacking on the case, since it sounds like there's a bigger fish to be had if they can pin this murder on a smaller one."

"Drug dealers," I said. "If it's drug dealers, then it's got nothing to do with our world, right? Maybe that's why I've felt so detached from Sherry Burton's murder. I feel terrible that it happened, and that it happened here makes me feel vaguely responsible, but I've been able to hold it at a distance after the initial shock of finding her. Now I realize it's affecting people I know very deeply." I told her about our visit to River's house with Laney. "She was so sentimental about her time with Sherry and upset about her death. Even Bryan Mason, who I don't think anybody would describe as a sensitive soul, seems genuinely disturbed."

"Formative years," Esme said. "That's when we were all searching for our identity."

I nodded, thinking of Gavin's reminder that we'd been in the same puppy pack in school. He'd been among the herd of kids who'd come to my house to study, or for pizza and movie night. Or sometimes my dad would organize us into a battalion for some volunteer project or other. Gavin and I hadn't been best buddies or anything, but we'd been schoolmate friends. By high school we'd drifted apart. Gavin had started hanging around with a racier crowd, headed by Bryan Mason. Laney had left us behind by then, too. It was nice to rekindle those friendships now that we'd all found ourselves.

Correction: all of us but Gavin, the lost boy.

sixteen

"THANK YOU," RIVER SAID WHEN I HANDED HIM the report. "You two have lived up to your reputations. I'm looking forward to seeing that scrapbook." He turned to Jennifer. After a moment of silence, she felt his eyes on her and straightened.

"Oh yeah, thanks," she said, and I believed she kinda, sorta meant it.

"I don't know how this is all going to work out," River said, "but now that I know old Sam a little"— he nodded toward the photo album on the table—"I wouldn't much mind having him resting out there on the hill. So it'll be okay either way it goes."

"You're a kind soul, River," Esme said.

Luke harrumphed. "You didn't see him dealing with the workers who improperly installed the solar panels on the workshop this morning," he said. " 'Kind' was nowhere in his repertoire."

River grinned. "I guess I do get a little hot under the collar when people disrespect the vision," he said.

I remembered then how River had been the morning we'd discovered Sherry Burton's body. He'd come stomping across his yard loaded for bear. It had scared me a little, but then finding the girl was dead had made me forget how angry he'd been.

River wasn't all laid-back hippie. I'd heard that from several people who knew him well. He'd had a tough time of it in his war, Vietnam. He'd come back with emotional and spiritual baggage.

A crash came from the direction of the workshop, and we all jumped.

"Oh Sweet Mother, what now?" River said, heading for the back door.

"You see to that, Dad. I'll take this over to Ron," Jennifer said, picking up the report from the table. "I really did mean it, you know," she said, turning to Esme and me. "Thanks, both of you."

"Glad we could help," Esme said, and I had hopes of the wall coming down, the doves let fly, swords being beaten into plowshares. Or at least the Christmas truce I'd read about in one of Samuel's letters, when the German and Allied soldiers in the trenches simply decided among themselves not to fight on Christmas day and sang carols, played touch football, and showed one another family photos before resuming their places in the fighting the next day.

Luke walked us outside and we could hear River giving the workmen a dressing-down for their careless handling of a workbench they were unloading.

"We're headed out to see your grandmother," I told Luke. "Have you seen her?"

Luke nodded. "I went out there, but she didn't know who I was. Grandma Lottie didn't like kids much, and she especially didn't like having to take care of us. I think it was more to do with her relationship with our mother, if you could call it a relationship. If you look up 'dysfunction' in the dictionary, our family photo will probably be there."

Esme was standing next to me and I could hear her breath coming in small puffs. "Luke," she said, her voice sounding a bit strained. "Do you remember when there was a well out here? Right about in here," she said, taking a few paces.

"No," Luke said, tilting his head. "Not a working well. Grandma Lottie's house was on well water, but there was an electric pump house, not an old-fashioned pulley-and-bucket type. There was a flower bed where the well had been, though, and she was very particular about it. We'd catch hell if we messed with it. Which was strange, now that I think about it. There were no flowers anywhere else on the property other than wildflowers. She thought growing flowers was a frivolous waste of time. Actually, she thought pretty much everything was a frivolous waste of time. But she said if you were going to put the work and money into growing something, you ought to be able to eat it."

River stepped out of the workshop and cupped his hands, calling for Luke to come help. Once he'd trotted off I turned to Esme. "Are you getting something?" I asked.

"Plenty," Esme said. "Oh, Sophreena, I don't know what it's all about, but something terrible happened here. Right here on this spot."

"At the well?" I asked.

Esme took in a deep breath. "Yes," she said. "There are people—three, I think, maybe four. There's shouting. It's dark and something terrible is happening. There's fear and panic. It's all coming at me so hard I can't breathe. I need to get out of here."

We turned to see Jennifer standing three feet away. Her body was rigid and her eyes wide. "Oh, dear God," she muttered, "you're deluded. You need help. You both need to go. Now." She turned and went back into the house.

Esme let out a groan. She lifted a hand and seemed about to call after Jennifer, but then she let the hand fall. Her shoulders slumped and she looked totally defeated. I'd never seen Esme like this and it unraveled me.

"Oh, Esme, I'm so sorry. I should have been watching. I didn't hear her come out. Let's not worry about her. It'll be fine, just fine. No problem." I was chirping inanely, and couldn't seem to stop.

"You know it will surely not be fine, Sophreena. Or if you don't, you should. She'll have this all over town before nightfall. Esme Sabatier, the crazy old conjure woman. And the first thing she'll do is go straight to Denton. I might as well go home and start packing my things."

"Don't be ridiculous, Esme," I said. "People here know you. They're not going to turn their backs on you because of what she says."

"You've not lived with this as long as I have, Sophreena. It won't be good." She looked out across the yard toward my car. "I can't go with you to Cottonwood. I'm sorry. I just don't feel up to it right now."

"I won't go either," I said. "I'll stay with you."

"No, I need some time," Esme said. "You go on. I'm going to have a walkabout, then go to Claire's. I've been meaning to get out here to hang some curtains for her anyhow. You go take care of your business."

"Our business," I called as I watched her walk away. I had a lump in my throat and I was blinking back tears. I quickly swiped at my eyes as I saw Luke approaching.

"Crisis averted," he said, jerking a thumb toward the workshop. He gazed out to where Esme was trudging along, struggling with her heels. She stopped and took off her shoes and continued on her way in her bare feet. That's when I realized how bad this was. If Esme was forsaking her shoes, what was next?

"Where's she going?" Luke asked.

"To Claire Calvert's," I said, trying to sound casual. "She just remembered she'd promised to help her with something. I guess I'm on my own. I don't suppose you'd want to go out to Cottonwood with me to see your grandmother? I'm taking all the things that were in that bundle from Sadie. You might learn some things about your family, assuming you're interested."

"Sure," Luke said. "I would like to know more about the family. I was told next to nothing about our history growing up. I know zip about my father's side. And by father, I mean genetic donor. I never met the man. He planted the seed but didn't wait around for the harvest. Same goes for Sherry's dad. Mom really knew how to pick 'em. So, yeah, I'd like to know more about the family. It would be nice to find there were some shining lights somewhere up in the family tree."

"Every family I've ever traced has a mixture of shining lights, steady signals, dim bulbs, and burnouts," I said. "But I believe we all ought to know our own history. After all, it's made us who we are. It gives us things to live up to and things to live down, things to honor as traditions and things to work to reform."

"I've got plenty of reform projects," Luke said. "Maybe I can find some of the other stuff to go with it." He offered to drive his car and I took him up on it so I could leave my car for Esme. I put the keys in the glove compartment and texted her. I transferred the box containing the photo album, the letters, the memo book diaries, and other artifacts to Luke's trunk. As he raised the lid, I had a fleeting thought of Gavin finding his trunk full of Sherry Burton's belongings. What a shock that must have been.

"Root beer?" Luke said as I placed a six-pack of the brew on the far side of the trunk, as far away from the artifacts as I could get it.

"I'm not above bribery, or tempting her with drink," I said. "She likes root beer."

"Still?" Luke said. "She used to brew a homemade version from the sassafras trees that run along the edge of the woods down by the creek."

"I don't think I've ever had homemade root beer. Was it good?" I asked.

Luke pursed his lips. "Grandma wasn't big on sharing, but I swiped a bottle one time. It was good, but not good enough to get smacked for. I didn't try it again."

"If you can get your grandmother to tell us the story of what happened to Samuel Wright, I'll buy you a case of the best," I said as I climbed into the passenger seat.

"I'll hold you to that offer," Luke said as we started

down the long gravel driveway. "I think the things I missed most during the last year were hamburgers and Cokes, which is weird because I'm essentially a vegetarian."

"Forbidden fruit?" I said.

"Yeah, except I had all the fruit a person could ever want," he laughed, and nodded in the direction of Claire's house. "So Esme and Claire Calvert are friends?"

"Yes. They work together sometimes. Esme tutors kids through a program at her church and the Literacy Council provides resources and referrals. At least that's how they met, but now they're close personal friends, too."

"Ms. Calvert's a nice woman," Luke said. "Or at least she was nice to the little snot-nosed punk I was when we stayed here in the summers. She'd loan me books and give me snacks, and one time, when it was a rainy day and she saw I was outside, she set up this big canvas tent at the corner of her yard and said I could use it as my headquarters. That was her little joke 'cause the tent was army surplus."

"Sounds like a kid's dream," I said.

"It was," Luke said. "She left it up and I took some of my stuff out there and I had it fixed up pretty cool, until Sherry found out about it and knocked it all down."

"So I take it you and Sherry didn't get along?" I said.

"Most of the time she didn't acknowledge my existence," Luke said. "With us it wasn't the Hansel and Gretel syndrome, the two of us together against the wicked stepmother, or grandmother in our case. It was survival of the fittest. She'd have sacrificed me in a heartbeat if it gave her an advantage. Otherwise she totally ignored me, which made me want her attention more than anything. I was an awkward kid and didn't make friends easily. I wanted to hang out with Sherry and her pals, but that was not gonna happen. So I spied on them constantly. I got pretty good at it, too. But anyhow, she didn't smash the tent because she didn't like me, she smashed it because Claire Calvert had given it to me."

"She didn't like Claire?" I asked, frowning. "Who doesn't like Claire Calvert?"

"Sherry," Luke answered with a sigh. "Ms. Calvert took it upon herself to come over and talk to Grandma Lottie about Sherry. She told her about Sherry and her friends hanging out down by the creek, getting up to no good. And she told her, too, that based on her talks with Sherry, she thought it would be good if Sherry got some counseling."

"I don't suppose I need ask how your grandmother reacted to that."

"Grandmother Lottie didn't give a rip what Sherry

did, but she was livid about being shamed by a neighbor. Sherry got it bad. Grandma Lottie gave her an
old-fashioned switching like she'd threatened a million
times before. We didn't think she'd ever actually do it.
Sherry was fourteen years old and if she'd realized what
was coming she'd have run, but Grandma was quick.
She grabbed Sherry and tied her hands to the back
porch rail with a piece of clothesline and whipped her
with a switch off a peach tree. She striped her across
her legs and behind. It hurt, I'm sure, but mostly Sherry
was humiliated and blistering mad. At Grandma, of
course, but we were always mad at Grandma, that
wasn't anything new. She was furious with Claire Calvert. She blamed her for all of it."

"That's horrible, but I'm sure Claire had good intentions. She'd like to see you, by the way," I said. "Maybe
you could stop by and say hello sometime."

"Uh," Luke said, "yeah, maybe." He flipped down
the sun visor, squinting his blue eyes against the
midafternoon sun. His skin was so brown from his past
year in the tropics, his eyes were icy in contrast.

He ran his hand through his newly clipped hair and
shook his head. "Naw, naw, I couldn't face her."

"Why not?" I asked, watching as his face went
through a series of grimaces.

"Guilt," he said. "I feel guilty about what happened
to her."

"You? What do you have to feel guilty about? Oh no, tell me you weren't the one who made that phone call, Luke."

"No!" he said sharply. "It wasn't me. But I didn't stop Sherry and her posse from making it. I swore to myself I'd never tell. But Sherry's gone now, it can't hurt her, and as for the others, I don't know them. Actions have consequences. My whole life has taught me that."

"Would you tell me about it?" I asked.

"I'd like to tell Claire Calvert, but I'm too much of a coward, so yeah, I'll tell you. Like I said, Sherry hated Claire Calvert after she got that whipping. And she really did think Claire was having an affair, or at least that's what she said after the fact, but maybe she was trying to make herself feel better. Anyhow, I told you I'd gotten pretty good at spying on her and her friends by the end of the summer. I got close enough that night to hear them hatch the plan to call Quentin Calvert and get him to come home and catch Claire in the act."

"Oh no," I said with a groan.

"Oh, yes," Luke said. "One of the guys put up some protest. I think Quentin was related to him somehow, but Sherry convinced him that was even more reason for him to want the husband to know what was going on. Sherry was a good manipulator, she got them all whipped up. They all climbed on their bikes and pedaled off to find the nearest pay phone. I stayed right up there in my tree perch wondering what I should do. I thought of telling Grandma Lottie, but then I was afraid there would be another episode with the switch. And I thought of going to Claire's and warning her, but it didn't seem like I should show up at her door if she was, well, you know, in the middle of something. So I did nothing. Absolutely nothing. And Claire Calvert ended up in a wheelchair."

"You were a child, Luke," I said.

"I was a kid, but I was never really a child," he said. "Not the way we grew up. I knew something bad would happen. I didn't figure on how bad, but I should have at least tried to stop them."

"How did Sherry feel about it?" I asked. "Afterward, I mean, with the ways things turned out."

Luke shrugged. "Didn't seem to affect her at all. I wouldn't say she was happy about what happened to Claire; she wasn't that vindictive, but she didn't seem to think she had any responsibility in it. That's how she claimed she felt anyhow, though I suspect it bothered her more than she let on and that the weight of it got heavier over the years, because she'd mentioned it from time to time."

A million thoughts were rushing through my head about how this involved Gavin, Bryan Mason and, oh, dear God, Laney.

"Sherry was running away from something," Luke said, "that's for sure. But she could have run to any-where. I think she made a beeline for this place be-cause she wanted to make amends. She'd been working to clean up her act, or so she said in the letters she left me. She was pretty much a mess when I left a year ago and I couldn't get routine mail during that time, but she sent a few letters to my old apartment and I read them after I got back. There was stuff in there about making things right, nothing specific, but she said she wanted a clean slate. I think maybe she was in one of those recovery programs. And she told my old roommate she was getting ready to start a new life."

"Did she mention anything specifically about Claire or the incident?" I asked.

"No, like I said, just general stuff, but I think what happened back then must have been high on her list."

"Did you tell Jennifer any of this? Or River?"

"No," Luke said with a sigh. "I wanted to, but I couldn't figure out how to get into it. And then River offered to let me stay with him and I really like the guy and I didn't want to rock the boat. Selfish, I know. And Jennifer? Man, she always seems like she's ready to tear into me about something. I guess we got off on the wrong foot with me breaking into the house, but I mean, what's a break-in or two between friends, right?"

"Would you mind if I told her about it? Or told Denny Carlson? You met him; he's the other detective on your sister's case. This might be important to the investigation."

"You tell him, if you think it might lead to something. I don't quite see how it could, but I guess you never know, right? I'll try to screw up my courage and talk to Jennifer about it afterward; maybe she'll have had a chance to cool down by then."

"Do you think your grandmother knew about any of it?" I asked.

"She might have suspected," Luke said. "I heard she gave some money to the Literacy Council when she sold the place to River. Grandma Lottie was not exactly the philanthropic sort. I'd say that was guilt money, not that she probably thought she did anything wrong, but maybe because she felt the weight of family obligation or whatever. She was weird that way."

"It doesn't bother you that she didn't leave the place to you and Sherry?" I asked.

"I wouldn't have expected it," Luke said. "I doubt it would have occurred to her to do that. As I said, we weren't really a family unit. I grew up not having a clue about what it meant to belong to a family."

"If it's any consolation," I said, "most of the families I research have gone through some bad spells. And no matter how things have gone in generations past, you'll be the kind of father you make up your mind to be when you have your own family."

"So you don't think I'm doomed to keep repeating all this misery?" Luke asked with a wry smile. "How about you, what was your family like?"

"My parents were fantastic," I said. "I always felt loved and supported and they were both great role models. A generation back, though, things were a little dodgier. There's a part of my biological heritage I don't know anything about, since my mother was adopted, and it was a closed adoption, a locked-and-bolted closed adoption."

"But your mother was a happy person?" Luke asked.

"Oh, yes, she was very happy and comfortable with herself, though she always did wonder about the people she came from. That's actually why I got into the business."

"I've sometimes wondered," Luke said, "if it was because she was adopted that Grandma Lottie was always such an insecure person, but I know that's too simplistic."

"Yes, it is," I said. "I've known lots of adoptees and I'm sure you have, too. As a group, they're no more or less screwed up than the rest of us. But I don't doubt it could be a factor, depending on the circumstances. I need to warn you, Luke, I'm going to push to get your grandmother to tell me what happened to your great-grandfather. It may not be pretty."

"I'd like to know," Luke said. "And maybe it's twisted, but I feel closer to him after looking at that photo album than I ever did to my grandmother, who is still alive. Is that strange?"

I smiled. "I just trace 'em; you have to figure out how to feel about 'em."

I spent the rest of the drive to Cottonwood on the phone with Denny, relating what Luke had told me about Sherry and her cohorts making the phone call to Quentin Calvert all those years ago.

"I see," Denny had said. "I'd say that needs some looking into. Would you ask the young lad if he might have a few minutes tonight to talk to me about this?"

I did, and though Luke flinched, he said, "Sure."

"Is Jennifer there with you?" I asked, wondering if she had indeed gone straight to Denny to tell him what she'd overheard Esme say at River's place.

"Nope, it's her day off, why?"

"No reason," I said. "I just figured she needs to know about this, too."

"We're partners, Sophreena. What I know, she'll know."

"And vice versa," I whispered under my breath.

*   *   *

Miss Lottie was her usual uncharming self. On my previous visits I'd thought of her demeanor as amusingly
eccentric, but after all I'd learned about her, there was
nothing amusing about her. She was just an old, embit-
tered human being.

Still, there's this little Pollyanna streak in me that
believes it's never too late for redemption. Not as long
as a person is drawing breath, which in Miss Lottie's
case meant she'd better get a move on.

Luke approached her bedside as he might a buzzing hornet's nest. "Hello, Grandma, it's me, Luke. Luke
Mitchell."

It wasn't lost on me that a grandson oughtn't be required to give his full name for a grandmother to know
who he was, but this situation seemed to require it, and
possibly a photo ID as well.

"Oh, no sir," Miss Lottie said, her lips pinching into
a thin line across her sallow face. "I told your mother,
I'm too old for this. I can't be chasing younguns all over
creation. My knee hurts and I've got canning to do. The
garden's coming in. She's the one that tramped around
and got you, let her look after you."

Luke raised his eyebrows at me and turned up both
palms.

I felt terrible. Blithe as he was about his grandmother,

I could tell it was hurtful, even now as an adult whose education had doubtless taught him much about human interactions and dysfunctions.

"Miss Lottie," I said, forcing some insincere sweetness into my voice, "I brought you some root beer." I put the frosted glass I'd requested from the lunchroom on her tray and filled it to the brim. She grabbed the glass before I could finish pouring and put it to her rubbery lips.

"This is awful," she pronounced. "You call this root beer? It's weak as water."

"Best I can do," I said. "Drink a few more sips and maybe it will get better. Then we can look at these things I've brought you. I have an album here with some pictures of your father and your mother."

"Pictures?" she asked, her interest seeming to pick up. "Where'd you get pictures of my folks?"

"From the attic at your old house," I said. "I found the album in a bundle Sadie left for you."

"Sadie?" she said. "You don't say one ill word about Sadie. You dare not or I'll climb right out of this bed and thrash you."

Luke threw up his hands and stepped back, distancing himself from the woman.

"Everybody who ever knew her said she was a wonderful woman," I said soothingly. "And she wanted to make sure you had these pictures and letters." I held up the stack. "See? And there are some little diaries here. Miss Sadie wrote down everything—"

"Wrote down?" Miss Lottie croaked, her voice coming out like a donkey bray. "She wrote down what happened? Why in creation would she do that?"

I looked at Luke and he gave me a "go on" motion. "I don't know," I said to Miss Lottie, "maybe she wanted to make sure you remembered."

"How could I forget? That's not something you forget, ever. Don't mistake me, there's lots I don't remember. I'm old and I know my mind's going. But I remember every single second of that night."

Luke opened his mouth, but I shook my head at him. I'd seen how the old woman's spine had stiffened and I knew she was gathering her resolve. Better to go slow and see if we could soften her up some more.

I opened the photo album. "I especially like this picture of your parents on their wedding day," I said, smoothing out her bedcovers and putting the album in her lap. I handed her the eyeglasses from the bedside table and helped her get them hooked over her ears. She adjusted them with shaking hands and then looked at the picture, lifting her head to see through her bifocals.

"That's them?" she said, more a question than a statement. "I never seen this picture before. That looks like my daddy, all right, but I don't know if that's my mother."

"You never saw this picture?" I asked.

"That's what I said," Miss Lottie snapped. She started to turn the pages, her blue-veined hands still shaking. She examined each picture for a long time. "I never saw any of these before, but that one, that's for sure my daddy," she said as she stopped at a card cabinet photo of Samuel Wright in his uniform. She ran her hand over the page in a gesture that could have been loving remembrance or else a check to see if the photo was real. "Where'd you get these?" she asked, squinting her rheumy eyes.

"From the attic at your old house. Sadie left them for you," I repeated, trying to summon some patience. "They were wrapped up in a bundle of cloth, with your name written on it."

"Then why have you got 'em?" Lottie asked, jabbing a clawlike finger at me. "You stole 'em."

"She didn't steal anything, Grandma," Luke said with a long-suffering sigh. "You sold the house and everything in it, remember? These things don't belong to you anymore. And the new owner and Sophreena were both nice enough to make sure you got them back because they thought you might enjoy seeing them." He gave me a sidelong glance and muttered, "As if you could enjoy anything."

"You haven't seen these things before?" I asked her again.

"I never went up in that attic after Sadie died," Lottie

said. "I couldn't have got up there even if I'd wanted to. I told you, my knees are bad. I couldn't manage those steps. Wasn't nothing up there but junk anyways."

I didn't bother to tell her one man's trash was another man's treasure. How I wished I had an attic full of stuff that could help tell my family story. The few things that had come down to me from my mother's family could fit easily into a shoe box.

We spent the next hour going through the items with the old woman, and gradually, oh so gradually, she began to soften.

I read her a few of the letters and showed her the little memo books Sadie had written in like a diary. I read the entries from when she and her father came to live at the Harper place, and Lottie got a dreamy look.

"Sadie was a mama to me from then on out," she said. "And a better one nobody could ask for. I don't hold her to account for what happened. Not a bit of it."

"'Course not," Luke said. "I think she knew that. Didn't she say that in her diary?" he asked, giving me a wink.

Okay, this was thin ethical ice, but I really, really wanted to know what Sadie Harper wasn't being blamed for. "I think I do remember that," I said vaguely, flipping through one of the memo books.

"Didn't she write down all that happened that night?" Luke asked.

The ice was getting thinner, but there was no going back now. "I don't know if she wrote down everything," I said, which was true as far as it went. "But from what she wrote it was clear she was troubled about it," I said, framing the comment carefully.

There was dead silence in the room and Lottie was looking tired. I was exhausted and about to throw in the towel, when Luke spoke, his voice soft.

"I never asked much of you, Grandma," Luke said. "But the man was my great-grandfather, and I'd like to know what happened. Would you tell me?"

"I said I'd never tell," Lottie said, lifting her chin. "And I never did."

"You never did, as long as Sadie was alive," Luke said. "But you can tell me now. I'm family."

"Family!" Lottie snorted. "Accidents, that's what Marla calls you, both of you. If I tell you what happened, you'll tell Sherry and then it'll be all over town. Then what'll become of Sadie?"

"I won't tell Sherry," Luke said, drawing a ragged breath. "You have my word."

"Well," Lottie said, considering, "you're not one much to lie, I'll give you that. Not like your sister, who'd lie when the truth would do just as well."

"That night?" Luke said, trying to nudge her back on track. "What happened?"

Lottie squinted at the window where the slanting

sun was coming in through the blinds, casting the room in golden light. I got up to close it but stopped when she spoke. "Leave it," she said. "I want the light for as long as I can get it."

We waited and finally Miss Lottie spoke, her voice so soft I had to step close to the bed to hear her. "Sadie's gone, isn't she?"

"Yes, she's gone," I said. "She passed more than thirty years ago."

Miss Lottie nodded. "It can't hurt her now. There was a half-moon that night," she said. "I was always partial to a half-moon when I was a youngun. Liked squeezing my eyes nearly shut to make out the whole round of it if I stared at it for a long time. Couldn't abide ever looking at a half-moon after that night. Aunt Sadie and Uncle Oren had gone to bed but I wanted to watch the moon, so I took my quilt to the window. I wanted my doll baby to see the moon and while I was showing her, I saw Daddy out in the yard. He'd been fidgety for a few days. That's what Sadie called it, fidgety. Uncle Oren called it shell shock. I had no idea about what that meant back then. I had it in my child's mind it had something to do with turtles. Daddy couldn't sit still and he'd prowl around, talking to himself. When he was like that I couldn't make him better. It was like he didn't even hear me or see me, like he was somewheres far off and him not there at all, just his ghost self.

"I saw him out the window, he was running across the yard, all bent down like there was something out there he might hit his head on if he didn't stay low, 'cept there wasn't nothing. Just wide-open yard. Right about then a hooty owl called and Daddy fell on the ground and made a noise. I was scared he'd hurt hisself so I went to see after him. I stopped at the well and got the bucket and the ladle from where it was sitting on the edge of the well. I could barely carry it, and I spilled lots, but there was some still left and I figured Daddy might need a drink of it. He was all curled up in a ball with his hands over his head and yelling like a banshee. I reached down to touch him and he cried out like the devil himself had grabbed at him. He looked up at me and yelled something I didn't understand. He grabbed me and started running for the well. Sadie and Uncle Oren came out just then, both of them in their nightclothes. Daddy hollered at them. 'Get down, get down,' he kept hollering, 'mustard gas, mustard gas,' which I thought was silly. I knew what mustard was and I knew what gas was and they didn't go together. But Daddy was scaring me and I started crying and trying to squirm down but he held me fierce tight and ran with me. It was hurting my legs and I started bawling."

She stopped there, and for a moment I thought she wasn't going to go on. I wasn't sure she even remembered we were in the room. But then she turned from the window and looked first at me, then at Luke, and her face contorted.

"He tried to put me down the well," she said. "He tried to kill me. He went out of his head. Afterwards Uncle Oren said he probably saw that metal bucket shining in the moonlight and it took him back to something that happened to him in the war. That was a deep well and I was screaming and crying and trying to kick away and cling on all at the same time. I knew I was fighting for my life. I couldn't see the water, all I could see was that dark hole in the ground, and I knew, because I'd thrown pebbles down there before, that it was a long, long way down and if he got me in there I'd die. I didn't know how to swim and I had the idea that the hole went all the way down to the middle of the world. Sadie was yelling at Daddy and grabbed aholt of my legs and Uncle Oren was trying to prise Daddy's hands off me, but Daddy snatched me backwards, whipping my head around till it made me dizzy. He came around with his fist and hit Uncle Oren so hard I thought he'd kilt him. He was on the ground and not making a noise anymore, but the rest of us were making plenty. Sadie was screaming and Daddy kept yelling 'Get down, get down' and was trying to get me into the well. Sadie was clawing at Daddy, trying to get me free. I was slipping; I could feel it. Daddy had let my legs go and I was dangling in the opening. I kicked as hard as I could trying to get my foot over the ledge of the well but my little legs were too short. I grabbed at Daddy's shirt and held on as tight as I could, but he reached up and started peeling my fingers back so I'd let go. He broke this one," she said, holding up a crooked pinkie. "I couldn't even scream anymore by then; my voice was gone. The next thing I knew I heard a loud, awful sound and everything let go. Somebody had an arm around my waist and I fell back on the ground with Sadie, both of us crying and panting like dogs. Sadie got me up and pushed me toward the door, telling me not to look back but to go in the house and lock the door and stay there until she told me to open it.

"But I did look back. Uncle Oren was groaning and starting to try to sit up, but Daddy was still, lying there beside the well on his belly. Something was bad wrong with his head. The rusted old pulley Uncle Oren had left on the ledge of the well when he'd put in a new one was on the ground beside Daddy, covered in something dark and shiny. I'd never known anybody who died, and I'd surely never seen a dead person, but I knew Daddy was dead."

"She saved you," I said, though I hadn't intended to speak.

"She saved me that night and lots of nights after that, from bad dreams and black thoughts, from blaming myself or blaming Daddy. She hung on tight. But there was a piece of me that went down the well that night and I never did get whole again. And neither did Sadie."

"God," Luke whispered, "I wish I'd known all this back then. No wonder . . ." he started, but his voice trailed off.

We visited with Miss Lottie for a while longer, looking through the photo album with her again and trying to leave her with happier memories. I went out to the desk to let the charge nurse know she'd had an emotional afternoon and that she might need extra attention that evening. When I came back Miss Lottie was dozing, the photo album open on her lap. Luke was sitting by the bed, holding her hand.

He looked up and saw my smile and gently pulled his hand away. "Doesn't change anything," he said quietly, "but it sure explains a lot."

seventeen

IT WAS FULL DARK BY THE TIME WE LEFT COTTON-wood. I called Esme to see how she was holding up and braced myself for a tirade, but she sounded calm, too calm. There was an air of fatalism in her voice. I didn't like the sound of it one bit.

"I liked you better cranky," I told her. "Buck up, Esme, it doesn't matter what Jennifer thinks. Plus, you were right."

"Right about what?" Esme asked.

"Lots of things," I answered, aware of Luke beside me in the car. "Miss Lottie told Luke and me about what happened the night Samuel Wright died. Oh, Esme, it's a god-awful story, like something out of one of those dark Gothic tales."

"That it was dark, I already knew," Esme said. "I've got the headache to prove it."

"I'll be home in a bit; Luke's gonna drop me off," I

said, hoping that would convey the message to Luke that I wasn't going to invite him in. I needed some time alone with Esme.

"No, have him take you back to River's. You'll need to get your car," Esme said. "The curtains were the wrong size and Claire and I went out to exchange them. But they had to do a special order, so she dropped me at home."

"Okay, see you in a few," I said, clicking off and giving Luke the update.

We talked the rest of the way back to Morningside about the story Miss Lottie had told us. Luke was right—it didn't change anything, except maybe his perceptions of his grandmother, and maybe of himself. But sometimes that can be a very big deal. I could tell he was processing it all, both as a grandson and as a scholar. I could identify with this phenomenon, as this was what I was going through as I found out more about my mother's adoption. My grandparents had wanted a baby very badly, and they'd gotten one, also very badly.

On the one hand, everything that happened in the past was what had brought me to where I was today. Wishing some things had been otherwise seemed like a cosmic game of Jenga. If even one block got pulled out of the tower, where would I be? Would I be? If Mom hadn't been adopted from the Marshall Islands, she probably wouldn't have ended up in the States and she'd never have met my dad. I'd never have been.

Similar thoughts had to be going through Luke's mind. If Miss Lottie hadn't been subjected to that horrifying incident as a child, she might have grown up a different person altogether. There were so many ways that could have gone, but probably none of them would've led to Luke's existence.

As Luke turned off onto the county road for River's place, we were suddenly away from the town lights. With neighbors spread out on their multiacre plots, we'd abruptly gone pastoral. The headlights swept the woods, closing in on either side of the highway. The asphalt snaked around curves and up small hills and down into shallow dips in the land. We crested a hill and hit a straightaway. I could see the entrance to River's driveway situated about halfway between us and the next series of curves. As we passed a thicket of pines, Luke pointed out my window. "That's the short-cut I was talking about. Grandma didn't take care of the driveway and it was an invitation to sink to the axles in mud. There's a clearing in there where we'd leave our cars when we came here after we were grown. There's a path that leads right to the kitchen door."

"I didn't realize you continued to visit after you were old enough to drive," I said. "I guess I had the impression you didn't have much of an attachment here."

"We didn't," Luke said. "I didn't, anyway. Sherry came back a few times to visit. Honestly, I think she came to see what she could get out of Grandma," he said. "I never caught her at it, but I'm guessing she probably pilfered a few things from the house. I came down a couple of times when she was here 'cause I was at Georgetown, and it was easier to get here than down to Miami to see her. Despite everything, I still wanted to see her. She'd gotten nicer to me as we got older. We came maybe three or four times."

"And you stayed with your grandmother?" I asked.

"I did. I'm not sure where Sherry stayed. With a friend, she said, but I don't know who."

"Do you think Sherry would have parked in there that night?" I hesitated, trying to think of how to phrase the question. "The night she came out here?"

I could see Luke's frown of concentration limned by the dashboard lights. "You mean the night she was killed? No, I don't think Sherry drove here. Her apartment manager tells me her car is still in the garage down there. I'm assuming the repo men will be around for it soon; I seriously doubt it was paid for. Sherry lived her life on the delayed payment plan, financially and in every other way, too."

Luke put up a hand to shield his eyes as a car that had been parked along the roadside switched on its headlights and pulled out into the road, coming toward us. "Geez, high beams, jerk!" he muttered, and I grabbed at the dashboard as the car crossed over the centerline and into our lane. It was coming fast, very fast.

I screamed, or thought I did, then realized I'd only made a mewing sound. I pushed my feet into the floorboard and bent down. Luke swerved and I got slung sideways. Luke caught my nose with his elbow as he put both hands on the steering wheel and turned sharply onto the narrow shoulder. The car bounced along, gravel pinging against the underside and vegetation scraping at the body. I was jostled around until I found myself looking out the back window at the receding taillights of the other car. My seat belt engaged and I felt it dig into my shoulder as the car jounced along. I tried to get my hands up to brace myself against the headliner, but that only served to bang my hands painfully against the roof. I tried tucking down and turning sideways as I felt the rear tires going into a skid. We traveled a few more feet before the rear end of the car went into the ditch and the engine stalled. When we came to rest, I was looking through the windshield at the stars.

There was a quiet like no quiet I've ever heard, or rather not heard, before.

"Are you okay?" Luke asked, his hands still clamped around the steering wheel.

"I think so. You?"

"I'll let you know as soon as I can take inventory," Luke said, his voice little more than a whisper.

I don't know how long we sat there, but when we finally started to move, it was slow and awkward. I had trouble unlatching my seat belt. Once I was free, I struggled to get out of the car on the ditch side because gravity kept insisting that the door stay closed. I had to hold it open while climbing out onto the sloping ditch bank. Weeds snaked around my feet and rocks set my ankles turning.

Luke was having his own troubles on the driver's side; his seat belt had locked and he couldn't get the release button to work. I climbed up onto the roadbed and went around to try to help, and after considerable banging and prying with a screwdriver Luke produced from the glove compartment, we finally got him out.

We didn't know whether to call the cops and wait by the car or walk on to River's house and wait for them there. I looked up and down the lonely stretch of road and voted for option number two. "That wasn't an accident," I told Luke, "and the driver could come back for another go at us."

We started our limping trek toward River's driveway, keeping well over to the side of the road, ready to leap the ditch at the slightest hint of danger.

But the driver didn't come back, and by the time Denny and Jennifer got there, River had checked us both over, doctored our scrapes and bruises, and distributed ice packs.

I called Denny direct, even though I knew he was off duty. He must have been with Jennifer because they both showed up minutes later. While Jennifer had gone back to her old sullen self, Denny seemed completely normal. Maybe she hadn't had a chance to tell him what she'd overheard Esme say.

"Can either of you tell us anything about the car, anything at all?" Denny asked.

"It was a dark color," I said. "And a regular car."

"Yeah, not a wagon or an SUV, a sedan," Luke added. "I was so busy trying to keep us out of the ditch I didn't catch much else, but it was definitely a dark-colored sedan."

"Me either," I said. "I was busy being scared out of my wits. I tried to get a look at the plate after it had passed, but we were being bounced around and I couldn't focus."

Only I had seen something. I just didn't know what. I'd seen something that might be important but I couldn't get it all sorted right then. Too much stuff was buzzing around in my head, plus my nose was throbbing like the dickens.

Denny and Jennifer drove us back up to where the car had come to rest, and Denny called in the highway patrol investigator to come do the calculations. More flashing lights, more questioning, and steadily stiffening muscles were putting both Luke and me into a bad humor before it was all done.

When at long last everything was documented, River and Luke examined the damage to the car and determined it would run. They drove it up into River's driveway. Denny and Jennifer walked me back toward the house, and as we approached their car Denny said, "Sophreena, let us take you for a cup of coffee."

"We called in, we're still on duty," Jennifer pointed out.

"Yeah, and I'm dead tired," I said, though I regretted having to agree with her.

"Not a suggestion," Denny said, and grabbed my arm, escorting me to the car and placing me in the backseat, cupping my head to keep me from hitting it on the door as if I were the prime suspect in some heinous crime.

He drove in silence to the all-night pancake house out near the expressway, which at that moment hosted a few bleary-eyed truckers and a party of teenagers sucking down Cokes and shooting straw papers at one another.

Denny guided us to a booth on the opposite side of the establishment and went to the men's room. I had to resist the impulse to put my head down on the gray-speckled Formica table and take a nap. I'd told him absolutely everything I could think of, what did the man want from me? Did he not believe me? Or maybe he didn't believe Luke. Maybe he wanted to question me alone.

Jennifer slid into the booth opposite me. She had a weird expression on her face. I couldn't read it. Triumph? Worry? Indigestion?

Right at that moment I didn't care what Jennifer was thinking about me or Esme or anything else. I just wanted a hot bath and a long sleep.

When Denny came back, an older waitress with hair an unlikely shade of red hied over and took our order, not bothering to hide her disappointment when we ordered only coffee. Cheap-ticket table.

Still Denny didn't speak. He moved the syrup container and the jam and jelly rack so he could rest his arms on the table and waited for the waitress to come back and pour our java. After she walked away he lifted his cup first to me, then in Jennifer's direction. "Here's to y'all," he said, and took a noisy slurp.

"Look, Denny," I said. "I've told you every single detail I can remember. I have absolutely nothing to add. And I'm really, really tired. Could you just take me home?"

"I will shortly," Denny said. "This little tête-à-tête is more in line of a personal conversation between you and me and my partner," he added, turning in Jennifer's direction, "so I guess it's not really a tête-à-tête."

Jennifer leveled me with a look and I wanted to smack the smugness from her face.

"I can explain," I said. "Esme and I were—"

Denton held up a hand. "My meeting," he said. "I get to do the talking. Did I ever tell either of you about my great-aunt Leonie? No, I'm sure I haven't. Well, she was my grandmother's sister. My grandmother helped raise me, did most of the hands-on work, truth be told. Not because my mother didn't care, but because she was working all the time, trying to make a life for me. Aunt Leonie lived right next door to Granny, so I saw a lot of her growing up."

"Much as I'd love to hear about your family, Denton," Jennifer cut in, "we're supposed to be on duty here."

Again I found myself reluctantly in agreement with Jennifer. I was so tired I could barely manage to sit up in the booth, though the coffee was starting to put a little starch in my spine.

Denton gave Jennifer a look that made her scoot back a little in the booth and I decided this was no time to argue with him.

"This will only take a few minutes and it's important or we wouldn't be here," he said, his demeanor calm but very firm. "Aunt Leonie was a very ordinary woman in lots of ways. To look at her you'd have thought she was just a sweet old lady. But the thing is, Aunt Leonie knew things. She knew things she oughtn't by rights to have known. You get what I'm saying?"

Jennifer sniffed. "You're saying she was some kind of psychic or something? You know I don't believe in any of that stuff."

"No one is asking you to," Denny said. "I'm not trying to convert you. I'm just sharing an experience I've had in my life. I loved and respected my aunt Leonie. She was a humble soul who never used what was special to her in any way except to help people. Now, Jennifer, you've told me things you overheard Esme say this afternoon, and we need to get some things straight among the three of us."

I turned to glare at Jennifer and she shrugged. "He needed to know he's involved with a crazy woman," she said.

I tried to rise, but lucky for me the booth prevented the maneuver, since I had no idea what I would've done if I'd gotten to my feet. Again, Denny lifted a calming hand.

"Here's the thing," he said. "I know you told me out of concern for me"—he turned to Jennifer—"and I thank you for that. But let me be clear. I know Esme Sabatier. She is many things, but crazy is not one of them."

"No, she's not crazy at all, she just—" I began, but again Denny cut me off.

"I am a grown man and Esme is a grown woman and we are getting along fine and dandy. If she has things she wants me to know she will tell me, in her own way and in her own good time," he said. "In the meantime, neither of you is to mention anything about this episode to anyone, in particular not to Esme. Do I make myself clear?"

Jennifer leaned forward and I thought she was about to argue, but after a glance at Denny's face she nodded.

"Clear," I said, but I wasn't happy about it. If Esme knew about Denny's great-aunt, it would change things. Now he was swearing me to secrecy, which was so unfair. All I'd have to do is tell Esme that Denny knew and he was okay with it and everything would be smooth sailing.

"I can see what you're thinking," Denny said with a knowing smile. "I've got a little bit of a gift myself. But I mean what I say, not one word."

"Not a word," I said with an exasperated sigh. "But I don't like it."

eighteen

I GOT HOME A LITTLE AFTER NINE AND THE HOUSE was dark and quiet except for the light we leave on in the kitchen. Esme had apparently already gone up to bed. This was not a good sign. Esme and I are both night owls. Wired on the two cups of coffee I'd sucked down during Denny's lecture, I rousted her from her warm bed and lured her down to the kitchen with the promise of a juicy story. I brewed up some chamomile tea while I waited for her to get into her robe and slippers and come down.

Once we'd settled over our tea, I recounted the story Miss Lottie had finally divulged about how Samuel Wright died. Then I told her about somebody trying to run Luke and me off the road.

"Why in heaven's name are you telling me that second? You should've told me that right off. Are you sure you're okay? Look here at me. Oh, your poor nose. Why in the world would somebody do that?" she asked, putting her hand to her chest. "Was it a drunk driver?"

"I'm okay, though I'll be sore tomorrow. And no, I don't think it was a drunk driver. This was deliberate. Luke swears he can't think of anybody who'd be after him, but I've got to wonder if maybe Sherry's troubles in Miami followed her here. Maybe somebody thinks Luke knows something, though he swears he doesn't. Not about her business down there, anyway. But I've got something else to tell you."

I shared what Luke had told me about the fateful prank call Sherry and her posse had made that set up the chain of events leading to Claire Calvert's accident all those years ago.

Esme's face contorted. "All that happened to Claire because she expressed concern about a troubled teenage girl? When I get to the Pearly Gates I'm gonna have a long list of questions I want answered."

"Me, too," I said. "Such a stupid, spiteful goof, and it caused so much pain. I did some dumb things when I was a kid, but I hope nothing that caused any real harm. Can you imagine? Poor Laney, she must feel so ashamed. She was so emotional when we visited River's place. Now I'm realizing that it wasn't all nostalgia. What a load of guilt that must have been all these years."

"But she didn't feel guilty enough to come forward during all this time," Esme said, her lips pinched. "And how about the two boys? Never a peep out of either of them."

"No," I said with a sigh. "Up until a few years ago Bryan was still thinking he'd make it big as a professional golfer. I'm sure he wouldn't have wanted anything to tarnish his image."

"What about Gavin? He certainly didn't have to worry about his image," Esme said.

"No, but Gavin wouldn't have wanted his part in it to come out. Remember, Quentin Calvert is his uncle."

"I knew Gavin came over to cut Claire's grass and do little odd jobs around the house," Esme said, "but I just assumed she paid him to do it. I never knew they were kin."

"Maybe she does pay him," I said. "Or maybe he does it out of regard for her, or out of guilt. In any case I'm going to have some questions for Gavin first chance I get. I can't tell you why, but I've got a hunch that was his car that ran us off the road."

"What do you mean you can't tell me why?" Esme said.

"I mean, I don't even know myself why I believe it was him, or his car anyhow. I really didn't get that good a look at it. But his car is the right size and shape, and it's dark gray. It fits our general description—along with a hundred other cars in the area. But there was something I can't quite . . ." I snapped to attention as it came to me. "Sticker in the back window—a Wolfpack decal. Gavin went to NC State briefly. I think I caught a glimpse of that decal."

"Are you sure?" Esme asked.

"Not remotely," I said with a grin. "But Gavin doesn't know that."

"You should call Denny," Esme said. "Let him have a talk with the boy."

"No!" I said, the word coming out sharper than I'd meant it to. "No, Esme, I really don't want to do that. Gavin's got enough problems and I don't want to get him in any more hot water if it wasn't him."

"Gavin heats up his own water, Sophreena. He'll end up in trouble one way or the other."

"I don't want to believe that," I said. "I'm gonna go talk to him tomorrow."

"I don't like that idea," Esme said. "I'm going with you. I'll stay in the car, but if it really was him that tried to run you off the road, you don't know what he might do."

"We'll see," I said. "In the meantime, let's both get some sleep."

Esme caught my hand as I passed by. "Is there something you aren't telling me?" she asked.

"Probably," I said, skirting the question. "I'm so tired I'm probably leaving out a lot of details. We'll talk again in the morning."

"All right, darling," Esme said. "I'm so thankful you're okay. You get some sleep. We need to talk, but it'll wait until tomorrow."

Esme was still morose when she came down the next morning. She was dressed in her church finery, but she was clearly downhearted.

"Is Denny going to church with you?" I asked.

"I didn't call him," Esme said.

"Really, Esme," I said, tiptoeing along the razor's edge of my promise to Denny. "I don't think Jennifer will say anything to Denny."

"Unless she gets struck dumb, she'll say plenty," Esme insisted, then turned abruptly to look at me. "Do you know something I don't?"

"I daresay I know a lot of things you don't," I said, trying for a grin.

"Yes, you daresay," Esme said, narrowing her eyes at me. "Are you going to church?"

"Not today. I'm going out to see River this morning to fill him in on the story of how Samuel Wright died. I'm sure Luke has told him the gist of it, but since this was our gig, I'd like to give him our take. I have some information about the unit Samuel served with and I found a diary online this morning that was written by a member of that unit contemporaneously. There are some bloodcurdling descriptions of what they went through. I think that might help put what happened to Samuel into perspective."

Esme nodded. "I'll probably see Claire at church and I think I ought to tell her what we've learned about who made that phone call."

I frowned. "I don't know," I said. "I mean, I think Luke might like the chance to tell her himself."

"She's got a right to know," Esme protested.

"Yeah, she does, but please, just hold off and let me talk to Luke first, will you?"

Esme nodded. "I'll wait a little while. But if he hasn't spoken to her by nightfall, I'll be telling her."

"Fair enough," I said. "And speaking of nightfall, I won't be here for dinner. Jack and I have a date."

"A real date?" she asked, her eyes lighting up.

"A real date," I assured her. "He's taking me to Olivia's for dinner."

"'Bout time. Hallelujah and longtime comin'!" She continued to smile, but I could see a hint of sadness in her eyes, too, and I knew she was back to stewing over the situation with Denny. But, curse Denny's hide, there wasn't much I could do about it. Not if I wanted to stay in his good graces.

As soon as Esme was out the door, I ran upstairs and pulled on a pair of jeans and a T-shirt and headed for Gavin's apartment. I wasn't worried about Gavin being dangerous and I hadn't actually agreed to wait for Esme. She'd be ticked, but if it wasn't this, she'd be ticked about something else, and I was tired of dancing around her. I wanted some answers.

It was ten o'clock on a Sunday morning and I had every reason to believe Gavin would still be in bed, but I mashed the doorbell anyway, and held it down for a while for good measure. I wasn't the least bit concerned about his beauty rest.

Finally he opened the door, looking none too well. His hair was sticking up in spikes and he was glassy-eyed. I waved my hand in front of his face. He was having trouble focusing and I hoped it was only because I'd awakened him from a sound sleep.

"We need to talk," I said, pushing past him into his apartment. It was shockingly tidy. I'd expected to find a grungy space littered with pizza boxes and empty cans, but it was neat as a pin. The furnishings were sparse, but of decent quality, and he had some well-chosen framed prints on the walls. It threw me. I had to take a moment to adjust.

Meanwhile, Gavin was holding his head as if it might fall off his shoulders and frowning at me like I was an alien who'd dropped into his living room. "Soph-reena? What are you doing here? Has something happened? Is Joe okay?"

"Joe?" I asked. "Yes, as far as I know, Joe is fine."

"Well, then, what the—" Gavin held up a hand, then hustled toward the back of the apartment. I could hear him "worshipping at the porcelain throne," as the partyers in my college days used to call the morning-after ordeal.

He came back out a few minutes later, cradling his head in a wet washcloth. "Why are you here?" he asked again.

"Not that you asked for my advice, Gavin, but should you really be out drinking and partying, considering you're still on probation?"

"I wasn't," he said. "I must be coming down with a bug or something."

"Where were you last night, Gavin?" I asked.

"Out," he said. "Why? Oh God, what's happened now? What are they looking to pin on me? Whatever it is, I didn't do it, I swear."

"Did you drive your car last night?" I asked.

He dragged the washcloth down his face and brightened somewhat. "No. My car's been sitting out front, right where I left it when the cops released it to me after they got Sherry's things out of my trunk. I biked to work."

"How'd you go out last night if you didn't drive?" I asked.

"A friend picked me up," Gavin said.

"A friend?" I said.

Gavin was getting aggravated and I could see he was going to start arguing, so I tried to head him off at the pass. "Look, Gavin, I'm trying to be a friend. Some things are happening and you need to answer my questions so I can help you. Who was the friend?"

"A woman," he said.

"You're seeing someone?" I asked.

"What are you, my mother?" he snapped, cradling his head in his hands.

"Thankfully, no," I said. "Just hang in a minute more, and I'll explain. Who is this woman? Were you with her all evening? What time did you get home?"

"Her name's Francesca. And if you want to know, she asked me out. I'm not a total loser, you know. She made me dinner, then we went to a late movie, then back to her place for a while. I got in about midnight."

"Do you ever let anyone borrow your car?" I asked.

"No, nobody," he said, getting up to go to the front door. "I'm telling you my car has been parked right there." He pointed out the door, then frowned. He walked out to the end of the sidewalk, hobbling a little as his bare feet found pebbles, and stared at the car, a strange expression creeping onto his face. There was red dust on the tires and fine gravel was stuck in the treads. The bottoms of the door panels were likewise dusted in red. Otherwise the car was spotless and polished to a high sheen.

I looked in the back window. Sure enough, a Wolf-pack decal.

"You didn't run me and Luke Mitchell off the road last night?" I asked Gavin.

"What? No!" he said. "Wait, who's Luke Mitchell?"

"Does it matter?" I asked, irritated that my question hadn't hit home with Gavin. "He's Sherry's brother."

"Oh yeah, that kid. I forgot he had a different name," Gavin said, and again clutched at his head. "You're not making any sense, Sophreena."

"Could anyone else have used your car to run us off the road?" I asked.

"You keep saying run you off the road," Gavin said. "You mean like bad driving or on purpose?"

"On purpose," I said firmly.

Now Gavin wouldn't look at me. I pushed. "Gavin, I'm trying to help you."

He rounded on me and I saw fire in his eyes, a white-hot anger that made me step back. "You're not trying to help me," he hissed. "You're just like all the others. You're trying to put something on me I didn't do. What's the use, once you've got the rep you're into it, you can never get out. Everything you try just makes it worse. Just leave me the hell alone!"

*   *   *

As I drove to River's house, I was shaken. I'd rarely seen Gavin lose his temper.

A lot of people regard Gavin as a dimwit, and I understand why. It's a persona he cultivates to keep people's expectations low. He was a below-average student in school, but I happen to know he's a really smart guy. He always scored well on standardized tests, like off the charts, teachers-whispering-to-one-another-in-wonderment scores.

Was he playing me? Was going on the offense his defense? Did the anger come from being caught and cornered? Or had he really had no idea? Was he that good an actor?

With all that had happened in the last twenty-four hours, I hadn't had much time to process what Luke had told me about the phone call that led to Claire Calvert ending up in a wheelchair. It had caused great harm then, but it still wasn't over. Even all these years later, it was still hurting people.

If this became public, Laney Easton was in for some deep embarrassment. Even if she hadn't been the instigator, she'd held guilty knowledge for all these years. And she and Claire were friends and worked together frequently. Then there was Bryan. He needed to be well connected and well regarded among those well off enough to belong to the country club set. This wouldn't be good for him either.

Gavin was Quentin Calvert's nephew. He definitely had some explaining to do if this came out.

Still, while it might be painful, it didn't seem the kind of thing a person would commit murder to forestall, right? Surely this long-ago mischief by a bunch of immature kids couldn't have anything to do with Sherry's murder.

Or, if it did, there were stronger candidates than the kids themselves. Claire, for instance. Ridiculous, but just as a mental exercise, I made a list of those who'd have the strongest motives for retribution. Claire was top on the list, but even supposing she was able to do it, she wouldn't have. Then there was Quentin. If I were in his shoes, I'd be angry upon finding out some snot-nosed kids, my own nephew included, had put all this in motion. In addition to everything he'd suffered personally, it appeared he still loved Claire and would be angry on her behalf. And then there was Nash Simpson. Clearly he had a lot of unresolved issues about his part in Claire's tragedy.

But how could they have known? As far as I knew, neither man had any connection with Sherry Burton. Then again, as far as I knew didn't extend very far.

Next I did some mental sparing about whether to report my suspicions about Gavin, or Gavin's car, to Denny. Despite his weird behavior this morning, Sherry's things in his trunk, it possibly being his car that had run Luke and me off the road, I was still convinced he had not been involved with Sherry's murder. I'd known him a long time and I didn't think he had that in him. Or maybe it was only wishful thinking. Maybe he was counting on me to believe him for old times' sake. Maybe. Maybe. Maybe.

And Luke Mitchell? Was there something strange about him showing up the way he did? Was he the good guy he seemed? Had he really turned up here to answer his sister's distress call, or were there other motives involved? And as for our little detour into the ditch last night, if it was intentional, were they after Luke or me? Who would have known we were together in that car? Well, any number of people could have known. It wasn't like it was a secret assignation or anything. Luke claimed he had no idea who'd want to harm him, and he'd seemed genuinely perplexed. In fact, he'd looked at me in an almost accusatory way, as if I'd brought the incident down on his head. And maybe I had, but if so, I was as clueless as he was.

The answer to each of these questions was the same, too many unknowns to solve for x.

River and Luke were sitting in lawn chairs in the backyard, a pitcher of tea on the ground with a paper towel draped across the top to keep the bugs out. River beckoned me over to the chair they had waiting for me and poured me a plastic cup of the tea, which I downed in a few unladylike gulps.

Luke had already told River the story Miss Lottie had related, so I built some context for it by reading passages from the diary kept by the young man who'd been in Samuel Wright's unit. He described the conditions in the trenches and the horror of the things the soldiers faced every moment of every day.

"You come back from war with demons in your knapsack," River said.

"Personal experience?" Luke asked.

River nodded. "People tell you to forget about it and move on, but I don't ever want to do that. That's why I changed my name."

"River's not your given name?" I asked. "I just figured you had hippie parents."

River laughed. "Not hardly. They were conservative as they come. Up until Nam I was Robert Victor Jeffers, Bobby to my friends. But Vietnam changed everything. I think I already told you I was a medic. We did patrols in the Mekong River Valley. The first thing a downed man would ask me when I went to tend to him was 'Am I gonna die?' I'd always say, 'Yeah, someday, man, but not today in this River Valley.' One guy saw the R.V. on my dog tags and decided it stood for River Valley, and the nickname stuck.

"'Course my promise was a lie. A lot of them died. And all these years later I still don't know why they had to die, or what they died for. All I knew for sure when I came home was that I didn't want to forget any of 'em, so I had my name changed legally so I'd hear it every day and remember."

"Did you have any PTSD issues?" Luke asked.

"Still do," River said, his gaze fixed on the horizon. "Nightmares now and again, and I'm no fan of Fourth of July fireworks. Hearing the whump of helicopter blades makes my blood race, too. But that's nothing compared to what it was when I first came back. I wasn't fit to be around people. But I was lucky. I had a wife who understood and supported me, and then we had a daughter. When your life gets full of good stuff, it can help keep the demons at bay. That's what this land is for me now, a way to stay grounded, literally in this case."

The phone rang inside the house and River struggled to get his lawn chair out of the lounge position. "I gotta get that. I'm expecting a call from my contractor."

"So, how are you feeling after our little game of chicken last night?" Luke asked once we were alone.

"My nose hurts, I have bruises on my shoulder from where my seat belt grabbed, and I'm stiff, but otherwise fine. You?"

"Sore hip and I feel ninety years old, but when

I think how bad it could have been, I think we got lucky."

"Yeah, listen, Luke. I wanted to talk to you about something. About what you told me about that phone call your sister made to Claire's husband—"

"My sister and her pals," Luke corrected.

I nodded a concession. "The thing is, I think Claire has a right to know. I have to tell her."

Luke smiled a sad smile. "She already knows," he said. "I went over to see her this morning. I told her everything and apologized for keeping it to myself all this time. It was rough, but if there's anything I've learned during my experience this past year, it's that human beings need to be able to depend on one another if they want life to be better for everyone. She didn't say she forgave me, but she said she'd work on it. I hold that as an honorable and honest response. I told River the whole story last night. He's extended his home to me and I want to be up front with him. The truth will set you free and all that."

"Set you free or get you run off the road," I muttered.

"You think it had something to do with that?" Luke frowned. "How could it? I'd never told a soul until I talked to you about it yesterday in the car."

"I don't know. I'm just trying to think of anything that might have targeted us."

Luke frowned. "My guess is, something from Miami followed Sherry here and whoever she was running from thinks I know something about her business. I don't, but that's the only thing I could think of that makes any kind of sense. I'm pretty sure she was dealing drugs. She wasn't a user, or at least I never saw any sign that she was, but I can see how she could justify it to herself to sell. She always wanted what she wanted, you know? I don't know that for sure and she never confided in me, but I'm not stupid. She had way too much money for a bartender and I don't think she had a sugar daddy."

"So you think she got involved in a deal that went bad somehow?"

"Yeah," Luke said hesitantly. "Or what I'd rather think is that she was trying to leave that life. She did write those things in the letter she left me about wiping the slate clean. But maybe that's just what I want to believe."

"A lot of that going around," I mused.

Esme was puttering around the kitchen when I got home. She'd shed her Sunday clothes in favor of a pair of turquoise slacks and a colorful tunic. No belt, no earrings, no necklace, flat sandals. Something was definitely wrong. Her movements, usually swift and efficient, were now listless.

"Esme, please tell me what's going on with you," I pleaded, unable to keep quiet any longer.

"I'm fine, Sophreena," Esme said, her tone contradicting her words.

"Is that F-I-N-E as in fouled up, insecure, neurotic, and exhausted?" I asked.

She flapped a hand at me. "You're about as funny as a toothache. Now, go on and let me finish up in here."

I looked around but couldn't see anything that especially needed finishing and I didn't like that she wanted to get rid of me. "Did you talk to Claire this morning?" I asked.

"Yes, she told me Luke came to see her. She says she'd like to have some time alone today to think on things and talk with Quentin about it. She's taking a couple of days off work; she's a bundle of emotions. I'll go over tomorrow morning."

"I wonder how Quentin will take it," I said.

"Me, too," Esme said. "But Claire claims Quentin has come a long way, that he's got control of his anger issues through the counseling he got in prison. She's more worried about Nash Simpson. And you know what else about good ol' Nash? I saw him at Top o' the Morning earlier. He drives a dark green sedan. Doesn't have a Wolfpack decal in the window, but it does have one from a gun group with a big old perching bald eagle smack in the middle. Might look pretty similar at a quick glance on a dark road."

"Sheesh," I breathed. My mind started to immediately sort through a stack of what-ifs. Had Nash Simpson somehow learned about the phone call? But how? What if it was Luke he was after? But why? Luke hadn't been a party to the prank. But he had known about it and kept quiet all these years. Had I ever done anything to earn Nash Simpson's wrath? I didn't think so; I hardly knew the man.

The doorbell rang, interrupting my ruminations, and both Esme and I turned to look out the kitchen window. We couldn't quite see the porch at that angle, but we saw Denny and Jennifer's unmarked car parked at the curb.

Normally this would have sent Esme into a primping spasm, but all she did was strip off her rubber gloves while muttering what I was pretty sure was a really naughty word in French. She threw the gloves on the counter and started toward the door with a heavy sigh. Not good.

I followed her out into the hall and watched as she presented Denny and Jennifer with a decidedly unwelcoming greeting. "I'm busy," she said simply.

"Good to stay busy," Denny said, undaunted. "But we need to talk with Sophreena a minute, please."

He gently pushed his way past her and motioned

me to the family room, Jennifer falling into step behind me in case I decided to bolt. Which I felt inclined to do after seeing the look on Denny's face.

"Tell me what you thought you were doing," Denny began, after compelling me to sit, "going to question Gavin this morning without even telling me you believed it was him in that car last night. What were you thinking?"

"I thought I told you to wait for me," Esme added, coming up beside Denny.

I looked at them, standing side by side, both of them doing everything but shaking a scolding finger in my face, and I burst out laughing. "Sorry, Mommy. Sorry, Daddy," I said. "Listen, I didn't believe it was Gavin in the car. I had only a vague hunch. So I went over to talk to him, that's all. I wasn't meeting him in some dark alley at midnight. Wait a minute, how'd you know about it anyway?" I turned accusing eyes on Esme.

She looked indignant. "I didn't tell him," she said. I turned to Jennifer, wondering if I'd said anything about where I'd been when I was at River's house, but I didn't think I had.

"He called me," Denny said. "Gavin told me about your conversation, and the more he got to looking at his car after you left, the more he started to think somebody had taken it. Gavin's a creature of habit;

I mean, really ingrained habit. He hangs his keys on the same peg of a three-peg rack in his kitchen. Same peg every time. Only this morning, they were hanging on the wrong peg. And the seat and mirrors in the car were adjusted wrong. He thinks somebody's trying to set him up."

"I think so, too," I said. "And anyhow, he's got an alibi. He was with a date last night during the time we were run off the road."

"Francesca Creswell," Jennifer said. "She goes by Frankie. She works at the golf course. Only she says she can't alibi him for the whole time."

This surprised me—both the information and the fact that Jennifer was sharing the information.

I was mulling over my response when Denny's cell phone buzzed. "It's the chief," he said to Jennifer. "I'm going to step out to take it. I'll be right back," he said, turning to give me another hard stare as he left the room.

The three of us waited in uncomfortable silence. Esme continued to stare at the doorway where Denny had gone out. We could still hear his muffled voice, and the look of longing on Esme's face made my chest ache.

The silence dragged on for what seemed a long time until finally Jennifer broke it. "Listen," she said, "I know I haven't always been the friendliest person since you've been seeing Denton." She took a step toward the doorway, trying to get Esme's full attention. "The truth is, I was jealous of the fact that he talked to you about our cases and asked for your advice. I didn't think it was appropriate. He should have been discussing the case with me, just me. But then my dad pointed out that I talk to him about cases all the time. I use him for a sounding board because I know I can trust him. I'm realizing now it's the same with you two. And as for the other thing, well, I don't believe in that stuff, but if you do, it's your own business."

Esme turned to her and I braced myself for a snarky comment. Instead she heaved a great sigh as if exhaustion had overtaken her. "Don't trouble yourself," she said, "it's nearly over."

Before we had a chance to ask her what she meant, Denny was back. He swept the room with a glance, and Jennifer and I both examined our shoes. Neither of us had violated his edict, but somehow I still felt guilty.

"Okay," Denny said, "I want both of you to hear me on this. We're working on something and I can't have you getting tangled up in it. Stay away from Gavin Taylor and Bryan Mason. And I don't want you talking to Laney Easton, either. You got it?"

"I got it," I said. "So I take it this is about that phone call to Quentin all those years ago. You know Claire's concerned about how Nash Simpson is going to take it if he finds out."

"I'd be more worried about his wife," Jennifer said. "She's a wildcat and she's still convinced Claire was trying to steal Nash away from her. Like he's a hot prize."

Denny pinched the bridge of his nose and muttered something under his breath. "It's not a question of whether he learns about this, but when and under what circumstances. I think it's best to bring in all the parties tomorrow and talk to them and see if we can control the fallout," he said, turning to Jennifer. "We need to get back out there, we've got a lot of ground to cover."

As we moved out of the room, I watched Esme. There was very little animation in her face and she moved like her feet were made of lead. At the front door Denny turned and pointed a finger at me. "You remember what I said. No contact." Then he reached over and touched Esme on the shoulder. "I'll call you later," he said, giving her a wink.

"That's fine," Esme said with about the same enthusiasm she might have offered a door-to-door vacuum-cleaner salesman.

The door closed and Esme shuffled off toward the kitchen to continue putzing around. It hurt me to the core to see her this way. I wanted grumpy Esme back. The only thing keeping me from breaking my pledge to Denny was the fact that Jennifer hadn't broken hers. If I blabbed to Esme now, I'd prove every bad thing Jennifer had ever thought about us.

Instead I went upstairs and started getting ready for my date with Jack. It was four thirty in the afternoon and he was picking me up at six. I've never taken more than a half hour to get ready for anything. I wasn't exactly sure what to do with all that prep time.

I was planning to wear the dress I'd bought for the wedding. I don't hold much with this idea that you can't be seen in society in the same dress twice in a season. For what I'd paid for this one, I planned to get all the use out of it I could. I might be mowing the lawn in the thing before all was said and done. I hung it in the bathroom to steam out the wrinkles.

I showered, then rubbed my hair nearly dry with a towel and left it to curl as it dried. I knew better than to try to bend it to my will. I put on a little blush, a smear of tinted lip ointment, and a couple of strokes of mascara. For me this was heavy-duty preening. I donned my new dress and slid my feet into my new shoes. I tried a few poses in front of the mirror. I felt a little weird, but I looked pretty freakin' good.

I came downstairs and had a flashback to prom night as I went into the workroom to show Esme. She clapped her hands and held them to her chest, grinning like a proud mama. "You look so pretty!" she exclaimed, walking a circle around me to get a view from every angle.

"You don't have to make it sound like a miracle,"

I said with a pro forma harrumph. But I was secretly thrilled to see Esme smile, whatever the cause.

She was smiling, but when I looked closer, I saw there were tears brimming in her eyes. I would have pushed her then, and probably would've ended up breaking my oath to Denny, but Jack's voice in the front hall saved me.

"Hey, Soph! You ready?"

"Back here," I called.

Jack had taken a little care tonight as well. He had on a pair of pressed khakis and a dress shirt, and he smelled of an aftershave I really liked.

"Wow," he said when he caught sight of me. "You look really . . ." He paused, searching for a word. "Really different," he finally finished.

"Oh, you sweet-talkin' dawg, you," Esme said with an exasperated sigh.

"You look beautiful," Jack amended. "But we might want to take your car. I'm in the pickup, which seemed like a better choice than my motorcycle, but neither really works with that dress."

On the way to Olivia's, neither of us could find anything to say, or we'd both start talking at once. Olivia's had been open only a short time, but it was clear it was going to be a smashing success. Though the trappings were fancy, it was a welcoming and comfortable place. Jack and I were greeted by the restaurant's owner, Daniel Clement. I'd gotten to know him well while researching his family history for his mother, and based on his grin, I had a hunch he was in the gossip loop about Jack and me. As he showed us to our table, he told us what he had planned for Marydale and Winston's reception, which would be his first big catering job. Daniel had been a dissatisfied lawyer in a former life and I admired how he'd had the courage to leave a career that was making him miserable to pursue something he loved. People can change if they have the will to do it and the support to sustain it.

After we'd studied the menu and made our selections, Jack leaned across the table and whispered, "You really do look beautiful, Soph."

"Thanks," I said, "you're not so bad yourself. I feel a little strange. This is all very special, but next time let's just order in a pizza, okay?"

Jack laughed. "Sure, but this is our first real date and it should be special. Speaking of which, I got you a little something to mark the occasion." He handed over a slender box.

I hesitated. It had never occurred to me to bring him a present. Jack read my mind. "It's not a big deal. I just wanted to get you something. Go on, open it."

I tore off the paper and lifted the lid off the box, pulling out a delicate silver chain with a small round pendant disk etched with a branching tree, similar to the one on the locket Winston had gotten for Marydale.

"Not as romantic as a heart," Jack said, "but it looks like the family trees you draw for people, so I thought it would suit you better."

I put the necklace on and knew I'd never want to take it off. I'd had it for two seconds and already it was precious to me. Which made me think of Laney finding her bracelet at River's house. She'd been so happy to get it back. Though when I thought about it more, what she'd actually said was that James would be happy.

"Do you think it's possible for a couple to have an equal relationship?" I asked Jack.

"Yeah, sure," he said, each word drawn out. "Is this because you didn't get me a present? Or you don't like the necklace?"

I smiled. "You know I love it," I said. I told him how it had made me think of Laney and James. "She's such a strong, confident woman, and yet when I've seen her with him it seems like she sort of folds in her wings and turns everything over to him."

Jack laughed. "Believe me, Soph, I have no expectations that you'll fold in your wings. Maybe it's the age difference with them, or something about their political careers; that's got to be touchy. Or maybe they weren't friends first, like us."

Our food arrived and from there on out the evening was grand. We ate and chatted aimlessly about whatever crossed our minds, and all the things I'd always loved about our easy friendship came back, only with an extra bonus.

Jack insisted on walking me to my front door when we got back to my house. "You know," he said, "if we really were coming home from the prom, your dad would probably be peeking out the window to see if I kiss you good night."

"Don't worry, I'm sure Esme's got that duty covered," I said, and we immediately heard footsteps shuffling around inside.

Jack kissed me. It was a very nice kiss, an extremely nice kiss.

"We said we'd take it slow, right?" he asked as he pulled back to look at me.

"Yes, we did," I agreed.

"What the hell were we thinking?" He gave me a crooked smile. Then he kissed me again, lightly this time, and called out good night as he jogged to his truck.

Dee called me the next morning, rousting me from some very interesting dreams. "Can you come down to the police station?" she asked.

"Do I need to bring bail money?" I muttered. "What have you done, Dee?"

"Ha-ha," she said. "I'm down here with Laney.

Denton called her yesterday and asked her to come in this morning on an official matter. She's got no idea why she's here and she's a little ticked about it. I don't want to put you on the spot, but do you have any idea what this is about?"

"Don't put me on the spot, then, Dee," I said. "It'll all be clear soon. It won't be particularly pretty and Laney's not going to be happy, but it may be a relief in the end."

I debated whether my going down there would violate Denny's order. He said not to talk with Laney, but he didn't say I couldn't be there for her after this all came out. I told Dee I'd be there right away.

Dee was sitting with Laney on a bench in the tiny front lobby when I got to the station. She raised her eyebrows at me, but I shook my head.

Laney was checking her watch. "I've got a full day," she said. "I hope this doesn't take much longer. I hate to keep people waiting. And because they're keeping me waiting, my schedule is going to get jammed. You really don't have to wait with me, Dee." She looked up and saw me approaching. "Sophreena, what are you doing here?"

I glanced at Dee, who gave me a rueful smile. Apparently she hadn't told Laney she'd called me.

"I needed to see Denny about something," I lied. "And you?"

"Well, Denton called me yesterday and asked me to come down. They said they needed my help. I assume it's village business, though I wonder why it was Denton calling and not the chief. In any case, they're making me cool my heels. Sit down," she said, patting the bench beside her.

I sat. I felt duplicitous, but at the same time I truly believed this would help Laney in the long run. It must have been a terrible secret to carry for all these years. But for the immediate future, it was going to be like taking nasty medicine in hopes of a cure. I wished I could brace her for what was to come, but I couldn't. I was already technically in violation of Denny's order.

We all turned as the door opened and Gavin stepped inside the lobby. He squinted to let his eyes adjust to the interior lighting. He spotted us and gave a quick nod, then checked in at the desk. The desk officer hit a button and the door buzzed open. Gavin disappeared into the business end of the station.

"Oh no," Laney said, once the door closed behind him. "I hope he hasn't done something dumb again. Poor Gavin, he just can't seem to stay out of trouble. I worry about him."

Next came Bryan Mason. He went through the same adjustment as he passed through the doorway out of the bright morning sunlight. He looked around and spotted us. Laney smiled and gave him a little wave. His expression was hard to read, but if somebody had forced me to label it, I'd have called it hurt, which wasn't an emotion I'd normally associate with cocky Bryan Mason. He went to the desk and was immediately ushered to the back.

"I wonder what's going on," Laney said.

"So do I," Dee said, looking across at me.

Just then the door opened again and Luke Mitchell came in. He nodded at me and was approaching the desk when the side door opened and Jennifer beckoned him to come through. She stepped out into the lobby, still holding the door open. "Sorry to keep you waiting, Ms. Easton. We'll be with you in a few minutes."

"Okay," Laney answered, glancing at her watch again. "But do let me know if it's going to be much longer. I'll need to cancel some appointments."

I longed to tell her she should go ahead and cancel everything for the rest of the day, maybe for the rest of the month. This was going to be such an embarrassment for her, even though she'd been only indirectly involved.

"Do you know that guy who just went in?" Laney asked.

I nodded. "Luke Mitchell, Sherry Burton's brother."

"Oh, my God, do you think this has something to do with her murder?" Laney asked, wide-eyed.

"I don't know," I answered, honestly this time. I'd thought it was about the prank call, but maybe the two things were related somehow.

The parade continued. A young woman came in, looking around nervously. She went to the desk and I heard her give her name—Francesca Creswell. So this was Gavin's date. She was petite, with a beautiful figure, long chestnut hair, and dark eyes. She was gorgeous. And she'd asked Gavin out?

Laney's frown deepened when she saw the woman. "Do you know her?" she asked. "She looks familiar, but I can't place her."

"I don't know her," I said, "but I think she works at the golf course."

"Yes," Laney said, "that's where I've seen her." She went back to thumbing at her cell phone, texting her secretary to cancel her morning appointments.

The next person to enter was James Rowan. He spotted Laney and came over, bending to peck her cheek. "What are you doing here?" he asked.

"I'm here to see Denton," she said. "Village business," she added. "But something's come up for them and I've been moved to the back burner."

"I think the something that's up is what I'm here for," he said. "I'd best get on back and find out what it's about. See you tonight?"

"You bet," Laney said, and I noticed her hand went

instinctively to her bracelet. She was worrying it, twisting it around her wrist.

A few minutes later, Nash Simpson and his wife arrived. Both ignored us completely and went straight to the desk, complaining loudly about having been called in and demanding to know why. The desk officer buzzed them in and they disappeared into the black hole of the back offices.

"Wow, it must be getting crowded back there," Dee said.

"It must," Laney said with a forced laugh. The bracelet action had picked up, and I thought maybe she was finally catching on to what this was about. If not, the next visitor to the station should have tipped her. Quentin Calvert came in, his face stony. Given his life experience, police stations probably seemed like the gateway to hell. He was directed inside and I sincerely hoped they were going to put him in a different room from Nash Simpson, or else the cops might need to don riot gear.

The dime finally dropped for Laney when Esme came in the door, pushing Claire Calvert's wheelchair. Laney's breathing went ragged and I could see the panic in her eyes, but she put up a good front. She greeted Claire like the old friends they'd been, and to Claire's credit, she was cordial in return, if a bit cool.

Claire was taken to the back and Esme settled in the chair opposite us to wait.

We sat in silence for a few long moments, then Laney spoke, her voice soft. "You know, Dee, you were lucky Marydale didn't let you hang out with us when Sherry was here. Be grateful she cared enough to look out for you. Don't get me wrong, I loved being with Sherry, I really did. She was absolutely her own person and she didn't care what others thought of her. I always cared way too much what other people thought of me." She gave a rueful laugh. "Still do. But Marydale was right; she was a bad influence. She could talk you into doing things you knew you shouldn't do. Things you might come to regret."

She was still twisting away at her bracelet and I thought back to the afternoon she'd found it in the seat of her car. There had been red mud stuck in the links. Had she dropped it? I replayed the scene in my head. No, she'd started to get into the car, then squealed and turned, with the bracelet in her hand, holding it up so we could see. How had it gotten muddy stuck down in the car seat?

I looked over and saw Esme studying Laney. It was a peculiar look.

Dee was pressing Laney about what she meant by regrets, but I was only half listening, since I already knew.

We waited for what seemed like hours but was really only twenty minutes or so. Suddenly the door from the back pushed open with some force and James Rowan strode into the lobby, his face pale and his mouth set in a horizontal slash. Laney got up to go to him, but he brushed past her. She grabbed onto his sleeve, but he jerked away and kept walking without a backward glance.

Laney chewed at her lip and I could see she was struggling to force back tears. "We'll talk later," she said, her voice unsteady. "I'll explain everything. I was just a kid."

I could see Jennifer talking to the desk officer and I wished she'd come get Laney and let her get this over with.

"But you weren't a kid last week," Esme said, staring down at her hands. "Were you, Running Deer?"

Laney looked at Esme, her face contorting. "How did you—"

"Isn't that what she called you, your friend Sherry?" Esme asked.

"Yes," Laney said uncertainly, "but how did you know that? Oh, let me guess, Gavin, or Bryan? So we had silly tribal names, so what? We were kids," she said again. "Just kids."

Esme kept talking, and I saw Jennifer coming up behind her. I tried to signal Esme that we weren't alone, but she seemed to be somewhere else. I couldn't reach her.

"Remember the promise you all made?" Esme asked. "It was kids' stuff, yes, but you meant it. You joined hands and chanted: *A pledge is a pledge and a promise is a promise. If either is broken, a curse be upon us.*"

"How did you . . ." Laney began, her lips trembling. "It was Gavin, wasn't it? I always knew he was the weak one. It was so long ago. We were children," she wailed.

Esme continued as if she hadn't heard. "She called herself Walks by Night. I have a message from her; it's for you. She says she gave you a chance. She warned you that you could never hope for a good life unless you wiped the slate clean and atoned for the harm you'd caused. But you didn't give her a chance, did you? She's dead."

Tears were streaking down Laney's face and dripping onto her lap. She didn't seem to notice. She squeezed her eyes shut and after a very pregnant pause she began to speak in a rasping whisper. "I didn't mean to hurt her. She wanted to go out to the spot down by the creek where we used to meet. Sacred ground, she called it. And she wanted to go at the time we used to meet back all those years ago. She roamed around for a while, then told me she was going to Claire Calvert to tell her about making the phone call. We argued. It was all well and good for her if she wanted to turn over a new leaf—she was a drug dealer, did you know that? She was running from some people in Miami, but she didn't tell me that when she asked if she could stay with me. She brought that danger into my home with no regard for my safety."

All of us sat in stunned silence. Jennifer was standing totally still and I could see she was debating whether to interrupt, no doubt analyzing the legal ramifications of this impromptu confession.

"I love this town," Laney went on. "I love the people, I love Claire," she said, hiccupping a sob. "Sherry would be somewhere far away in another week. I'd still be here in Morningside. I tried to make her see it would ruin me, but she didn't care. She was going to tell Claire right that minute. The vigil people were just clearing out and Claire's lights were still on. I grabbed her and we fought. I didn't realize until later I'd lost my bracelet. She took off running and I ran after her. I didn't mean to hurt her; I only wanted to stop her. I had to stop her. She was the one who made the call, but I knew we'd all get the blame. We'd all promised we'd never tell and now she was going back on it. And what would it have helped, really, to have it come out now? James had already been criticized for talking Quentin Calvert into that plea bargain. He wouldn't want that in the news again. And I knew if he found out I had any part in what happened, no matter how small a part, it would be bad." She looked up then, her eyes pleading. "And it is bad. It's very bad. You saw him."

"But Laney," Dee said, her voice catching, "you killed her?"

"I didn't mean to," Laney said, sobbing now. "It was an accident. It was starting to rain and I was chasing her, trying to get her to listen to me. I grabbed at the back of her shirt and we both fell. She hit her head on something, I guess. It was an accident, a freak accident. I saw she was dead and I panicked. I just left her there."

"Oh, Laney," Dee said.

"It gets worse," Laney said, folding her arms across her middle and rocking. "I should have called for help. She must not have been dead like I thought, because when she fell we were down in the middle of the field. The only thing I can figure is that she came to at some point and somehow made her way up to that grave before she died. If I'd called 9-1-1, she might still be alive. Her life is over, and now so is mine."

I'd walked to the police station but I crawled into Esme's SUV for the trip home. I was emotionally spent. I felt sad and angry and betrayed, like the world's biggest sucker. How had I not seen this sooner? The business with the bracelet had bothered me, but I'd ignored it. And now I saw clearly that Laney's attempt to rekindle our old friendship had only been a ploy to get information about the investigation.

Esme drove in silence until we were in our driveway, then she switched off the motor and drew in a long breath.

"I've never had that happen before," she said, sounding so tired she could hardly push the words out. "When I went over to Claire's this morning I decided to walk down to the creek just so I'd have a better picture of where those kids used to gather. Sherry came to me so clearly it nearly knocked me off my feet. I've never gotten any kind of message from someone so newly deceased, and I've never gotten anything that word-for-word precise. It scares me. I know I've complained in the past about how wishy-washy the messages can be, but I want that back now."

"Maybe it was a one-shot deal," I offered, "because you're so close to Claire or because Sherry Burton was so determined to clear the slate."

Once we were in the house, Esme trudged straight up the stairs to rest and I wandered around, stewing. I wanted desperately to talk to Jack, but he was still at work. In the end the emotional exhaustion got me, too, and I fell asleep on the family room couch. When the doorbell woke me I looked out the window and saw the gold and magenta hues of twilight.

Denny was standing on the steps, a cone of flowers in his big hands. He held them out to me. "I know you and Esme had a hard day. We're supposed to have supper together tonight, but if she's too tired, I'll understand. She's not answering her phone."

"I'll go check," I said, shaking my head to clear the cobwebs.

Esme was in a chair, staring out the window at the sunset. She'd been crying, I could tell. "Give me a few minutes," she said. "I'll come down."

Denny rose when I came back into the family room and delivered her message. "I'm really sorry about how things turned out, Sophreena," he said. "I know Laney's a friend."

"What can you tell me?" I asked, knowing there were boundaries he wouldn't cross, not even with Esme and me.

"She's made a complete statement," he said. "James Rowan recused himself from the case, which is the right thing to do, but probably for all the wrong reasons. Anyway, she'll probably be arraigned tomorrow or the next day and I expect she'll be released on high bond. Her folks have the money. As far as the charges, I can't tell you anything about that 'cause I don't know. It's a strange case."

"With lots of loose ends, it seems to me," I said, frowning.

Denny nodded. "All I can tell is we're working to sew it all up."

Esme came in just then, and clearly they weren't going to supper, as she was in yoga pants, a cotton top, and bedroom slippers. Not a smidge of makeup. She stood, rubbing her hands together. Then she crossed her arms over her chest and drew in a shuddering breath.

"It's good you're both here," she said. "I've got something to tell you," she said.

Finally, I thought. She's finally going to tell Denny about the gift. But why did she want me here?

And then she dropped the bomb.

"I'm so sorry, Sophreena, but I'm leaving here. I've got to go," she said, her voice catching.

I felt as if someone had punched me in the stomach, leaving me breathless and stunned. "You can't," I said, looking to Denny for help.

He was maddeningly calm. "Tell us why, Esme," he said.

"It's time," Esme said with a deep sigh. "Oh, Sophreena, we always knew this was a temporary thing," she said, stepping over to take me by the shoulders. I could see tears pooling in her eyes and her voice was so soft I could barely hear her. "It's time I moved on."

"I didn't know it was temporary," I protested, shrugging off her hands. "You never said 'temporary' partner,

Esme. You're just going to walk out on me? On our business? On our friendship? I trusted you more than I've trusted anybody since my parents died," I said, anger now flaring up, "and now you're just going to leave? How could you do that? Just because you're scared to tell . . ." I caught myself just in time; I was still aware of the pledge I'd made to Denny. "Just because things aren't perfect doesn't give you the right to leave me in the lurch. We've got clients lined up. We've got obligations."

Esme put her hand on her hip and gave me an eye roll. "Oh, for pity's sake, Sophreena, I'm not leaving the business, I'm just moving out of the house."

"What?" I said, feeling my anger subside. "Moving? Where are you moving? An apartment?" I turned to Denny. "Is she moving in with you?"

"No, I am not, Sophreena!" Esme said. "I bought a house. Mrs. Etheleen's place. I need to be on my own and so do you," she said. Then she turned to Denny. "I should have told you my plans, too," she said. "But it was important to me to make this decision all on my own." Turning back to Sophreena she said, "I've dreaded telling you. I know I've been cross these past weeks, but I guess I was heartsick over the idea of the separation. This is going to be a big change for us."

"Well, kudos for the way you told me, Esme," I said testily. "Now it's my turn to be cross. You scared me half to death, announcing you were leaving like that. And as far as change? Esme, I can see Etheleen Morganton's house from the front door, it's not like you'll be going to the moon."

"That's right," she said, "and the best part of all, I'll have a freestanding garage with a big old room over it. It would make a good family history resource center, at least until we can find a bigger space."

"Well, that all sounds great," Denny said, rising. "I don't believe I'm needed here. I'll be going along and let you two get things sorted out."

"I'd like you to stay," Esme said. "We need to talk. There are some things about me I haven't told you and I think it's high time I did. Sherry Burton was right about the need for a clean slate before you can move on to a better place in your life. Sophreena, give us some privacy?"

"I'd be delighted," I said. As I passed Denny, I gave him a big grin. He smiled back, but I also saw a hint of trepidation in his eyes.

I arrived at Jack's condo twenty minutes earlier than we'd arranged and thought of letting myself in. I had a key from the many times I'd watered his plants and fed his fish when he was away. But with the change in our relationship, it suddenly seemed presumptuous.

It turned out to be irrelevant, since he pulled in about three minutes later, as I was carrying on the debate with myself. While he made me a grilled cheese sandwich and tomato soup I spilled everything that had happened. He listened, injecting "oh," a "wow," or an awed whistle once in a while.

"I feel really bad about Laney's situation, but really angry with her, too. And I still don't know how any of this ties in with Luke and me getting run off the road, or with Gavin finding Sherry's stuff in his trunk."

"But you have faith in Denny. If he says they're working on it, then you'll get answers eventually, right?"

"Right," I said with a sigh, taking the first bite of gooey goodness from my sandwich.

"And as for Esme moving out, maybe she's right, maybe it's time," Jack said.

"Yeah, I think so," I said, unable to suppress a smile. "I'll miss her, but some privacy might be nice."

I met Dee for coffee the next morning and as we stood in a line that snaked all the way out the door, I spotted Bryan Mason at the far back table. He was sitting with the Francesca woman. Something about the scene made my blood boil and I imagined I actually heard gears clicking in my head.

On Gavin's best day he's an average-looking guy.

Cute if you like scruffy guys, but nothing that would cause a gal to swoon. And this woman had asked him out? No, surely not without an ulterior motive. And what would that have been? To get him away from his apartment and his car? And what of Bryan's uncharacteristic concern for Gavin? I had a hunch his goal had been the same as Laney's—access to information on the investigation.

Well, now I wanted information. And since they had Laney's statement, I figured I was released from my promise not to talk to Gavin or Bryan.

"Get me a cup of medium roast and an apple fritter, would you?" I said to Dee, pressing money into her hand.

"Sophreena, don't . . ." she called as I walked toward the tables, but I didn't stop.

I approached Bryan's table with purpose and planted my feet. "Hello," I said. "Fancy seeing you two together. You know, Bryan, Gavin's got enough problems without you messing with him. Or you, either," I said, turning my ire on Francesca Whozit.

Bryan gave me an amused smile. "What are you talking about, messing with him?" he asked. "I haven't done anything but try to help him."

"Help him right back into jail!" I said.

Bryan gave me a perplexed look, but I didn't buy it for a moment. "You're obviously upset about something.

Sit down, Sophreena. Have a cup of coffee with us. Do you know Frankie?" He held out a hand in her direction, all Mr. Charm.

"Cut it, Bryan," I said. "I know you had something to do with—"

Dee grabbed my arm hard. "I got us a table," she said.

I pulled my arm away. "I'll be there in a minute, I'm not done here," I said.

"Yeah, you are," Dee said in a singsong voice. She nodded curtly to Bryan and the woman and dragged me off bodily. Picking up our pastries and coffee from the table, she continued to the sidewalk, her hand around my arm like a vise.

"What are you doing? Fine, I won't talk to them. Where's my coffee?" I asked, trying to wrench my arm away.

"No coffee," Dee said. "Keep walking." When we came alongside a florist's van, suddenly Jennifer stepped into our path. "Thanks for your help," she said to Dee and took her turn at the vise grip on my arm like it was a relay baton. "Probably be best if you go on home, we'll call you later," she said to Dee. And with that she practically threw me into the van.

"What did I tell you?" came a deep voice from the front seat. "Did I not say, clearly, Sophreena, don't talk to either of those fellas? Was I not specific?"

"Yes, Denny, you did," I said, rubbing at my arm. "But that was before you solved the case. And those two were sitting there looking all smug and it just got to me, that's all. I know he had something to do with—" I stopped abruptly as I looked around the van. A guy was sitting on the floor in the back, headphones clamped askew to his head so that it left one ear free. He was staring at a computer screen. Two computer screens, actually.

He glanced up and nodded at me. "Jerry," he said. "I'm a technician."

I craned my neck to see the screens. One was a video feed of the table where Bryan and Francesca were sitting. The other was an up-and-down squiggle that I surmised was an audio feed.

"You may have just screwed up an operation it took us weeks to put into place," Denny said through clenched teeth.

Jerry raised his voice so Denny could hear him. "Actually this may have worked in our favor. He was Joe Smooth before, now he's rattled. We may get something yet."

Jerry tapped a key and suddenly the van was filled with voices. I looked a question at Jennifer.

"We flipped Frankie," she said. "She's wired."

"I didn't sign up for this," Frankie was saying. "I want no part of it. You told me Gavin was guilty, that he killed Sherry, and that you were just trying to make sure the blame fell where it should without getting us involved. Now Laney Easton has confessed and the police are asking all kinds of questions."

"Stay cool," Bryan said. "It'll all be okay. It's all over with now. All we have to do is go low-key for a little while. Our suppliers are a little skittish, but it'll blow over in a few weeks and it'll be business as usual."

"Business as usual?" I asked, but my question only earned me a shushing from the three of them.

"Not for me, it won't," Frankie insisted. "I'm out of it. Out of the whole business."

"No, you're not," Bryan said, his voice dead calm. "You're in up to your pretty little eyeballs. I'm very disappointed in you, Frankie. You had only two things to do that night. Two things," he repeated, holding up two fingers. "One, keep Gavin out of sight and tank his alibi, and two, put his keys back. You totally screwed up one out of two."

"You didn't tell me you were going to run somebody off the road, or I would never have helped you."

"A little self-aggrandizing," I said. "But she's working it, isn't she?"

Jerry nodded and grinned at me, but Denny and Jennifer shushed me again.

I could see Bryan starting to shift in his chair. They were little metal bistro chairs and not the most comfortable under any circumstances. He leaned in toward Frankie, causing the back legs of his chair to tilt off the ground. He reached across to place his hand on hers. To a casual observer, it would have looked like a gesture of affection. "Listen to me," he hissed. "This is not the kind of thing you can resign from, Frankie. Don't act stupid; it doesn't suit you. If I'd wanted Gavin's car for anything legit, I'd have asked to borrow it."

"I want out," Frankie said, pulling her hand away. "Out of all of it."

"And last week you wanted the same thing I want. I want enough money so that I can quit my job and stop licking other people's boots. And at this point I don't care what I have to do to get there. And you'll be right by my side, helping me, every step of the way."

"You don't own me, Bryan," she said. "And you'd better remember, I know everything about your operation."

"You should," Bryan laughed, "you helped me set it up. Without you and Sherry, I'd never have realized I was sitting on a prescription drug gold mine. Seems rich folks have a lot of anxieties. And as for owning you, Frankie, you'd better remember I've already killed once to protect our enterprise. Who's to say I wouldn't do it again if I felt everything was on the line?"

"What?" Frankie said, and I really believed the shock this time.

"Laney never was any good at finishing what she started," he said, his voice down to a growling whisper. "She called me in a panic after she and Sherry fought and, as usual, she expected me to clean up her mess. But when I got there, Sherry was very much alive and thoroughly pissed. She was going to tell not only about what happened all those years ago but she'd gone all righteous prig about our deal. She was the one who told me how to do it, for God's sake. And there she was, screaming all this nonsense about how I needed to cleanse my soul and how being involved in the drugs had ruined her life.

"So," he said, throwing up his hands and leaning back in his chair, "if it was ruined anyhow, what good was it? Right there by that open grave in the middle of a driving rain. Two problems solved, or so I thought. I guess the cat was already out of the bag about that phone call to Quentin Calvert when we were kids. I took care of it. I let Laney go on thinking she'd killed her, which worked out well, incidentally. But, good friend that I am, I did help her get Sherry's things out of her place. I figured Gavin would end up back in jail for something anyhow, eventually. And it might as well be something that would help me out. I was gonna tip off the police anonymously, but the idiot called them himself."

"What do you have against the brother?" Frankie

asked. "Were you trying to kill him when you ran him off the road? Were you going to pin that on Gavin, too? My God, Bryan."

Bryan shrugged. "I thought maybe Sherry told him stuff about us. I wasn't trying to kill him, I just wanted him to move on and figured I'd give him a little encouragement. Look, Frankie, I'm not a monster, I'm just a guy who's tired of getting the short end of the stick. I'm telling you all this," he said leaning in close again, "to let you know I mean what I say. Nothing is going to stand in my way. Nothing and no one."

"You really killed her?" Frankie said, her voice shaking.

"I didn't have a choice," Bryan said, leaning over to cup her hand again. "I didn't want to do it, just like I wouldn't ever want to hurt you, Frankie. But yes, I really killed her."

"That's it!" Denny said. "Keep it rolling, Jerry. Jennifer, let's move in."

nineteen

WINSTON AND MARYDALE'S WEDDING WAS JOYOUS.
The weather bestowed its blessing, allowing the ceremony to be held in the garden as Marydale and Winston had wanted.

Winston's concerns about how the families would
blend seemed to have been a waste of anxiety. During
the reception Dee and Brody abandoned all sense of de-
corum and began chasing Winston's youngest grandkids
around the backyard to a chorus of laughter and squeals.

Marydale and Winston each looked resplendent
and seemed to be enjoying every moment. This was
very different from other weddings I'd attended, where
the tension that ramped up during preparations spilled
over into the big day and every minor glitch was cause
for a freak-out.

Winston flubbed his lines during the vows, causing
Marydale to get the giggles. Marydale's two Westies,

Sprocket and Gadget, were honored guests, at least until Sprocket peed on the best man's shoe, much to the amusement of the grandchildren, and some adults, too. A mother bird got worried about so many people close to her nest and took a couple of dive-bombing runs at the wedding party. Still, everyone kept right on smiling and enjoying themselves.

Most especially Denny and Esme. They were the happiest I'd ever seen them. Esme even allowed some public displays of affection from Denny, an arm around her waist, an adoring eye lock, gestures she'd never have permitted a month ago.

Coco brought River as her plus one and I had the chance to ask if he'd heard from Ron Solomon about what was to be done with Samuel Wright's remains. "Ron said I could probably make a case for having him moved, but it didn't seem right somehow," River said. "We'll keep him there, only this time with a proper grave marker," he said. "I'm at peace with that idea and Luke's pleased. I hope his sister would be, too."

"And what does Jennifer think?" I asked.

"Jennifer's in a good place," River said, smiling and shaking his head. "Or leastwise, she's working toward it. She's never allowed herself to be happy since her mother died, but she's mellowed out here recently. I don't know what did it, but I'm not gonna overthink it. I'll just take it as a gift from the cosmos."

"How are she and Luke getting on?" Jack asked. "Last time I talked to Luke, he was thinking maybe he should look for other quarters."

"That's changing, too," River said. "Fact, the two of them have gone out to the mountains on a camping trip with some of Jenny's other friends. They're at Sliding Rock. I'm thinking the water may be pretty cold this early in the season, but if I know those two, neither of them will admit they can't take it. I expect they'll come home with blue lips and frozen fannies."

"Sounds like there may be a little something developing there," I said.

"No, nothing like that," River said. "But if things did go in that direction, I wouldn't have any objection. I've grown quite fond of the boy. But it's nothing romantic between them, they're just becoming friends."

"Friendship romances are the very best kind," Jack said, punching me playfully on the arm.

"Well, you two oughta know," River said. "Them, too," he added as Marydale and Winston stepped up on the back porch so everyone could see for the official cake cutting. They thanked everyone for coming, Marydale cried, Winston stammered, the dogs yipped, and everyone clapped and hooted and lifted glasses of champagne to toast the newlyweds.

I reached up to touch the pendant Jack had given me and ran my fingers over the embossed tree that represented life, growth, and family. Things were changing. Marydale and Winston were married now. Esme was back to her old self, still bossing me around, but with good humor again. She'd closed on the house and would be moving out soon. I'd miss her, but she'd be only a half a block away, and she was right, it was time. She and Denny were past the last obstacle keeping them apart, and Jack and I were finding our way in our newly defined relationship. Who knew what life would bring in the months and years to come, but after the ugliness of the past weeks, there was plenty to celebrate. As I looked out over the crowd of well-wishers, a feeling of deep contentment came over me. I wasn't thunderstruck, but I was most definitely awestruck. I touched my champagne glass to Jack's. "To new beginnings," I whispered.